"Are you going to the garden party?" Arthur surprised himself with the question.

"Me?" She looked equally startled. "No, I told you, I don't go to social engagements."

"Neither do I usually, though if it's because of your scar, then that's ridiculous."

"No more than becoming a recluse to punish yourself for something you couldn't help."

He let one side of his mouth curve upward, acknowledging the hit. "Then shall we both make an exception?"

"Why?" Frances kept her gaze averted. "Why should we go? We don't need to prove anything."

"No, we don't need to, but I suppose I want to." He looked at her profile in the sunshine, resisting the urge to draw closer. "You've made me want to join the world again, Frances."

"Oh." If he wasn't mistaken, her cheeks darkened again.

"You can wear your veil if you want to, but..."

"I don't want to."

"Good. Then we can go and support each other, and if anyone stares, they'll have me to deal with."

JENNI FLETCHER

———

*The Viscount's
Veiled Lady*

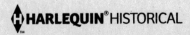

Recycling programs
for this product may
not exist in your area.

ISBN-13: 978-1-335-63495-5

The Viscount's Veiled Lady

Printed in U.S.A.

www.Harlequin.com

Jenni Fletcher was born in the north of Scotland and now lives in Yorkshire with her husband and two children. She wanted to be a writer as a child but became distracted by reading instead, finally getting past her first paragraph thirty years later. She's had more jobs than she can remember but has finally found one she loves. She can be contacted on Twitter, @jenniauthor, or via her Facebook author page.

Also by Jenni Fletcher

Harlequin Historical

Married to Her Enemy
Besieged and Betrothed
The Warrior's Bride Prize

Whitby Weddings

The Convenient Felstone Marriage
Captain Amberton's Inherited Bride
The Viscount's Veiled Lady

Visit the Author Profile page at Harlequin.com.

For Helen (and all the sisters who argue).

Also for my writing friends, especially the Unlaced Ladies, who stop me from getting lonely.

Historical Note

Whitby jet is a semi-precious black gemstone that has been used in jewellery-making since the Bronze Age. It is renowned for being both lightweight and incredibly hard, as well as for taking on a vibrant shine when polished. Formed from the fossilised remains of Araucaria trees (early ancestors of modern monkey-puzzle trees) it can still be found in a stretch of shale along the North Yorkshire coastline, now known as the Heritage Coast.

Examples of Whitby jet were displayed at the Great Exhibition in 1851 and it became popular after the death of Prince Albert in 1861 when Queen Victoria went into a state of semi-permanent mourning. Mourning itself became particularly ritualised during this era with widows forced to become almost living memorials to their deceased husbands.

By the 1870s, the demand for Whitby jet was at its height. Around 1,500 jet workers were employed in approximately 200 jet workshops throughout the town, but, unfortunately, it was a boom industry that lasted for around a century and then fell out of favour, partly because of cheaper imports and partly because it failed to keep up with changes in fashion. Jet mining itself was made illegal in the late nineteenth century to prevent coastal erosion.

As a result, many traditional methods of carving have been lost and modern jet workers are largely self-taught. I'm grateful to Hal and Imogen Redvers-Jones at the Whitby Jet Heritage Centre for answering my questions about Victorian jet-carving techniques and to Botham's of Whitby for providing so much delicious research!

Chapter One

Whitby, North Yorkshire—July, 1872

'You want me to do *what*?'

Frances Webster dropped the piece of jagged black stone she was polishing on to the table with a thud.

'I want you to visit Arthur Amberton for me.' Her sister Lydia draped herself over a *chaise longue* by the window, somehow managing to look both spectacularly beautiful and sound utterly shameless. 'It's not as if I can visit a bachelor on my own, is it? I'm a respectable widow.'

'And I'm a respectable spinster. That's worse.'

'Yes, but you're always wandering along the beach by yourself. Anyway, it's different for you.'

'Why?'

'Oh, don't be so tiresome.' Lydia shot her a look that suggested the answer ought to be obvious. 'You know perfectly well why, Frannie.'

'No. I'm sure I do not.'

Frances gritted her teeth at the hated pet name. She suspected her older sister did it on purpose, as if she were still a child to be ordered around and not a woman who'd turned twenty-two that past spring. It was also obvious what *why* referred to. Lydia was forever dropping hints about her scarred appearance without ever going so far as to actually refer to it directly. Well, if she had something to say, then for once she could just say it out loud.

'I mean it doesn't matter if anyone *does* see you with him. It's hardly your fault, I know, but you're not exactly the kind of woman a gentleman would dally with, are you? Your reputation would be perfectly safe.' Lydia heaved a sigh. 'It's such a pity when you used to be so pretty. If only you'd married Leo when you had the chance—'

'Enough!' Frances raised a hand, deciding that she'd heard quite sufficient after all. 'You're right. I'm sure my face would repel any man.'

'Well, I wouldn't put it quite like that.'

Not in her hearing perhaps, Frances thought icily, though what her sister and mother said about her behind her back would probably convince her to wear a bag over her head for the rest of her life. They both thought of her facial scarring as the worst misfortune that might have befallen her on the very morning of her eighteenth birthday, but then both of them were beautiful. In her mid-fifties, their mother was still a strikingly attractive woman, with only the faintest touch of silver in her dark hair and an almost unnaturally smooth, porcelain complexion. Walking side by side with her eldest daughter, the pair of them were capable of turning every male head in Whitby.

Of course there had been a time, not so long ago either, when *she* wouldn't have looked so out of place beside them. With only a six-year gap in their ages, both she and Lydia had inherited their mother's fine looks and statuesque figure, though it had taken her own curves so long to appear that she'd thought they weren't coming at all. She'd been a late bloomer; though when she finally had, she'd shown signs of surpassing even her sister in beauty, or so their mother had once told her to Lydia's furious chagrin.

Her accident had put paid to all of that, however, so that now, although they shared the same oval face, dark eyes and chocolate-coloured hair, they were hardly two sides of the same coin any more, rather two different coins altogether, one lustrous and shiny, the other dinted and tarnished.

'Now will you take a message for me or not?' Lydia was starting to sound impatient.

'No, and I can't believe you're even suggesting it! John's only been dead for ten months.'

'Exactly!' If she were remotely offended by the insinuation, Lydia gave no sign. 'Ten whole months. How much longer am I supposed to remain in mourning?'

'A year and a day in full mourning and another year in half-mourning, you know that. The Queen's been wearing black for over a decade.'

'I'm not the Queen!'

Frances swallowed a sarcastic retort, vaguely amazed that her sister was aware of the fact. Most of the time she acted as if she had a sovereign right to command everyone around her. If it had been up to Lydia, no one would have spent more than a week wearing black.

'I can't understand what good it does to imprison me in my own home!' Lydia jumped to her feet abruptly, starting to pace up and down the parlour in frustration. 'Mama hardly lets me go anywhere or see anyone.'

'Only because it's not seemly for you to go visiting yet.' Frances gave her a sympathetic look, for once in agreement. Forcing widows to remain trapped indoors with their grief didn't strike her as the best way of helping them to overcome it either. Not that Lydia seemed particularly grief-stricken.

'It's ridiculous that I'm supposed to act as if my life is over. John was already half-dead when I married him. He was past sixty when we met.'

'I thought you said that age didn't matter in a love match.'

'I said that?'

'Yes, before you got married.'

'Oh.' Lydia looked sceptical. 'Well, I suppose I did care for him, as much as he could have expected me to anyway, but I don't see why I have to waste my best years in mourning now that he's gone. I'm sure he wouldn't have wanted it either.' She stopped pacing in front of a mirror and pressed her fingers against her cheeks, tugging the skin gently upwards. 'I'm only twenty-eight. Wearing black crepe makes me feel old.'

'We're all tired of wearing black, Lydia, but those are the rules. At least you've no need to worry about money.' Frances tried to sound reassuring. 'John left you a good legacy.'

'Barely a third of what he was worth.'

'But he left the rest in trust for Georgie.'

'With his lawyer holding the purse strings. As if *I* can't be trusted.'

Frances dipped her head to hide her expression. The terms of John Baird's will, though by no means churlish towards his young bride, suggested he'd understood her better than anyone had realised. With Lydia in control of his fortune, their son George would have been lucky to see so much as a penny on his majority.

'Maybe he thought you wouldn't want to be bothered with such details.'

'I don't see why. Georgie is my son. It's not right that somebody else is looking after his future. John used me very badly.'

'Mmm...' Frances picked up her stone and polishing cloth again with a sigh. Lydia's memory in regard to her deceased husband was becoming more and more selective by the day. But then John Baird hadn't been quite the catch she'd been hoping for when she'd made her come-out, not compared with a certain eligible viscount anyway, a man they'd all thought had been lost at sea...

'In any case, I wouldn't remarry until after a suitable period.' Lydia settled back on to the *chaise longue*. 'But if I have to wait until I'm out of mourning then Arthur might marry somebody else and then where will I be? I missed my chance six years ago. I won't miss it again.'

'Marry?' Frances stopped polishing abruptly. She'd been working on that particular piece of jet for half an hour, smoothing away the rough edges and imperfections so that now, in the light of a flickering candle, she could see her own eyes reflected in the surface. They looked sad even to her. Quickly, she put the stone aside, dropping it into a small wooden box filled with sawdust.

'You mean you *still* want to marry Arthur?' She asked the question softly, wondering why she hadn't guessed the truth sooner.

'Of course! What did you think we were talking about?'

'You only said that you wanted me to take him a message.'

'To persuade him to call on me, yes.'

'Why can't you just write?'

'Because I already have.' Lydia's expression turned sullen. 'He sent a note back saying he was too busy to renew our acquaintance. You know there was a time when that man would have crawled over hot coals for me and he calls it an acquaintance!'

'You did marry somebody else, Lydia.'

'Only because I thought Arthur had drowned! What was I supposed to do?'

'Maybe wait more than a week before getting engaged?'

'*Wait?*' Black eyes glittered with anger suddenly. 'I'd already spent *years* waiting for Arthur to persuade his father to accept me. It was humiliating enough having to keep our engagement a secret, but then he had to go and fall off his boat and abandon me. He left me to become an old maid!'

Frances fought the urge to roll her eyes. As she recalled, Lydia couldn't have behaved any less like an old maid. She'd had more than enough spare suitors to choose from, not that Arthur had known about any of them. He'd been aware of her other admirers—in truth, it would have been nigh impossible to miss them—but he'd never known quite how serious some of those other flirtations had been. That had been one small mercy when he'd gone missing, though now Frances wondered how he'd felt when he'd come home and discovered just how quickly he'd been replaced...

'I'm sure you were very hard done by, Lydia.'

'How was I to know that he'd come back nine months later and I'd be stuck with John? Do you know, Arthur didn't even visit me!'

'How could he? You were married.'

'Well, all right, but I'm a widow now and he's still

unattached, and now that his father's dead there's no one to object. I don't see why we can't resume our engagement. It's quite romantic when you think about it, as if it were meant to be all along.'

'Yes. How convenient of John to die when he did.'

Lydia shot her a petulant look. 'I wouldn't expect you to understand about love.'

'I never said that I did.'

'And Arthur did love me.'

'Yes,' Frances conceded wistfully, 'he did.'

That part was undeniably true. She'd never seen a man so in love as Arthur Amberton had been with her sister. She'd still been in the schoolroom at the time, but to this day she remembered the way he'd gazed so adoringly at Lydia, as if she were the Juliet to his Romeo. Once upon a time, she'd hoped some man might look at her like that one day, though the chances of it seemed unlikely now.

Arthur Amberton had been the very epitome of everything she'd imagined the perfect gentleman to be: intelligent, charming and exquisitely mannered, albeit with a faint air of sadness about him. Dashingly handsome, too, with wavy, chestnut hair and intense, ochre-coloured eyes. He'd been considerate towards her, too, always taking the seat next to hers in the parlour when it was empty and asking about her art as if he were genuinely interested in her hobbies, treating her like an adult and not just a child, unlike the rest of Lydia's admirers. She'd tried her very hardest to think of him as a brother, especially after Lydia had confided the secret of their engagement, but in truth she'd been more than a little in love with him herself, wicked as it had felt at the time. When he'd been lost at sea, she'd felt as devastated as if she'd been the one he'd left behind. She'd never understood how Lydia could have forgotten him so quickly, but then her sister had never been one to put all her eggs, let alone her heart, in one basket.

'From what I've heard, however, it turns out I had a lucky escape six years ago.' Lydia propped an arm behind her head. 'Apparently the family fortunes were in a terrible state back then.'

'Lydia!'

'Oh, don't be so naive, Frannie. Love has to survive on something, you know.'

'Well, if he's so poor, why do you want to marry him now?'

'Because he's not poor any more, silly. His brother's marriage to Violet Harper restored all that.'

Frances reached into her pocket for a new stone, examining it for flaws as she tried to unravel the tangled machinations of her sister's mind. She vaguely remembered hearing that Violet Harper, the shipbuilding heiress, had married Arthur's twin brother Lance a few years before, though she couldn't see how that helped Lydia…

'I don't understand.' She gave up finally. 'How does that affect Arthur?'

'Because it was her money they used to develop and expand their iron mine. It's become quite successful, so I hear, and Amberton Castle's been almost completely refurbished. Not that Arthur resides there himself, the vexing man. He lives in some woebegone old farmhouse on the edge of the Moors, but the property's all still in his name.'

'How do you know?'

'Because I make it my business to know.'

'Oh…' The tangles smoothed out suddenly. 'And if

you were to marry him, you'd insist on him moving back to Amberton Castle?'

'Of course. For his own good.' Lydia gave a self-satisfied nod. 'It's the family home and he's the Viscount.'

'But if his brother and sister-in-law have spent their money on repairing it…?'

'Then I'm sure they could afford to make alternative arrangements as well.'

'Naturally. What a pity Arthur doesn't want to renew your acquaintance, then.'

'He just needs to see me!' Lydia shot bolt upright, glaring as if the words themselves had stung her. 'If I could be in the same room with him for ten minutes, then I could convince him to propose again, I'm sure of it.'

This time Frances didn't even try to stop her eyes from rolling. The worst of it was that Lydia was probably right. She'd never had any problem convincing men to do what she wanted. Usually she only had to snap her fingers for them to come running. It was frankly amazing that Arthur Amberton had managed to resist her appeals for this long, but then people said that he'd changed during the nine months of his mysterious absence. No one knew where he'd been or why he'd been away for so long. There were rumours that he'd spent time on a fishing boat, though surely that was unlikely.

'Well, I'm not going.' She put her foot down obstinately. If Arthur didn't want to see Lydia again, then she certainly wasn't going to force him. 'And I don't know why you think I could persuade him anyway.'

'Because he's always liked you. He was forever wandering off to talk to you.'

'Was he?' Frances felt her cheeks flush guiltily.

Sometimes it had seemed as if he'd deliberately sought out her company, but then she'd always assumed that had been wishful thinking on her part. 'I'm sure he was just being kind.'

'Of course he was just being kind,' Lydia snapped, 'but it was rude of the pair of you. I used to feel quite aggrieved.'

'Then I'm sorry.'

'You could still make it up to me.'

'No!'

'Think about poor Georgie. Don't you think he deserves a stepfather?'

'Of course he does.' Frances narrowed her eyes suspiciously. Lydia had always been quick to recognise other people's weaknesses and the three-year-old boy was definitely hers.

'And don't you think a viscount would make a worthy stepfather? Think of all the advantages. Not just to him, but to poor Mama and Papa as well.'

Poor Mama and Papa? She stiffened at the implication. 'What about them?'

'Well, they must have expected to have us both married off by now and yet here I am, back under the same roof, and it's not as if you're ever going to leave. It must be a lot to deal with at their age when they might have expected a bit of peace and quiet. If I married Arthur, then it would make life easier for everyone, don't you think?'

Frances bit down hard on her lip. She couldn't deny that. For everyone except Arthur himself, that was...

'And you could come and live with us at Amberton Castle, too, if you wanted.' Lydia's voice took on a wheedling note. 'Georgie much prefers you to his nurse and he'll need a governess.' She waved a hand dismissively. 'If you're not too busy playing with stones, that is.'

That did it. Frances put both her hands down on the table, pushing herself to her feet. 'I am *not* playing with stones. I'm making jewellery. Which some people think I'm quite good at, incidentally. I made four pounds last week.'

'Why, whatever do you mean?'

'Just that I took a few of my best pieces to Mr Horsham and he bought them from me.'

'The jeweller? You mean you're in *trade*?'

Frances hesitated for a moment and then smiled. It hadn't occurred to her to think of it that way before, but now that Lydia had said it, she supposed it was true. Carving beads and cameos out of the jet she collected on the beach was just one of her many artistic pursuits, but she enjoyed it. If she could make a reasonable amount of money from selling her pieces, then perhaps it could be a means of becoming independent, too, a way to live without feeling like a burden or embarrassment to others. Then she could be *the artist* Frances Webster instead of *that poor, scarred girl*...

'Yes.' She pulled her shoulders back, fuelled by a new sense of ambition. She was in trade. And pretty happy about it, too.

'Do Mama and Papa know?'

The happy feeling vanished at once. Since the accident, her parents had allowed her far more freedom than most women her age, but when those activities involved trade, she had a feeling even they might not be quite so tolerant.

'Perhaps I ought to tell them...' Lydia's rosebud mouth curved into a smug-looking smile. 'After all, they have a right to know when you're sullying the family name.'

'I'm not sullying anything!'

'That is *unless* you're prepared to deliver one little message for me?'

'All right, Lydia, you win.' Frances dropped back, defeated, into her seat. 'What do you want me to tell him?'

Chapter Two

Frances weaved a slow and reluctant path along the beach, stopping occasionally to pick up a pebble and skim it across the tops of the oncoming waves. She didn't bother to count the bounces. Her record was fourteen in a row, but today the stones felt like lead weights. She was dragging her feet so heavily that if she didn't hurry then the tide would be all the way up to the cliffs before she could make her escape back to Whitby, but at least she knew the tempestuous North Sea and its shoreline well enough to know exactly how much time she had.

Besides, she reassured herself, her errand wouldn't take long, just a few minutes to deliver the message and get a response. For her sake, she hoped it was a yes, if only to prevent Lydia from sending her back again. For Arthur Amberton's sake, however, she hoped it was a definitive no. Family loyalty aside, she couldn't help but feel that he'd been the one who'd had a lucky escape six years before. He might have been head over heels in love with her sister, but he hadn't known her at all.

Frances's stomach had been performing a series of unwanted contortions at the prospect of seeing him again, her emotions torn between excitement and dread. After his surprise return, she'd hoped to catch a glimpse of him in Whitby, if only to reassure herself that he was truly alive and well, but to no avail. According to the local rumour mill, he rarely came to town, let alone attended social functions, and after a while she'd given up hope.

Which was, she'd eventually decided, for the best. As much as she'd wanted to see him, she'd had absolutely no desire for him to see her. If they'd met again, then she would have had to explain the veil that she habitually wore out of doors and then listen to the inevitable words of sympathy and reassurance. She was heartily sick of those words, shallow platitudes that meant nothing, especially from men, though perhaps not from Arthur...

Would he have behaved any differently from Leo if he'd been in the same situation? she wondered. She didn't want to believe that Arthur would ever have been so fickle, but he was still a man, and men seemed to value beauty in women above all else. Lydia was living proof of that and Arthur had been smitten with Lydia... In which case, yes, he probably *would* have behaved like Leo after all!

She stopped short, shocked by the direction of her own thoughts. They sounded bitter in her own head and she didn't want to be bitter, even if it was hard not to be sometimes. Besides, what did it matter how Arthur would have behaved? What did it matter what he thought of her veil? This visit had nothing to do with *her*. She was there to talk about Lydia, that was all.

She tossed her last pebble into the sea and then started up the sandy slope towards a gap in the cliffside. According to Lydia, Arthur's farm was located just before the small fishing port of Sandsend, half a mile from the shore and accessible along a gorse-lined path from the beach.

She made her way along it, skirting around the perimeter of the village to join a dirt track on the other side. It was steeper than she'd expected and rutted with holes that made walking difficult, so that she was panting by the time she reached the edge of the Moors, where lush green fields gave way to brown heathland. Breathless, she stopped at a wooden gate, taking a few moments to admire the view. From this vantage point, she could see the sea spreading out like a shimmering turquoise carpet all the way to the horizon beyond. It was a beautiful position for any dwelling, even a 'woebegone, old farmhouse', though as she trudged on through the gate and around the side of a small woodland copse, she could see that it was anything but.

Far from dilapidated, it was clearly a working farm, a scene of well-organised chaos with giant bales of hay stacked along one side of a three-storey stone house and what looked like a newly built log store on the other. It was hardly deserted either. On the contrary, there seemed to be animals everywhere: pigs in a sty, goats and sheep in two separate pens, at least two dozen chickens and five lazy-looking cats roaming wild, not to mention a pair of horses peering out from over the top of a stable door.

Frances stopped in the centre of the yard and turned around slowly, searching for any sign of a human in the midst of so many animals, but there seemed to be no one, just a brown-and-white speckled dog sitting by the front door of the farmhouse, its head tipped to one side as if it were the one in charge. Judging by its short coat and piercing blue eyes, she guessed it was a sheepdog, though fortunately it seemed to be friendly as well.

She bent down to ruffle its ears, struck anew by the impropriety of her situation. She was an unmarried, un-chaperoned, uninvited lady, trespassing on behalf of her widowed sister in order to persuade a single gentleman—a viscount, no less!—to accept a request that he'd already refused! Only Lydia would ask such a thing. Only Lydia would expect it to work!

But she was there now and she might as well get the whole mortifying scene over with. Lydia was more than capable of carrying out her threat and telling their parents about her fledgling business if she didn't do what she wanted and her work was too important for her to risk that. She'd tell them about it herself eventually, once she'd earned enough to stand on her own two feet if nec-essary, but not yet. She had her own plans for the future and she'd reveal them when she was good and ready.

Bolstered by that conviction, she lifted her hand to the front door and knocked. There was no answer, though the door swung open on its hinges with a loud creak.

'Lord Scorborough?'

She called out his name, but there was still no an-swer. No sound at all, in fact. Tentatively, she took a few steps inside and along a darkened hallway, poking her head around another door into what looked like the kitchen. That was empty, too, though there was a large iron kettle steaming on the range. Perplexed, she lifted her veil and pulled it back over her bonnet for a clearer view. Clearly somebody was nearby, but why weren't they answering?

She felt a tremor of unease, resolving to go back out-side to search the yard again, when she heard the click of a door opening further down the hallway. Quickly, she turned around, ready to explain her intrusion, only to find herself face to face with a complete stranger wearing nothing more than a pair of short, cotton under-drawers.

'Oh!' she exclaimed aloud, sucking in a breath of panic as the stranger came to an abrupt halt, uttering a series of vividly descriptive expletives whose meanings she could only imagine. His legs and upper body were completely exposed so that, in the time it took for her to recover her wits, she had a close-up view of power-ful calves, a muscular chest and arms that looked to be around the same circumference as her waist.

'Oh!' She wasn't sure why she repeated the excla-mation, only that it seemed appropriate as she dragged her gaze to his face. His rugged appearance was almost as alarming as his lack of apparel. Close-cropped hair and dark stubble gave him the look of a convict. *Was* he a convict? His colourful language certainly wasn't that of a gentleman. She felt her palms break into a cold sweat, panic mounting as her heartbeat started to ham-mer erratically. The wrong farm! She must have come to the wrong farm, she realised, berating herself for the mistake in the split second before their eyes met and she spun on her heel and fled…

Arthur Amberton, the Fourteenth Viscount Scorbor-ough, had just finished bathing. He'd just stepped out of his bathtub, rubbed himself down with a sheet and pulled on a pair of under-breeches as an afterthought— an impulse for which he was now extremely grateful. Since he didn't keep servants and rarely had any visitors, he generally had no qualms about wandering around his own house completely naked, especially during the hot summer months, so that to find a black-clad woman standing in the corridor in front of him had come as an equal, and in his case somewhat uncanny, surprise to both of them.

She'd run away at the sight of him. Fled for dear life, more like… Which at least proved she wasn't a ghost, though now he supposed he'd have to go after her. Much as he resented any intrusion into his privacy, he really ought to find out who she was and what she was doing there, not to mention apologise for his less-than-enthusiastic greeting. Her end of the corridor had been dark, casting her face into shadow, but judging by the style of her clothes she was a lady.

He mounted the stairs to his bedchamber three at a time and pulled on the shirt and trousers he'd laid out earlier. He was supposed to be dining with his brother and sister-in-law that evening, though he would have preferred going to bed early instead. Working ten acres of land on his own meant he was usually exhausted by late afternoon, but at least it meant he was mostly too tired to think.

Dinner at Amberton Castle, however, was a standing weekly appointment, a compromise he'd made to stop Violet from worrying about him. His tiny sister-in-law's refusal to accept that he wasn't unhappy or lonely was more than a little irritating. He wasn't depressed, he didn't want or need companionship, and he especially didn't care for intruders.

He ran back down the stairs, jamming his boots on at the front door before charging out into the farmyard. He'd only been gone a couple of minutes, but already there was no sign of his mysterious visitor.

'Some guard dog you are.' He glared at Meg, his sheepdog-in-training, but she only wagged her tail enthusiastically. 'Which way did she go?'

It was a rhetorical question, of course. There was

only way she could have gone, back along the track that led to the village, unless she'd decided to take refuge in the pigsty. Quickly, he made his way towards the path, splashing his newly polished boots in the process, though he'd barely rounded the corner of the copse before he found her again, sitting in a muddy patch on the ground and clutching her leg.

'Are you hurt?'

She seemed to leap halfway into the air at the sound of his voice, twisting her head away to fiddle with something at the front of her straw bonnet. He slowed his pace, not wanting to alarm her any further, though she kept her face averted as if she were too embarrassed to look at him. Oddly enough, there was something familiar about that bonnet.

'I slipped on the mud.' Her voice sounded muffled.

'Farms have mud. You shouldn't have run away.'

'You shouldn't have scared me, walking around half-naked!'

'You ought to be glad it was only half.' He glowered at the back of her head, her refusal to look at him only increasing his irritation. 'And I don't believe there's a law against it in the privacy of your own home. Unlike trespassing, I might add.'

'Well, you should answer your door when somebody knocks!'

'For the record, I didn't hear you knock and that doesn't excuse you just walking in. It's my house!'

She swung back towards him at that, her face obscured by a black veil that appeared to be pinned to the hair beneath her bonnet. Was *that* what she'd been fiddling with? He grunted with exasperation. For pity's sake, surely she couldn't be so embarrassed. She hadn't even seen that much of him and it was a lot less than she might have… Still, there was something familiar about the voice as well as the bonnet, something that prodded his memory.

'I wish I hadn't walked in!' The eyes behind the veil flashed. 'I think I've sprained my ankle. Isn't that punishment enough?'

'Oh, for pity's sake.' He crouched down beside her. This day was just getting better and better. 'Are you certain that it's sprained? Here, let me look.'

'No!' She tugged her ankle away as he reached for it, putting her weight on the other foot as she tried to stand up instead. 'I can manage. Ahhh!'

'Sit down, woman, or you'll do even more damage.' He reached for her waist as she tumbled downwards again, but she jerked even further away from his touch, landing with a fresh squelch in the mud.

'I can't sit down…' Her voice was tinged with panic now. 'I have to go or I'll be late.'

'You were eager enough to see me a few minutes ago.'

'I was looking for somebody else, but it was a mistake. I shouldn't have come.'

Somebody else? His frown deepened at the words. Who had she expected to find there but him? 'Who were you looking for?'

'I…' She started to speak and then stopped. 'It doesn't matter.'

He folded his arms, not bothering to conceal a sigh of irritation. 'You know if you tell me, there's a fair chance I might be able to help.'

'Yes, but… Oh, very well.' She threw her hands up as if conceding defeat. 'I was told that Lord Scorborough lives here.'

'He does.'

'He does?'

The head twisted towards him again, but it was impossible to see past the veil. Who on earth was she? It was obvious she had no idea who he was, though he supposed he couldn't blame her for that. He didn't look much like a gentleman these days. He kept his hair cropped short for practicality's sake, to keep it out of his face when working, and he preferred being clean shaven to the current fashion for long moustaches and beards, but he hadn't shaved for a couple of days either. He'd intended doing so after his bath, had been boiling water for that very purpose when he'd found her in the corridor, so that he was probably looking more than a little weatherbeaten and bristly. It was no wonder she'd been so frightened. Still, he couldn't just abandon her there, no matter how much they might both prefer it.

'Come on. You're not walking anywhere on that ankle.'

'What…?' Her voice rose in alarm as he curled one arm beneath her knees and the other about her shoulders. 'What are you doing?'

'Nothing to sound so shrill about.' He lifted her up, liberally splattering his new clean clothes with mud as he carried her back the way that they'd come. 'I'm taking you inside so that I can bind that ankle.'

'I can walk!'

'No, you can't. You could try, but you'd probably break something.'

'I won't…'

'Believe me, I'm not thrilled by the prospect either, but I don't think either of us has a choice.' He kicked open the farmhouse door and carried her back through the hall to the kitchen, a curious-looking Meg trotting alongside as he deposited her in a tattered-looking armchair by the range and then reached up on to a shelf for some bandages. 'There. Now, what did you want with Scorborough?'

'It's private.'

'Private business with a viscount? Sounds intriguing.'

He deposited a roll of bandages on to the table with a thud. Her voice was still muffled by the veil and he had to fight the urge to tear it away. Wasn't she ever going to remove the blasted thing, even indoors? He might not have been in polite society for a while, but surely his appearance wasn't so shocking? At least not so much that ladies felt the need to cover their faces at the sight of him. He rubbed a hand over his stubbly chin. Just how fearsome exactly did he look?

'It's nothing like that!' She sounded indignant.

'Really?'

He folded his arms again, a new suspicion taking shape in his mind. Despite his somewhat chequered personal history, he was still a viscount and society still considered him a prize catch. He'd endured a number of probing visits from ambitious, matchmaking parents when he'd first moved into the farm, though thankfully they'd stopped when he hadn't returned the calls. The sight of him in his farm clothes might have had something to do with it, too, he supposed, but perhaps this woman was simply more determined than the rest.

'Really!'

She sounded so genuinely offended by the suggestion that he almost believed her. *Almost*. But he'd believed a woman once before and look where that had got him. He knew firsthand what good actresses women could be.

'Yet here you are, wearing a veil over your face and visiting a gentleman's house without any kind of chaperon? Forgive my scepticism, but to most minds that would suggest something of a personal nature.'

'How could it be personal when I thought I had the wrong house? I haven't even seen Arthur in six years!'

'Arthur?' He quirked an eyebrow in surprise. The way she said his name suggested they were already acquainted.

'Yes.' The veil face tipped downwards as if in embarrassment. 'But it's not illicit at all. I only came to deliver a message. He has no idea that I'm here.'

'On the contrary.' He drew up a stool and placed it in front of her, sitting down with one arm draped over his knees. 'He's fully aware of the fact. Allow me to introduce myself. I'm Scorborough.'

Chapter Three

'Arthur?' The veiled face leaned closer towards him. 'I didn't recognise you.'

He shrugged. 'If it's been six years, then I imagine you wouldn't, but now it seems you have the advantage. You say that we've met?'

'Yes, many times.' Her voice sounded almost excited now. Somehow that made it sound even more familiar...

'And you have a message for me?'

'Ye-es.' The excitement dissipated in one word. 'It's from my sister. Lydia Baird.'

He stiffened, all of his muscles tensing at once. Hearing the name, so suddenly out of the blue, felt as shocking as if he'd just been hit hard in the face. He could happily have lived out the rest of his days without ever hearing it again, but apparently that was too much to hope for, even in the privacy of his own home. Lydia Webster, as she was then, the woman he'd been secretly engaged to, who he'd been prepared to sacrifice everything for, who'd said that she loved him and seemed to mean it, too, right up until the moment when she'd broken his heart and stamped her dainty feet all over it...

Not that she knew what she'd done. He doubted she

had even the faintest inkling. The last time she'd seen him had been on a balmy mid-May afternoon when he'd left her parents' house determined to stand up to his father once and for all. He hadn't told her his intention and so she'd never known that he'd actually gone through with it, nor that he'd come back the next morning, eager to ask formal permission for her hand in marriage, only to discover just how false she truly was. That had been an occasion he would never forget and yet he'd had no one to blame for the shock but himself. He'd been warned about her often enough, not least by his brother Lance, but he'd never believed that she would betray him, not until he'd seen her walking arm in arm with another suitor, a man she'd clearly known *very* well, and all his hopes for the future—*their* future—had come tumbling down around his ears.

He hadn't accosted them. After the morning's argument with his father he'd felt too emotionally drained for another confrontation and so he'd gone down to the harbour instead. It hadn't been all because of Lydia— she'd simply been the last straw—but he'd felt as though he had the weight of the world on his shoulders. So he'd gone sailing and swimming and then…well, then he wasn't entirely sure what had happened. All he remembered was the feeling of being pushed to his limit, of simply wanting to leave and start all over again somewhere else.

With the blinkers so painfully removed from his eyes, he'd seen Lydia for what she was: a fortune hunter. She'd never wanted him, only his title, just as Lance and his father had said, and now it seemed she was in pursuit of it again. She'd already written to him twice in the past month on lavender-scented paper that had brought back a whole swathe of unwanted memories. He'd ignored the first and returned the second unopened, enclosing a brief note with what he'd thought was a suitably curt and definitive response. Apparently not. But then Lydia had never been one to take no for an answer.

'Arthur?' The veil tipped to one side again and he gave a small start, realising that he hadn't responded or, in fact, moved for a few minutes.

'What does she want?' As if he didn't know.

'She wants you to call on her.'

'Call on her?' His voice sounded more like a snarl and the veiled face recoiled instantly.

'Yes. For tea or…something.'

'*Tea?*' He hoped that his tone conveyed a suitable degree of contempt. He would rather have had dinner with the Kraken. 'Why?'

If a veil could have looked embarrassed, then this one would have succeeded. 'You'll need to ask her. I'm just the messenger.'

'Indeed.' He regarded her steadily for a few moments, trying and failing to see through the lacy fabric. What was she doing there? If Lydia was really so determined to see him again, then why on earth had she sent her sister? Why not simply come herself, especially in light of their former engagement? Not that he wanted her to, but it didn't make any sense…

'Why are you here?'

'I just told you.' Her head dipped, as if she were confused.

'Not that. I mean, why did Lydia send you to ask me?'

'Oh.' She hesitated briefly before answering. 'She didn't think it was appropriate to visit herself.'

'But it is for you?'

'No, only she was worried what people might think if they found out that she had come to see you.'

'What about your reputation? Wasn't she worried about that?'

'Oh, no.' The head shook almost violently. 'Mine doesn't matter.'

'Is that so?'

He leaned back, though he continued to look at her. Now *that* was interesting. For sanity's sake, he usually avoided thinking about the past, but he did remember a younger sister—Frances, that had been her name—a smaller, slighter version of Lydia, with bright eyes and a smile that must have been memorable since he did, in fact, remember it. She hadn't been out in society when he'd last seen her, though she'd often been sitting in her parents' parlour at teatime, usually occupying herself in a corner with some project or another. She'd liked making things, he recalled, or at least he didn't think he'd ever seen her without a paintbrush or needle or some other kind of crafting tool in her hand.

He'd liked her, too, that much he definitely remembered. He'd enjoyed spending time in her company while Lydia was surrounded by her usual crowd of admirers. There had been a natural, unpractised vivacity and enthusiasm in her manner that had made her face seem to glow whenever she'd spoken on a subject that she was passionate about, like art. It made him want to see her face again now. If she ever removed her veil, that was… Strangely enough, she was one of the few memories of that part of his life that *didn't* hurt, but what the hell could have happened to her if her reputation didn't matter? He found it hard to believe that her character could have changed so much in six years, but then people *did* change. He certainly had.

'Is your reputation so very bad then, Miss Webster?'

'Not bad, just different.'

'Different?' He echoed the word, feeling a sudden urge to provoke her, to goad her into taking her veil off to confront him. 'Then am I the one taking a risk in being alone with you? Perhaps I ought to be concerned?'

'What?' She sounded faintly shocked. 'No! Don't be ridiculous.'

'Am I being? You have to admit, the evidence is against you. You're a lady and I'm a gentleman, in name anyway. If anyone knew we were alone together, then it would place us both in a somewhat compromising situation. I might feel obliged to make amends and propose.' He lifted an eyebrow as she made a gurgling sound in the back of her throat, though whether it was one of protest or horror he couldn't tell. 'I'm surprised your sister didn't think about that.'

'She wouldn't think of it.' There was a bitter edge to her voice all of a sudden. 'Lydia doesn't consider me a person who *can* be compromised.'

'Because?'

'Because she just doesn't.'

'There must be a reason.'

'There is.'

'That being?'

'I *don't* want to talk about it.'

'And I don't appreciate people walking into my house without an invitation.' He narrowed his eyes pointedly. 'The reason, if you please, Miss Webster. I believe you owe me that much.'

'This!'

The cry seemed to burst out of her as she wrenched her veil back and he finally understood. She was scowling, her jaw thrust forward and rigid with tension, but his eyes were immediately drawn to the right side of her face, to the crimson-red cheek and wide, puckered scar running all the way down from her hairline to the corner of her mouth, as if something had gashed the skin open and left it permanently and irrevocably damaged. He let his gaze rest there for a moment before passing it over the rest of her features, so like and yet unlike those of the girl he remembered. What had happened to her? Not just to her cheek, but to *her*? The animated glow had been replaced by an air of defiant and yet pervasive sadness. Even so, scar aside, the resemblance to her sister was still striking enough to make him flinch.

'As I said...' her lips curled derisively '...not a bad reputation, just not one that anyone cares to protect. I suppose they can't see the point.'

'Forgive me.' He half-lifted a hand, but she waved it aside.

'There's no need to apologise. I haven't made anyone faint yet, but I've come close. You reacted quite well, considering.'

'No, I shouldn't have flinched. It wasn't because of your scar.' He rubbed a hand over his eyes, as if by doing so he could make her resemblance to Lydia go away. 'You just look so much like her.'

'Like Lydia?' She blinked. 'She'd be horrified to hear that.'

'It's Frances, isn't it?'

'Yes.' Her jaw relaxed slightly. 'Do you remember me?'

'Of course. We were friends.'

'A long time ago. A lot's happened since then.'

'To both of us, I think.' He lifted his hand again, a placatory gesture this time. 'I'm sorry.'

'I know. That's what everyone says.'

'Ah.' There seemed to be a depth of pain behind those words. 'It doesn't help much, does it? Sympathy, I mean.'

'Not really. I appreciate the thought, but sympathy doesn't fix anything. I have a scar. It can't be wiped away or mended. It's just how it is.'

'And you just want to get on with your life?'

She looked surprised. 'Yes.'

'Meaning you don't want to talk about it?'

'No.'

'Very well. In that case, Miss Webster, I believe we ought to concentrate on your ankle instead. If you'll permit me to take a look?'

'I really don't think—'

'But I do,' he interrupted firmly. 'This is my farmhouse and I intend to see that you're properly tended to. Now it's either me or a doctor and, if you'd prefer for nobody to know where you've been, I'd suggest you pick me. I can only answer for my own discretion.'

'All right. You do it.'

'Then may I?'

She opened her mouth as if to protest some more and then nodded instead, sitting very still as he reached down and lifted her foot carefully on to the stool beside him.

'I'll need to remove your boot.' He looked up, already untying the laces, and she nodded again, her undamaged cheek a noticeably darker shade of pink than it had been a few moments before.

'There.' He slid her boot off and pressed his fingers around the swollen ankle, feeling the heat of the injury even through her stocking. 'It's not broken, but it's a nasty sprain. It needs binding, but we'll need to remove your undergarments first. I can do it if you...'

'No!' Her voice seemed to have leapt to a higher pitch. 'I'll do it. If you could just...?'

She made a spinning gesture and he turned around obediently, staring out into the hallway as he listened to the rustle of her petticoats behind. It was a strangely enticing sound, one he wasn't accustomed to hearing, though as a rule he considered himself immune to the charms of womankind. He'd never been as enamoured of the entire female sex as his brother, had always considered himself a one-woman man, or at least he *had* before he'd decided he was better off on his own. Still, he couldn't help but imagine the actions taking place just out of sight. She must be drawing her skirt up, untying her garter, rolling her stocking down...

'Ready.'

'Good.' He cleared his throat before he spoke, though his voice still sounded uncharacteristically husky as he spun round again, trying to focus all his attention on the injury. Her ankle was red and swollen, though he could see the lower part of her leg now, too. As calves went, it was surprisingly shapely for someone he remembered as having a boyish figure. She really *had* changed in that regard, he thought, wrapping the bandage gently around velvet-soft skin. When he'd left she'd still been a girl, whereas now—he risked a glance up at a distractingly full bosom—now she was undoubtedly a woman. The thought was somewhat alarming, making his blood stir and his pulse throb in a way he hadn't felt for...well, for a considerable amount of time. Years, in fact. The years it had taken for her to grow up...

He tied the ends of the bandage more tightly than he'd intended, irritated by his own errant thoughts. Had he gone quite mad living on his own? She was Lydia's sister! He didn't want anything to do with Lydia—and that included her family—and he definitely didn't want to be thinking about her sister's legs, stockinged or otherwise!

'What did you mean about being late?' He asked the question to distract himself.

'Mmm?' She jerked her head up, looking somewhat startled. She must have been chewing her lip, he noticed, because it looked fuller and redder all of a sudden. Wetter, too, coated with a sliver of moisture…

'In the yard you said that you had to go or you'd be late.' He cleared his throat again, more forcefully this time. 'Late for what?'

'Oh, I forgot. I meant for the tide. The sea will be up to the cliffs in another hour. If I don't hurry, then I won't make it back to Whitby before dark.'

'You mean you walked here along the beach?'

'Yes.' She seemed nonplussed by the question. 'It's not far, but I really ought to hurry.'

'It's a good mile and I doubt you could hobble as far as the village tonight. You shouldn't put any weight on that foot for a few days.'

'A few *days*?'

She muttered a swear word and his lips twitched in amusement. He couldn't have put it any better himself.

'Well, Miss Webster…'

'I'm sorry.' Her expression turned guilty. 'I shouldn't have said that.'

'I've heard worse. I believe I actually said worse earlier.'

'Oh, yes—' her expression cleared again '—so you did.'

'Then I suppose I can't blame you for running away. Between that and my lack of clothing, I must have appeared like some kind of monster.'

'I thought you were a convict.' She dug her teeth

down hard into her bottom lip, turning serious again. 'But perhaps you might let me borrow your carriage? Just to take me to the outskirts of Whitby. I'll make my own way from there.'

'I don't have a carriage, only horses, and you won't be making your own way anywhere. I might not look like much of a gentleman, but I hope I still have better manners than that. I presume you can ride?'

'Yes.'

'Then I'll escort you home.'

'No!' She sounded positively alarmed. 'I mean, there's no need for you to put yourself out. I can go on my own.'

'I'm sure you can, but I'd like to have my horse back afterwards.'

'Oh...yes, of course.' Her expression wavered uncertainly. 'Then perhaps we could wait until dark and you might leave me in the street?'

He lifted his eyebrows, regarding her dubiously. 'Embarrassed to be seen in my company, Miss Webster?'

'No-o, but the truth is that my parents don't know anything about my coming here. They'd think it was shockingly indiscreet for me to call on you.'

'They'd have a point. It's unfortunate that your sister doesn't share their scruples, but it won't be dark for another few hours. Won't your parents be concerned if you're not home before nightfall?'

'Oh, no.' She shook her head with conviction. 'They're used to me coming and going, and Lydia will cover for me, I'm sure, under the circumstances.'

'Quite.'

He glanced down at his hand, surprised to find it still resting on her foot. He must have kept it there without thinking and now the feel of her skin beneath his fingertips was making him even more unsettled. Positively uncomfortable, in fact. Maybe his sister-in-law was right and he *was* starved of companionship. Not that this was the kind of companionship she'd likely had in mind. Even sitting so close to a woman now was making his collar feel uncomfortably restrictive. Or perhaps he was just used to wearing loose farm clothes. In either case, he ought to let go of Frances's foot. Now that he'd bound the injury, he really shouldn't still be touching her at all, especially when he was so acutely aware of the shapeliness of the legs beneath her petticoats. Except that pulling his hand away now would only draw more attention to it…

'Lydia only wants to talk to you.' Her voice sounded strangely breathless all of a sudden.

'So she sent you with a request that I've already refused, twice, without either your parents' permission or any care for your reputation?'

She shuffled in her chair, the movement of her foot beneath his fingertips causing an immediate, and this time unmistakable, reaction in his lower body.

'I didn't know that it was twice, but she said that she just wants to explain…about her marriage.'

He was actually glad to feel a rush of anger, dampening his other responses and finally giving him an excuse to pull his hand away. 'You mean to explain why she married someone else within a month of my leaving? *Can* she explain that, Miss Webster? Or are you going to tell me it was just her way of grieving?'

'She only wants…'

'She wants a title!'

He hadn't intended to shout, though he realised he must have as a heavy silence descended over the room, punctuated only by the sound of Meg's panting as she lifted her head from her paws and looked curiously between them. Miss Webster herself didn't say anything to either confirm or contradict his statement, only hunching her shoulders and dropping her gaze as if she wished she were somewhere else.

'I apologise.' He felt a stab of guilt for his outburst. 'But you shouldn't have come. Why did you? Just because she's your sister and she asked you to?'

'No...' she kept her gaze fixed on the floor '...but I couldn't refuse. I have my own secrets.'

'And your sister knows them, but your parents don't?'

She gave an imperceptible nod and he leaned backwards, mentally denouncing his former betrothed with a varied assortment of unchivalrous epithets. She might have been the last straw that had caused him to run away six years ago, but at that moment he was more than prepared to blame her for everything.

'Very well, then, we'll wait until dark if that's what you want. After that, I'll take you home out of sight of your parents and we'll say no more about it. As for Lydia, you can tell her my answer is and will forever remain no. Whatever she has to say to me, I've no desire to hear it. She can keep her letters and explanations, Miss Webster. She's put me off women for ever.'

Chapter Four

Frances winced, gritting her teeth against the pain as Arthur helped her into a saddle. Fortunately, the farm-yard had a mounting block or she didn't think she could have managed even with his strong hands around her waist, guiding her upwards. For a big man, he was sur-prisingly gentle, but it was hard enough limping, never mind climbing on to a horse. Much as she hated to admit it, he'd been right. She could never have made it back to Whitby on her own.

'Aren't we leaving a bit early?' She looked anxiously up at the sky. It was evening, but still as bright as mid-day. 'I thought we were waiting for dusk?'

'I have another engagement.' He slid her injured foot into its stirrup before quickly mounting his own horse. 'If you want to delay your return to Whitby, then you'll need to accompany me.'

Frances looked across at him with trepidation. It ap-peared to be more of an ultimatum than a question and she wasn't sure what answer to give anyway. They'd hardly spoken more than half-a-dozen words after he'd denounced her sister and, apparently, the rest of wom-ankind with her, sounding even more bitter about Lydia than she'd expected, so much so that he'd practically denounced her as a fortune hunter. He could hardly have given his answer any more definitively, though she suspected that would probably change if he ever *did* find himself in the same room with her. Her sister's personal charms rarely failed to achieve their desired result, though as to whether she'd get a chance to use them was another matter. Even if he hadn't been quite so adamant, according to local gossip, Lord Scorborough rarely left his estate. Which made the fact that they were on their way to some kind of engagement doubly surprising.

Then again, Frances thought, able to study him more closely now that she had her veil pulled down firmly over her face again, perhaps she ought not to be surprised by anything he did any more. Nothing about him was what she'd expected, including his reaction to her facial scarring. For the first few dreadful moments it had felt like Leo all over again, with him recoiling in horror at the sight of her, but Arthur's reason had been the very opposite of what she was used to. He hadn't seemed repelled by the scar itself, only by her resemblance to Lydia. It made a refreshing change. Not many people commented upon *that* any more.

Even so, she'd been taken aback by the changes in *him*. He bore only a passing physical resemblance to the slim and genteel man she remembered. He seemed— he surely was—bigger, as if he'd grown inches both upwards and outwards. The old Arthur had been tall and broad-shouldered, but still slender with pale, well-manicured hands and neatly trimmed, shoulder-length hair. There had been a slightly hesitant, self-effacing quality about him, too, whereas this man walked with an air of palpable confidence. The new Arthur was tanned and calloused and...well...rugged. There was really no other word to describe it. He looked as though he spent most of his life working outdoors and had the muscular physique to prove it.

She looked him up and down, struggling to reconcile the two versions. By his own admission, the new Arthur didn't speak or behave much like a gentleman any more, but at least he was dressed like one now, even if his jacket was more of the smart and functional rather than the formal-dinner variety. On the other hand, his boots had been repolished, his muddied shirt replaced and his cravat tied with elegant simplicity. He'd even shaved, though the effect was to give his jaw an even squarer and more chiselled appearance than when it had been bristling with stubble. All of his features seemed more defined somehow, as if her blurred memory of him had drifted into sharper focus. He looked like a man of energy and resolve, one who wouldn't bother himself with social engagements. All of which begged the question, *where* were they going?

'What kind of engagement?' she asked finally.

'Dinner.' He whistled for Meg. 'I hope you're hungry.'

'Dinner?' She dropped her reins again, appalled. She never went to dinner parties any more and, even if she had, how could he expect her to go to one *with* him? Never mind that seeing him again seemed to be having a strangely unsettling effect on her digestive system, but the whole point of waiting until dark was for them *not* to be seen together!

'Can't I wait here?'

'And muck out the pigsty?' He frowned over his shoulder. 'Why would you want to stay here?'

'Why?' She stared at him in consternation. There

were so many reasons. Surely he could guess a few of them! Besides the fact that a gentleman oughtn't to make such impertinent comments or ask a lady why she wanted to do anything! The old Arthur wouldn't have, but this new version seemed to have lost all of his tact along with his manners.

'You're starting to sound like an echo, Miss Webster. I repeat, why would you want to stay here?'

'Because I'm not dressed for dinner, for a start. Look, I'm covered in mud!' She gestured at her skirts and then blushed, belatedly realising that she was directing his attention straight to her posterior.

'So you are.' His eyes seemed to spark briefly before he lifted them back to her face. 'However, our hosts won't mind. They won't tell anyone they've seen you either, if that's what you're worried about.'

'But *who* are they? Do I know them?'

'I've no idea who you do or don't know, but I'm referring to my brother and his wife.'

'You mean we're dining at Amberton Castle?'

'Yes, and before you ask again, no, I'm not leaving you here alone.' He gave her a faintly sardonic look. 'There's really no need to worry, they don't bite. Or at least Violet doesn't. Lance has always been a bit more unpredictable.'

'But I don't go to dinner parties!' She had the horrible suspicion that she was wailing.

'Never?'

'No!' She shook her head, ardently hoping that he wasn't about to demand an explanation for that as well. Surely the reasons were obvious. It wasn't easy eating under a veil, but it was still preferable to being either ignored or gawped at. Dinner parties, like most social gatherings, were like a slow torture for her. Couldn't he guess that? But he only regarded her speculatively for a few moments before tugging on his reins and directing his horse towards the gate.

'Then you'll just have to make an exception this evening.' The words carried back over his shoulder. 'It's easier to ride straight to Whitby afterwards than come back and collect you.'

'But…' She stared helplessly after him, torn between a range of conflicting emotions. On the one hand, she'd always wanted to see the faux medieval castle that Arthur's father had famously built for his mother, though she'd never gone to any of the balls to which her family had always been invited. She'd been too young before her accident, and afterwards…well, balls were even worse than dinner parties. She could wear her veil more easily, but it made her stand out like a sore thumb, too. Never mind the chances of running into Leo. But she *did* want to see the castle, even if it would be more than her life was worth if Lydia ever found out. She'd turn green with jealousy and then bombard her with questions forever afterwards.

Ultimately, however, it wasn't her decision to make. She could hardly stay at Arthur's house and she couldn't ride off with his horse either. Which meant that she had no choice but to go with him. Just as he knew she didn't.

'We'll ride over the Moors.' He didn't as much as turn his head to make sure she was following. 'The weather's fine and it's a quicker route.'

That was one consolation, she supposed, picking up her reins again. She preferred the Moors to the coastal road. The wildness of the terrain made her feel closer to the elements, more a part of nature itself, where appearances didn't matter. There were also fewer people up on the tops and those few were more preoccupied with their work than with staring at her.

They rode steadily up the hillside on to a brown-and-purple plateau of heather and gorse interspersed with patches of cottongrass, tiny white flowers that gave the incongruous impression of snowdrifts in the middle of summer. Arthur rode ahead until the trail widened and then moved over to let her ride alongside, although he still didn't speak.

That was another difference about him, she realised. The old Arthur would have made polite conversation, would have mentioned the lovely weather they were having at least, but the new version seemed to prefer stoical silence. Oddly enough, however, she didn't feel uncomfortable with it. They seemed to be breaking all the rules of polite behaviour today, but somehow it felt refreshing and natural. Liberating even, with just the calls of a few seagulls and curlews gliding overhead to disturb the peace. The evening sun gave her a sense of well-being, too, warming her face through her veil as she tipped her head back and drew in a deep breath.

'Oh!' She glanced sideways for a moment and then came to an abrupt halt. The view behind and below them was magnificent, as if she were looking at three different landscapes at once: heathland, farmland and sea all merging seamlessly into one harmonious whole. There had to be a hundred different colours before her. 'I should come up here more often. It's breathtaking.'

'It is.' She heard him stop a few paces ahead, though when he spoke his voice sounded grave. 'It's hard to imagine a more beautiful place anywhere in the world, but I remember being desperate to escape. Even when I came back, I only wanted to leave again.'

She tore her gaze away from the scenery and looked

towards him in surprise. The sun was dipping towards the horizon now and in the gloaming light his eyes seemed to shine like amber jewels, blending in with the heathland around them, though they looked oddly expressionless, too. His manner and tone were jarring. He was talking about the nine months when he'd been away, she realised, when everyone had thought that he'd drowned, but his words made it sound as if he'd left on purpose, as if what had happened to him hadn't been an accident, as if he'd never wanted to come back. But why would he have wanted to leave, especially when he'd been engaged, albeit in secret, to Lydia? What could have made him so desperate?

'Escape?' She tried to keep her tone casual. 'I heard that you lost your memory when you fell off your sailing boat and were picked up by a whaling vessel.'

'Indeed?' His expression didn't change. 'That sounds exciting, but I'm afraid it's wrong in almost every respect. I didn't fall off anything, I didn't lose my memory and I rather like whales.'

'Oh.' There were so many implications to the statement that she could only focus on the last and most obvious one. 'You mean you've seen a whale?'

'Yes, to the north of Scotland, but they're no danger to us and I've too much respect for the sea than to hurt one of its most noble creatures.'

'I'd love to see one. I found a seal colony once, further down the coast towards Robin Hood's Bay. The whole beach was full of mothers and pups.'

'Ah.' He shook his head regretfully. 'Seals I'm not so fond of.'

'Why not? They're adorable.'

'They also bite through fishing nets, which need to

be sewn back together by hand. It's time-consuming, tedious and extremely pungent.'

'How do you know?'

'Because I *was* picked up by a vessel when I went overboard, only it wasn't a whaler, just a fishing boat from Aberdeen.'

'Oh.' She felt a murmur of disquiet. *Went overboard.* He'd spoken the words plainly enough, though he'd already denied having fallen. In which case...had he jumped? But, no, her mind shied away from that idea, surely he couldn't have.

'They took me on as a deckhand.'

'Meaning you worked on deck?'

'As the title implies.'

'But...' she drew her brows together '...you're a viscount.'

'True, but even viscounts have hands they can work with. When they're allowed to, that is. Believe it or not, I enjoyed the experience.'

'Enjoyed?' she echoed incredulously. How could he speak so calmly about it when she—*they*, she quickly corrected herself—had all been so worried? 'But we all thought you were dead! Then when you came back, we thought you must have been picked up by a whaler and carried north to the Arctic. That was the only possible explanation for why you were gone for so long.'

'Press-ganging?' He lifted an eyebrow, but she ignored the sarcasm, spurring her horse a few steps closer to confront him.

'If you were picked up by a fishing boat, then why didn't you come home straight away?'

'I just told you.' The eyebrow lowered again, joining its companion in a heavy, black line as his expression seemed to harden. 'I told you I didn't want to come home. I wanted to be lost at sea for a while.'

'So you deliberately abandoned your ship to join the crew of a fishing boat?'

'Something like that.'

'What about Lydia? You were engaged. Why didn't you want to come back to her?'

'I had a feeling she'd be all right. And she was, *wasn't* she?'

Frances felt a momentary misgiving. There was a taunting edge to his voice, almost as if he knew the truth about Lydia's other flirtations and was daring her to contradict him. But she had to. For the sake of sisterly loyalty, she had to.

'She mourned for you.'

'Yet it took her less than a week to engage herself to another man.'

'Ye-es.' She winced inwardly. There was no denying that part, though she'd hoped he hadn't known about it. 'But that doesn't mean she didn't care.'

'Doesn't it? Would *you* forget a man so quickly, Miss Webster? Presuming you truly loved him in the first place, that is?'

'No.' She found herself averting her gaze despite the presence of her veil between them. 'But Lydia isn't someone who can be on her own.'

'So I noticed. In fact, it was just about the last thing I noticed before I left.'

'What?' Her eyes shot back to his face. 'You mean you knew about John Baird?'

His lips twisted into something resembling a sneer. 'Not Baird, no. The man I saw her with was much younger.'

'Oh, yes, how silly of me, I meant…'

'Don't lie for her, Miss Webster, and don't feel bad for me either. I'm glad to know I wasn't the only man she was stringing along, though just out of interest, how many men *was* she secretly engaged to?'

Frances lifted her chin, resenting the accusation no matter how fair it was. 'You were the only one.'

'So she just kept a few suitors in reserve?' He gave a cynical-sounding laugh. 'A wise precaution as it turned out.'

'It wasn't like that.'

'If you say so, though it hardly matters any more.' He turned his horse about, digging his heels into the animal's flanks. 'In any case, I'd prefer that we kept this conversation between ourselves. Now come on, we don't want to be late.'

Chapter Five

They lapsed into silence again, though this time it felt more brooding than companionable. Frances let her horse fall behind, her mind whirling with everything Arthur had just told her. All this time, she'd assumed that what had happened to him had been an accident, but now it seemed that he hadn't just left deliberately. He'd *never* wanted to come back.

Worse still, he'd known about Lydia's betrayal. In six years, the idea had never occurred to her, but now it seemed the two things were inextricably linked. The bitterness in his voice suggested as much, though surely Lydia's behaviour on its own wouldn't have caused him to do anything quite so dramatic. He might simply have broken their engagement, not run away to sea. Yet he *had* run away, leaving his home, his responsibilities and his position as heir of Amberton Castle, so that everyone, his own family included, had assumed he'd had some kind of accident and drowned. His father had dropped dead on being told of the news. The thought made her shudder. No matter why he'd run away, the consequences had to be a terrible weight on his shoulders. No wonder Arthur wasn't the man she remembered. No wonder he didn't want to see Lydia again either.

* * *

After twenty minutes or so they descended into a valley, joining a bigger track that led towards a large, Gothic-looking mansion decorated with crenellations and turrets and arched, oriel windows, all festooned with cascades of trailing ivy. Frances caught her breath in amazement. Amberton Castle looked so authentically medieval that it was hard to believe it was all an illusion, a forty-year-old building designed to look like a real medieval stronghold and a royal one at that. Up close, it was just as impressive as its reputation suggested and even more hauntingly beautiful than she'd imagined. By rights it belonged to Arthur and yet he chose not to live there, a fact that only deepened the mystery around him. How could anyone choose *not* to live in such a fairy tale place?

At last they rode beneath a granite archway and she tugged on her veil, making sure it was firmly in place before they arrived.

'You should take that off.' Arthur leapt down from his horse and stalked towards her, lifting his hands up to help her dismount. 'You don't need it.'

'Yes, I do.' She slid down into his arms, vividly and uncomfortably aware of how broad his chest was in comparison to hers. Leo had never made her feel quite so puny. Then again, he'd never made her legs feel so unsteady either, though that was surely just an after-effect of the ride.

'No, you don't. Take it off.'

'No!' She stiffened at his imperative tone. He'd seemed sympathetic earlier, but clearly his mood had deteriorated during the ride. 'I prefer to wear it.'

'There's no need to hide.'

'I'm *not* hiding and it's none of your business. I can wear what I want!'

'There's nothing to be embarrassed about or ashamed of.'

'I didn't say I was either!' She lifted her hands to his shoulders and shoved, but he appeared immovable. 'And I don't recall asking for your views on the subject!'

'True, but you—'

'Arthur!'

A cheerful-sounding voice interrupted them, closely followed by its owner. Frances twisted her head away from her infuriating companion and gasped at the sight of his twin brother. With his neat, shoulder-length hair and smartly dressed appearance, Lance Amberton looked almost exactly the way she remembered Arthur, more like him than he was. The effect was so confusing that it rendered her momentarily speechless.

'I was starting to wonder where you'd got to.' If he'd witnessed them arguing, he gave no sign of it. 'But I see you've brought an extra guest for dinner, Arthur. A masked woman, no less.'

His mouth spread into a wicked-looking grin and it was immediately obvious who was who again. The old Arthur had never smiled like that and the new Arthur didn't appear capable of it. As far as Frances could tell, he didn't smile at all.

Still, she couldn't help but feel glad of his famil-iar presence beside her. She'd never met the notorious Lancelot Amberton before, but even as a girl she'd heard rumours about his wild behaviour, especially where women were concerned. She remembered Lydia being warned in no uncertain terms to stay away from him, though it was hard to believe anything particularly shocking of the eminently respectable-looking gentleman bowing in front of her.

'Captain Lance Amberton.' Arthur's voice seemed to hold a note of warning as he introduced them. 'Allow me to present Miss Webster.'

'*Webster?*'

'Miss *Frances* Webster.'

'Ah.' A fleeting look of horror turned into one of unmistakable relief. 'Then I'm honoured to make your acquaintance, Miss Webster. I'm sure that my wife will be delighted, too, only she's napping at the moment and I'd prefer not to wake her until she's ready. It won't be long, I'm sure.'

'My sister-in-law is expecting her first child in the autumn,' Arthur explained, 'and it's turned my recalcitrant brother into a mother hen.'

'Mother hen?' Lance shook his head as if he were genuinely aggrieved. 'If you're implying that I love my wife, then you're absolutely right, I do, and I refuse to apologise for it.' He extended his arm with a flourish. 'Now please allow me to escort you inside, Miss Webster. I believe I'd much rather talk with you than with this heartless brute.'

'She can't walk.' Arthur's voice cut across him.

'I can limp,' Frances protested.

'You shouldn't put any weight on your ankle.'

'It's not th—'

She'd barely started the sentence before he lifted her up again, ignoring her spluttered protests as he carried her across the courtyard and over the threshold of the castle, much to his brother's obvious amusement.

'I twisted my ankle,' she explained, profoundly glad of the veil hiding her flaming cheeks as they entered a large, oak-panelled and high-ceilinged hallway.

'Well, that explains it.' Lance followed behind them. He held a cane and walked with a slight limp, too, she noticed. 'I'm no stranger to injured limbs myself, Miss Webster, though I've never seen my brother behave so gallantly before.'

'I'm just being practical.' Arthur sounded gruff.

'I still don't need to be carried around like some damsel in distress.' She glared at him through her veil. 'Once is bad enough. Twice in one day is insulting. I could have managed perfectly well on my own.'

'In your opinion.'

'It's best not to argue with him once he gets an idea in his head,' Lance interceded. 'He's the most stubborn man you're ever likely to meet. These days anyway.'

'I'd still prefer to stand on my own two feet, injured or otherwise.'

'As you wish.' Arthur deposited her firmly, but unceremoniously, on the floor. 'Is that better?'

'Much.'

'Miss Webster.' Lance gave them both a distinctly penetrating look. 'Might I take your accoutrement? Our staff all appear to be hiding.'

'Yes, thank you.'

She started to unfasten her cloak and then felt another pair of hands take over, gently peeling away the folds and then lifting the garment from her shoulders. She half-twisted her head and felt her blush deepen. Arthur appeared to be utterly engrossed in the task, yet equally determined not to look at her.

'Apparently my brother wants to do everything this evening.' Lance gave something resembling a smirk, placing his cane in front of him and resting his hands on top. 'You seem to bring out his chivalrous side, Miss Webster. I applaud you.'

She cleared her throat, unable to think of an answer to that, gesturing towards her skirts instead.

'I ought to apologise for my appearance. I had a fall earlier and my dress came off somewhat the worse for wear.'

'Hence the ankle, I presume?' Lance nodded as if there was nothing more natural than arriving at dinner covered in dirty splotches. 'How unfortunate, but I take it that's how the two of you met? I do hope you're going to tell me my brother came to your rescue.'

'Yes, in a manner of speaking.' She untied her bonnet and pulled it away, taking care not to disturb the veil pinned to her hair, then passed that to Arthur as well. He took it and frowned, looking as though he were on the verge of saying something else before turning on his heel abruptly, carrying her things off to an anteroom.

'I heard that the house looked like a castle...' Frances looked around at the crests and tapestries covering the walls with admiration '...but I never expected anything like this.'

'Haven't you visited before?' Lance appeared unconcerned by her veil. 'Surely we've invited you to our summer balls?'

'Oh, yes, you've been very kind. My parents attend every year, but I don't go to balls.'

'Ah well, then, you're in luck. We're having a garden party instead this year. My wife is a stickler for tradition and insists upon our doing something, but I refuse to let her dance in her condition. I keep telling her to rest and she keeps telling me to stop worrying. We're quite the pair.'

He gave a strained-sounding laugh and Frances found herself wanting to offer some kind of reassurance. What was it he'd said earlier? *I love my wife and I refuse to apologise for it...* Apparently he was genuinely worried for her. Beneath the smile, there was a tightness about his face that spoke of some persistent anxiety.

'When is the baby due?'

'October, although I hope for sooner.'

'You do?' She couldn't conceal her surprise. It wasn't usual to hope for an early birth.

He nodded, his gaze flickering towards the staircase. 'My wife has a particularly small build. I worry about how she'll manage.'

'Oh, I see.' Frances drew her brows together sympathetically. Now she thought of it, she remembered once seeing Violet Amberton from a distance and being surprised by her excessively small frame. It was no wonder that her much-larger husband was worried. 'But you know, my sister has a tiny waist, too. Everyone was anxious when she was about to give birth, but it was all over in a couple of hours. She had a big, healthy boy and was out of bed in a week.'

'Then I'll hope for the same.' He took her hand and pressed it warmly. 'I appreciate the comfort, Miss Webster.'

'Lydia has a son?'

Frances cringed at the sound of Arthur's voice behind her. She hadn't heard his footsteps and the last thing she'd wanted was for him to overhear her talking about her nephew. Now that he had, however, there was no point in concealing the truth. 'Yes. You didn't know?'

'No. My interest in your sister ended a long time ago. I heard of her marriage, that's all.'

'Well, his name's George. Georgie.'

'You sound fond of him.' The words sounded faintly accusing.

'I am. My sister moved back to Whitby after she was

widowed and now we all live together in my parents' house. It's a pleasant arrangement, although sometimes I wonder if there are too many women for one little boy.'

'You're afraid of spoiling him?'

She hesitated before answering. It was hard not to lavish attention upon a three-year-old boy who'd lost his father and whose mother was obsessed with the idea of finding a new husband, but it seemed disloyal to say so.

'Perhaps, but I suppose that's preferable to neglect.'

'As long as it doesn't become stifling. Too much attention can be as bad as too little.'

'Indeed?' The solemnity of his expression made her hackles rise. 'And you have experience of raising boys, I suppose?'

'None at all, although I do have experience of being one.'

'And were *you* over-indulged, Lord Scorborough?'

'I wouldn't say so, no.'

'Were you stifled, then?'

There was a flash of something in his eyes, something piercing and intense like pain, at the same moment as a female voice spoke from the direction of the staircase.

'Lance?'

The man in question rushed across the hallway, his expression turning instantly from bewildered perplexity to tender concern as Frances watched in surprise. The Lance Amberton she'd heard rumours about had been wild and dangerous. This man appeared to be the world's most devoted husband. Evidently both brothers had changed.

'Good evening, Violet.' Arthur sounded as formal as

if he were presenting her to the Queen. 'Might I introduce Miss Frances Webster?'

'Miss Webster.'

The woman broke into a wide smile as she took her husband's arm and walked towards them. At ground level, Frances could see that her memory hadn't exaggerated. Violet Amberton was without doubt the tiniest woman she'd ever laid eyes on, with white-blonde hair and disproportionately huge eyes in an amiable-looking face.

'I'm sorry to impose upon your evening, Mrs Amberton.' She inclined her head, trying to convey a sense of apology through her veil. 'I'm afraid that I sprained my ankle and Lord Scorborough here rescued me.'

'And now he's brought you to join us for dinner?' The woman's gaze flickered between them, though her expression was inquisitive rather than calculating. 'I'm so pleased. If we join forces, we might be able to stop these two talking about mining all evening.'

'You mean you *don't* find iron smelting as fascinating as we do?' Lance put a hand to his heart. 'You wound me, my love.'

'Oh, but I'd never want to do that.' She leant her head against his shoulder playfully. 'But now I expect dinner is ready. I do appreciate your coming to dine with us, Miss Webster. If you can start a new topic of conversation, I'll be forever indebted to you.'

'I'm afraid that my dress…' Frances gestured downwards again.

'Oh, dear.' The tiny woman looked sympathetic. 'What a shame. I'd offer to lend you something, but I'm afraid you might find my clothes a little on the short side. Not to mention too wide.' She patted her bulging stomach and laughed. 'But it truly doesn't matter. I'm just delighted to have another woman to talk to. Please call me Violet.'

'Then you must call me Frances.'

'Then that's settled. Here.' Arthur extended his arm in a manner that was less of an invitation than a command, but Frances took it anyway, too touched by the other woman's offer of friendship to spoil the moment.

'Excellent.' Lance clapped his hands together. 'Now let's eat. I don't know about anyone else, but I'm famished.'

Chapter Six

Arthur swallowed a generous mouthful of port, wondering why he'd ever thought that bringing the woman to Amberton Castle was a good idea in the first place. Besides the inconvenience to himself, if his brother didn't stop giving him pointed looks across the table then he'd do more than kick him under it. Happy as he was to take Lance's mind off its usual preoccupation of worrying about Violet, his unexpected appearance with Miss Webster wasn't something he cared to discuss. Even with his brother. Even when the circumstances positively cried out for an explanation. Even now that the ladies had adjourned to the parlour and he had the distinct feeling that he wasn't going to be able to avoid the subject any longer.

'So…' Lance pushed a wooden-and-mother-of-pearl inlaid box towards him, opening the lid to reveal a row of thick, brown cigars. 'Are you going to tell me what's going on or do I have to guess?'

'There's nothing to tell.' Arthur selected the nearest cigar and lit it with a candle. 'But you can guess if you like. That ought to be entertaining.'

'All right.' Lance leaned back in his chair, inhaling

thoughtfully before blowing a cloud of smoke into the air above his head. 'In that case, I can only assume that you've decided to get revenge on the nefarious Lydia Webster by developing a tendresse for her younger sister. I imagine this is just one of a series of private liaisons.'

'Not very private since I've brought her here.'

'Ah, but naturally you've brought her here for my inspection and approval.'

'*Your* approval?'

'Knowing me to be an excellent judge of the female character, yes. I further presume that you're eloping in secret, which explains why she hides her face even while eating.'

'There's no tendresse.' Arthur snorted. 'This is the first time I've seen her in six years.'

'Then you ought to be more careful. Riding around the county with young, unmarried women is more my old style than yours.'

'It's nothing like that. She really did sprain her ankle.'

'Ah. Pity.'

'*Pity?*' Arthur almost spluttered on his cigar. 'She's Lydia's sister!'

'And we're twins, but that doesn't make us the same person. I like her.'

'As I recall, there aren't many women in the world you don't like.'

'*Past* tense and no offence taken, since you're obviously sensitive on the subject. I'm a happily married man these days, as you very well know.'

'Yes, I do and I apologise.' Arthur grimaced and then frowned at the table. It had been a low blow, reminding Lance of his misspent past, especially when he was now so utterly devoted to Violet. Why *was* he being so sensitive?

'Anyway,' Lance went on, 'there were a *few* women I didn't like. I don't recall ever saying anything positive about Lydia Webster, for example.'

'True. You called her a cold-hearted fortune hunter.'

'There you go then, but, married or not, I can still appreciate a woman of intelligence. I've no idea what your Miss Webster and Violet were talking about, but I don't remember Lydia ever taking such a keen interest in poetry.'

'Novels. They were discussing the works of Jane Austen.'

'Didn't she write poetry?'

'No, and it's not *my* Miss Webster.'

'Noticed that eventually, did you?' Lance chuckled. 'Does she look like Lydia?'

'Uncannily, except that Frances has a scar on one cheek. She had some kind of accident a few years ago.'

'And that's why she covers her face?' Lance sobered instantly. 'Then I'm sorry for joking.'

'You weren't to know. She hasn't told me what happened.'

'But you've seen it?'

'Yes.' Arthur blew a cloud of smoke out to hide his expression. Lance's gaze seemed altogether too perceptive all of a sudden.

'Maybe she doesn't like to talk about it.'

'She doesn't, but there's still no need for her to cover up like that. It's only a scar.'

'But it's her choice whether or not to show it. If she feels more comfortable wearing a veil, then it's none of our business.' Lance shrugged. 'Besides, I'd have thought you'd be glad she covers her face if she looks so much like Lydia.'

Arthur puffed out another smoke ring thoughtfully.

That was true. He ought to feel glad. Surely the last thing he'd want was to look at an almost mirror-image of Lydia all evening, yet he actually wanted to see Frances's face again. Why? It wasn't as if he felt any residual attachment to his former fiancée, that much he was certain of, but the fact that Frances felt the need to cover her scar bothered him. Was she embarrassed or had she been made to feel so unattractive? He didn't want her to feel that way…

'In any case,' Lance continued, 'you still haven't explained what you're doing with her. Don't tell me you found her limping around the Moors all on her own?'

'No, she came to the farm.'

'Your farm? Why?'

'I'll give you two guesses.'

'Lydia sent her?' Lance let out a low whistle. 'You have to give the woman credit for nerve. She's still fishing for a title, then?'

'So it would seem.'

'Well, it's taken her long enough. She's been widowed for almost a year. To be honest, I expected her to try something before.'

'She has. She's written twice asking me to meet her.' Arthur raised his cigar to his lips and then pulled it away again. 'How do you know how long she's been widowed? I didn't think you were so interested in Whitby society.'

'I pay attention to some things, especially things that might involve my family. I make it my business to know when my brother's being hunted.'

'Well, she's not going to catch me.'

'Don't be so sure. Women like that know how to get what they want and they don't give up easily. Only why on earth did she send her sister to you?'

'No idea. She must have thought a personal appeal would be more effective.'

'But she didn't visit you herself?'

'No. Too worried about her reputation apparently.'

'Thank goodness for that. So what message are you going to send back?'

'I said that I've already given my answer.'

'Mmmm…' Lance sounded pensive '…just stay on your guard. I wouldn't put anything past Lydia Web— what's her married name again?'

'Baird.'

'Lydia Baird. She's just the type to try to catch you in a compromising situation. Be careful she doesn't turn up on your doorstep.'

'One look at the farm and she'd probably change her mind.'

'It might be too late by then.'

'Which would be *her* problem, not mine. I won't be tricked into doing the honourable thing.'

'Won't you? We both know you're not as bad-tempered as you make out.'

'I'm incredibly bad-tempered and I refuse to be trapped into anything I don't want. I've lived enough of my life that way.'

'Glad to hear it.' Lance nodded approvingly. 'You do like her, though.'

'Lydia? Don't be ridiculous.'

'Nice try. You know perfectly well I meant Frances. You were looking in her direction all the way through dinner and you've just proven that you were listening to her conversation as well. You know you can't fool me when it comes to women.'

'Apparently I can since you're so far off the mark.'

'So you're saying that you *don't* like her?'

'I don't like any woman. I've learnt my lesson in that regard and it was a pretty damned painful one, too. From now on, I intend to leave the entire female sex alone and I'd appreciate them returning the favour. I only feel responsible for Frances, for tonight anyway.'

'If you say so.' Lance pushed his chair back and heaved himself to his feet. 'In any case, I've had a very enjoyable evening and so has Violet, I can tell. If I weren't *so far off the mark* I'd suggest you bring her again next week.'

'The next time she invades my privacy, injures herself and then compels me to take care of her, you mean?'

'You never know… So what's the plan for tonight? I presume you're taking her back to Whitby?'

'Yes, under cover of darkness. She insisted.'

'You know that's not the time most respectable ladies ask to be taken home?'

'Quite. Only she doesn't want her parents to find out where she's been. I think she intends for me to deposit her on the outskirts of Whitby and then hobble the rest of the way. It's ludicrous, of course. I'll have to see her to the door.'

'The same door where her sister lives?' Lance shook his head. 'Absolutely not. You might as well stick your head in the lion's mouth. Let me take her back in the carriage instead. If she needs an excuse, then she can say she twisted her ankle out walking and I found her. It's not such a long way from the truth, but this way you don't have to go and there's no risk of bumping into you-know-who.'

Arthur nodded absently. It was a better idea than his own, he supposed, though he felt strangely reluctant to give up the prospect of a night-time ride with

Frances. Despite the inconvenience, he realised he'd actually been looking forward to it...

'Ladies!' Lance swung the drawing-room door open with a flourish. 'I hope you haven't missed us too dreadfully.'

'Woefully, my love.' Violet laughed over her shoulder. She was sitting beside Frances on a red-velvet sofa, though only she turned around to look at them. 'But we managed to bear it somehow.'

'Minx.' Lance limped to his customary armchair. 'So what have you two been talking about?'

'Jewellery. Frances was just telling me that she makes it.'

'Indeed, Miss Webster?' Arthur moved towards the fireplace, resting one arm along the mantel so that he had a sideways view of her. Frances's eyes appeared to be riveted on the carpet, though he was pleased to see that she'd finally pulled back her veil, a development he could only put down to Violet's kind-hearted influence.

'Yes.' She looked faintly embarrassed to be the focus of attention. 'From the jet I find on the beach. Cameos and beads and brooches. Anything I can think of really.'

'Jet?' Lance hoisted his damaged leg on to a footstool. 'You mean the black stones that wash up on the shoreline?'

'Yes. That is, sometimes they wash up. Most of the time you can find them sticking out of the cliff face, where it gets worn away by the tide. Jet's a hard rock, but it's good for sculpting and it polishes beautifully. The lustre never fades and it's become very popular since the Queen started wearing black.'

'I'd love to see a few of your pieces.' Violet sat forward eagerly. 'Are you wearing any?'

'Oh, no.' She looked faintly startled by the question. 'I don't wear them myself. I used to make them as gifts, but recently I've...'

'Recently you've...?' Arthur prompted her as she faltered mid-sentence.

'Recently I've started selling a few pieces.' Her voice held a note of defiance as she lifted her chin to look him straight in the eye. 'You look very stern standing up there.'

'He never sits down in here...' Lance gave an exaggerated sigh '...but it's no good telling him, Miss Webster. Believe me, I've tried enough times.'

'I prefer to stand.'

'That's not the reason.'

'It's the reason I *choose* to give.'

Arthur lifted an eyebrow at his brother's challenging tone. They both knew exactly why he refused to sit down in the drawing room, in particular why he refused to take his father's old chair by the fireplace, but he had absolutely no intention of discussing the matter again now.

'Lance.' Violet gave her husband a pointed look. 'Arthur can stand on his head if he chooses.'

'Just as long as he knows he doesn't need to.'

'I do.'

Arthur gave his brother one last scowl and then turned his attention back to Miss Webster. Her comment about selling jewellery hadn't shocked him as she'd seemed to think that it might, but it did strike him as odd that she didn't wear any examples of it herself. On closer inspection, he noticed that all of her clothes were plain and unembellished, without any ornament at all, as if she were trying to draw as little attention to herself as possible. The image of her straw bonnet floated back into his mind.

'That's where I've seen you.' He snapped his fingers. 'Down on the shore collecting stones. You wear a straw bonnet and carry a wicker basket.'

'Yes.' She looked taken aback. 'But...when? I've never see you.'

'You said that I've changed.'

'True, but then I suppose we both have. We might easily have crossed paths and not recognised each other.'

'Perhaps we have...' He found himself almost smiling and cleared his throat hastily. 'Or perhaps I've just seen you from my boat.'

'You still sail?' She looked surprised again. 'Didn't your experiences put you off? I mean, after so long on a fishing boat...'

She clamped her lips together suddenly, as if she'd just remembered she was supposed to keep their conversation between themselves, and he turned his face towards the fire, grimacing inwardly as an awkward silence descended over the room.

As far as the rest of the world knew, what had happened to him was still a mystery, not to mention an accident. There were rumours, but since he'd neither confirmed nor denied any of them, speculation was *all* that they were. Only Violet, Lance and now Miss Webster knew the truth—and now Lance knew that he'd told her, too. What would he read into that? He could already feel his brother's eyes boring into the back of his skull. And *why* had he told her? He'd only met her, only renewed their acquaintance anyway, that afternoon. What had made him trust her so quickly? Bad enough that his own family knew how oddly he'd behaved. He didn't need the whole of Whitby knowing it, too. All it would take was for her to tell one person and the gossip would be all over town.

'My brother's a famously excellent sailor.' Lance came to her rescue, trying to lighten the mood, but Arthur turned around again, speaking over him.

'Quite the contrary, my *experiences*, as you call them, only made me more attached to the water. I told you, I didn't want to come back. Given the choice I'd still be somewhere in the middle of the North Sea.' He pulled his arm away from the mantelpiece decisively. 'But it's getting late. My brother thinks you ought to go home in his carriage and I agree. It's time for you to leave, Miss Webster.'

'Oh!' She sprang up as if she'd just been catapulted out of her seat, pulling her veil down with a sharp tug, though not before he saw the expression of hurt on her face, enough to give him a sharp stab of guilt. 'Yes, I'm sorry, I didn't mean to impose.'

'You're not imposing at all.' Violet shot her brother-in-law a recriminatory look. 'I've had a delightful evening. I can't travel much at the moment, but I do hope you'll come again and bring some of your jewellery for me to admire. I'm sure it's exquisite.'

'Thank you.' Her voice sounded faintly muffled behind her veil. 'I'd like that, too.'

'Oh, very well, then.' Lance heaved himself out of his armchair with a sigh. 'I was just getting comfortable, but since my brother is such a stick-in-the-mud, I suppose there's no rest for the wicked. With your permission, Miss Webster, I'll call for the carriage and escort you home myself.'

'I'll come, too.' Arthur took a step forward.

'No.' She made a move as if to forestall him. 'I've inconvenienced you quite enough already.'

'I never said…'

'But you're no inconvenience to me.' Lance made a gallant bow, pointedly blocking the way. 'In fact, I'd be honoured to escort you. As for you, dear Brother, under the circumstances perhaps you ought to go and mend your manners elsewhere.'

Chapter Seven

'Ride a cock horse to Banbury Cross…'

Frances bounced a giggling Georgie up and down on her knee, pretending to almost drop and then catch him again as her sister paced the length of the drawing room like a caged and increasingly irate animal.

'Is that *really* all he said?'

Lydia's cheeks were pink, though whether from anger, frustration or exertion, Frances couldn't tell. After eight days of being subjected to the same questions, however, she was getting used to deflecting the truth.

'Yes. I'm sorry, Lydia, but he said he'd already given his answer.'

'But you were gone for so long!'

'I told you, I sprained my ankle on the way home. It's hard to be quick when you're hobbling on one leg.'

'Well, it seems quite a coincidence that you were found by Captain Amberton.'

'It was, wasn't it? But it was over a week ago now. Can we *please* let the matter rest?'

Quickly, she turned her attention back to tickling Georgie under his armpits, ignoring the glint of suspicion in her sister's eye. Not that she was lying outright, she told herself, just not telling the whole truth. Besides, as it turned out, she hadn't needed to lie. Lance Amberton had done all the talking for her, escorting her to her parents' front door with a story about finding her at the side of the Sandsend-Whitby road that had almost convinced even her. He'd been charming and courteous, a perfect gentleman, in fact. Everything that his brother was not.

She'd tried her hardest not to think about *him* for the past week, a feat that hadn't been easy given the frequency of Lydia's questions, though overall she thought she'd done a reasonable job. She'd certainly consigned her ideas about the old Arthur Amberton to the past. Either her girlish memories of him had been mistaken or he'd changed so completely that the old version no longer existed. The kind, thoughtful man she'd remembered had been replaced by an ill-mannered, domineering brute. There was no danger of her wanting to renew her acquaintance with *him*, although she hoped to visit Amberton Castle again soon. That was the one good thing to come out of the evening. Violet and Lance had been considerate and welcoming, putting her so much at ease that she'd eventually felt comfortable enough to remove her veil, something she rarely did except with her own family. She'd enjoyed her evening with them far more than she'd expected, right up until the moment when Arthur had dismissed her as if she were just some inconvenience to be got rid of.

His rejection had been all too familiar, though it had felt doubly hurtful somehow, as if he'd attacked her when her guard was down. After all, he was the one who'd taken her there! He was the one who'd actually insisted that she accompany him! When he'd asked about her jewellery it had reminded her of their old conversations in her mother's parlour and when he'd *almost* smiled at her, she'd even started tentatively to wonder whether they might possibly be friends again. What a foolish idea that had been! But then why had she assumed he'd be any different from anyone else? Especially when he'd made it abundantly clear that she'd been nothing but a burden from the start. That was all she'd ever be to anyone, but the memory still hurt, as if he were Leo all over again...

'Well, it was very disappointing.' Lydia was still pacing up and down. 'When I saw you with a man, I thought you'd brought him back with you. I was in such a rush to put on my new lavender muslin that I tore the hem.'

'Lavender?' Frances rolled her eyes. 'Lydia, you know you can't wear lavender for another two months.'

'Oh, you sound just like Mama, but I doubt Arthur knows when John's funeral was exactly. He won't know if it's appropriate to wear or not. Lavender suits me.'

'Everything suits you, but, Lydia, maybe you ought to just let him go. He wasn't very polite when I spoke to him and I'm sure you'll have plenty of other suitors once you're allowed out of mourning.'

'I don't want other suitors!' Lydia's expression turned fierce. 'I *want* Arthur Amberton. Only perhaps I need to try a different approach.'

Frances's heart sank. 'What kind of approach?'

'I don't know yet, but he can't refuse to see me for ever. I'll find a way.'

'But he said that he doesn't want to see you.' She didn't know how much plainer she could make it...

'For now,' Lydia pouted, 'but we'll see about that.'

'If you say so.'

Frances lifted Georgie off her knee and stood up,

struck by a vague sense of foreboding. She was starting to wonder whether Arthur's blunt refusal to see Lydia was only making her sister more determined, provoking some contrary side of her character. Perhaps it would be better if he *did* meet with her after all. If he behaved as badly as he had the other night, then Lydia might actually be glad to relinquish the idea of marrying him. As it was, Frances had the discomforting feeling that her sister's interest was beginning to border on obsession...

'Where are you going?' Lydia looked up at her absently.

'Down to the beach. It's a lovely afternoon and my ankle's feeling much better.'

'Oh...that's good. In that case, would you mind taking Georgie for some fresh air? I thought I might make some calls.'

'Calls?'

'Yes, calls! I'm allowed to visit a few people, aren't I? As long as they're old and married and boring!'

Frances narrowed her eyes speculatively. 'You won't do anything foolish, will you?'

'Of course not.' Lydia sounded impatient. 'I know perfectly well what I'm doing.'

'That's what I'm afraid of.' Frances sighed and took hold of her nephew's hand. 'Come on, Georgie.'

The tide was almost at its lowest ebb, a good thirty yards from the cliff by the time they made their way down the slope of the promenade to the shore, Georgie toddling ahead with a bucket and spade clutched in his chubby hands. Frances had told his nurse to take the afternoon off so it was just her and him and a vast, unspoilt expanse of beach waiting to be decorated with sandcastles and seashell palaces, the way she liked it.

The weather was beautiful, too, one of those rare days when the sea was almost perfectly flat, so smooth that she could see the wakes left by the vessels and the sky bright and cloudless, with barely a trace of breeze to spoil the perfect mirror-shine of the water. It all looked so lovely that she felt a rush of sympathy for Lydia, trapped indoors in her mourning, but at least she and Georgie could still make the most of it.

She pulled her veil back to admire the view, enjoying the kiss of the sun on her skin. Georgie was used to her scar so he wasn't alarmed by the sight, and everyone else was either too busy or too far away to notice her. There were only a scattering of people anyway, just a few nursemaids and children, as well as a group of fishermen loading lobster pots into a boat on the shore.

'Picnic first?'

She spread a blanket over the sand and opened her basket to reveal two lemon buns, fresh from Mrs Botham's. The bakery had opened in Whitby seven years before and been an instant success, not least with Georgie who tucked straight into his bun with relish. Frances took a hearty mouthful as well, licking her lips to make sure she didn't lose any of the icing, and then stopped, struck by a strange, tingling sensation, as if something wasn't quite right. It wasn't the cake or Georgie. It was more like an awareness, as if somebody was watching her…

She looked up, straight into the eyes of one of the fishermen. And he wasn't just looking at her, she realised in alarm. He was saying goodbye to his companions and striding purposely up the beach in their direction as well, pulling his cap off to reveal a head of close-cropped hair that she recognised at once.

She swallowed her mouthful of cake with a gulp.

He must have been splashed by the waves because he looked conspicuously damp, his half-open shirt moulded to his chest and arms so that she could see the sculpted contours of the muscles beneath—of which, she couldn't help but notice, there were many. Even more than she'd appreciated the first time in his hallway. More than she ought to be staring at, especially when she wasn't wearing a veil. And it was too late for her to pull it down without him noticing!

'Miss Webster.'

He stopped in front of her, inclining his head slightly though his expression was just as stern as it had been when she'd last seen him standing on the doorstep of Amberton Castle the week before. Apparently neither his mood nor his manners had improved since.

'Lord Scorborough.'

'Might I enquire after your ankle?'

'You might.' She thrust her chin out belligerently. As answers went, it wasn't very polite, but she felt stubbornly determined to pay him back in kind. Even if her pulse just seemed to have trebled its usual speed.

'I hope it's feeling better.'

'Yes.'

'Good.' He nodded slowly, as if he were trying to think of something else to say. 'You managed to walk down here by yourself then?'

'Yes, except for my nephew here.' She gestured warily to the little boy sitting beside her. Being rude to her was one thing, but if he was rude to Georgie…

'So this young man is your escort?' To her surprise, his expression actually seemed to soften as he crouched down in front of them. 'Young Master Baird, I presume?'

The boy made a confused face and she had to stifle a laugh. 'He prefers George.'

'Master George, then. How do you do, young man?'

'I'm very well, sir.' Georgie opened up his fist to reveal the squashed remnants of his lemon bun. 'Would you like some?'

'That's very kind of you, Georgie,' Frances interceded tactfully, 'but you finish yours. Lord Scorborough can share some of mine if he wants.'

'All right.' The little boy rammed the last piece into his mouth and clambered happily to his feet. 'Can I build a sandcastle now?'

'Yes, but remember I like my castles to have at least three turrets and a moat!'

'Yes, Aunt Frances!'

She let her smile fade as he scurried away, acutely aware of Arthur still crouching in front of her. Was he looking at her? She couldn't tell. She was only conscious of the silence between them lengthening awkwardly.

'He seems like a nice boy.' Arthur spoke at last.

'He is.' She peered sideways, relenting slightly. 'Thank you for being kind to him.'

'Did you think that I wouldn't be?'

'No, but under the circumstances…'

'He's a child.'

'He's Lydia's child,' she answered significantly, 'and very dear to me.'

'Meaning that we couldn't be friends if I wasn't kind to him?'

'No, we couldn't, but then we aren't friends, are we?'

'We used to be. Maybe we could be again.'

She twisted her head to look straight at him that time, too shocked to make any attempt to conceal it.

'Is the idea so appalling?' His stern expression was back, even sterner than ever.

'Not appalling, no...' she chose her words carefully '...but surprising. The other night you only wanted to get rid of me.'

He grimaced. 'I wasn't trying to get rid of you, although I admit it must have seemed that way. The truth is that I don't find it easy to talk about my past, Miss Webster, and the conversation was hitting too close to home. However, that's still no excuse for ill manners. I was rude and abrupt and I've been told in no uncertain terms that I ought to apologise. In fact, I believe that I'm banished from Violet's company until I do. So...' he spread his hands wide '...please accept my apology.'

She held his gaze for a long, drawn-out moment. He'd come across the beach to apologise and he *seemed* sincere...and he'd been nice to Georgie... *Could* they be friends again? She didn't know about that, but she *could* forgive him.

'It's all right. I shouldn't have mentioned what happened.'

'No, I shouldn't have been so sensitive. You have every right to resent me for being rude. I only hope that you'll give me another chance.'

'I don't resent you.'

'And the second chance?'

'I'll think about it.'

'Fair enough.' He gestured towards the lemon bun in her hand. 'Now that's settled, are you going to offer me some of that or not? I believe you told your nephew that you'd share.'

She narrowed her eyes and tore off a chunk. 'A piece, but that's all. We're still acquaintances more than anything else.'

'Well, if that's the most I can hope for… May I?' He dropped down on to Georgie's empty space on the blanket before she could answer. 'Although you might call me Arthur. You used to.'

'That was a long time ago.'

'Not so very long. We're hardly in our dotage yet. How old are you anyway?'

She shuffled her bottom to the furthest edge of the blanket, but it wasn't far enough. He was still sitting barely a foot away, close enough that she could feel the body heat emanating through his damp shirt. Could he sense her heat, too? If he could, then he didn't seem unduly bothered by it, though that was probably because he still thought of her as a child, a kind of little sister at best. Surely the way he was speaking to her proved that. But at least her pulse seemed to be calming slightly.

'A gentleman ought not to ask such a thing of a *lady.*' She put particular stress on the last word.

'But I've never understood why not. Isn't honesty the best policy? I'm the grand old age of two-and-thirty, but since I remember you being in the schoolroom, you must be somewhat younger?'

'Twenty-two.'

'Really? You look older.'

'What?'

'In a good way, I might add. Your eyes especially. You have a wise face, Miss Webster.' He shrugged. 'That was supposed to be a compliment, only I'm out of practice in making them, I suppose.'

'Oh.' She turned her face away as he popped the piece of lemon bun into his mouth. 'In that case, you can call me Frances again, if you want.'

'I do want. This is delicious, by the way.'

'I know. It's my favourite of all Mrs Botham's cakes.'

'Have you tried them all?'

'Naturally. What self-respecting aunt would I be if I *hadn't* allowed my nephew to sample each one? Under strict supervision, I might add. Georgie and I have done extensive research. It's between these and the strawberry tarts.'

'Clearly I need to pay a visit to this bakery.' He frowned. 'What's so funny?'

'It's just hard to imagine you in a cake shop.'

'Why? Doesn't everyone like cake?'

'It just seems a bit frivolous for you, that's all.'

'Believe it or not, I can be frivolous on occasion.'

She looked him up and down sceptically. 'Give me one example.'

'How about sitting on a picnic blanket eating cake when I ought to be hauling lobster pots into a boat? Is that frivolous enough for you?'

'It's a start, though I think Whitby society might go into shock if you were seen in Mrs Botham's drinking tea and eating strawberry tarts.'

'I'll have to rely on you for supplies then.' He held her eyes long enough for her pulse to start fluttering again. Most people couldn't help but look at her scar, but his gaze was steady and unblinking. 'Maybe you could bring some to Amberton Castle, too. Violet hopes that you'll visit her again soon.'

'I'd like to, only it's difficult. I'd need the carriage to travel so far and if I told my mother where I was going then I'd have to explain the acquaintance. She doesn't know Violet and I have met.' Not to mention that Lydia would have a tantrum at the very idea…

'Ah…' he nodded '… I didn't think of that.'

'But I would like to see Violet again. I liked her very

much. She and Captain Amberton seem very happy together.'

'They are. Lance is a better husband than I could ever have been.'

'You?' She blinked. Had he been an option? The idea unsettled her for some reason.

He nodded. 'Our fathers wanted the two of us to marry. They even came to a secret agreement about it, around the same time I first met your sister, as it happens. I tried and tried to persuade my father to change his mind, but he wouldn't listen. Then, after I left, Lance inherited Violet, so to speak. She was just as thrilled by the prospect of an arranged marriage as I'd been, so much so that she tried running away, too, but Lance went after her.'

'And they lived happily ever after?'

'Eventually.' He sounded pensive. 'They were lucky.'

'Well, they certainly seem very happy and Amberton Castle is everything I imagined it would be. It's beautiful.'

'Still woefully inadequate as a castle, though.'

'What?' She drew her brows together as he heaved a pitiful-sounding sigh. 'What do you mean?'

'I mean there's no moat. Nary a bit of water in sight. You've just told your nephew that it was compulsory.'

'Oh…' She pursed her lips, resisting the urge to laugh. 'Well, it's not a *bad* castle.'

'Just not up to your exacting standards?'

'I can't help being a perfectionist.' She gave him a coy look. 'Perhaps you ought to dig a moat.'

'Perhaps I should. I don't mind admitting I'm pretty good with a spade.' He caught her eye and winked. 'Speaking of which, I have a sty that won't clean itself, more's the pity. Pleasant though it would be to sit here all afternoon, I ought to be getting back to work.'

'Yes…' She gave her head a small shake, trying to banish the strange fuzzy feeling his wink seemed to have caused in her chest. It wasn't unpleasant exactly, just unexpected. He wasn't smiling, but there was a warmth in his face she hadn't seen before and she wasn't sure how to react to it, only she didn't want him to notice anything different about her either. She didn't want him to see any reaction at all, especially since she shouldn't be feeling one.

'About Lydia…' She tried to get the conversation back on track. 'She was disappointed by your answer the other day.'

'She'll get over it.'

'But if you could just speak to her…'

'No.' He got up on to his haunches and looked straight at her. 'Do you picnic here often?'

'Ye-es. Georgie and I come two or three times a week.'

'Just the two of you?'

'Usually.'

'Only I thought I might come back on Friday afternoon. I'd like to have another of those buns, a whole one to myself this time, but since I don't want to cause a scene by going into the bakery myself, I fear I may be dependent on your good will. In any case, I'll be here if you decide to give me that second chance.' He brushed the sand from his trousers and stood up, though with the sun behind his back she couldn't make out his expression. 'Are you sure you can make it back up the hill on that ankle?'

'Perfectly sure.'

'I can carry her if she wants.' Georgie's small voice interrupted them.

'I'm glad to hear it, young man.' Arthur gave him an approving nod. 'In that case, I'll leave your aunt in your capable hands. Until Friday then, I hope.'

Chapter Eight

'You're in a good mood.'

Arthur glanced over his shoulder to find Lance leaning against the side of the pigsty.

'Am I?'

'You were whistling.' His brother's expression was more than a little inquisitive. 'I haven't heard you whistle since we were boys.'

'I've decided to take it up again.'

'Any particular reason?'

'I wasn't aware that I needed one.'

He stopped shovelling and rested an arm on the top of his spade. He was hardly going to admit that he'd been thinking about Frances. That afternoon had been the fourth in a row he'd gone looking for her and he'd been pleased and relieved by his eventual success. Firstly, because he'd wanted to apologise to her for his behaviour at Amberton Castle and, secondly, because he'd needed to work out why he couldn't stop thinking about her. Ever since that afternoon when she'd appeared like some kind of apparition in his hallway he'd been finding it harder and harder to concentrate.

At first he'd wondered if it was because of Lydia,

worrying that the old, weak part of him might be drawn to her because of their physical resemblance, yet the moment he'd laid eyes on Frances sitting on the beach, he'd known that that wasn't true. He'd wanted to see *her* and after half an hour spent in her company, the urge had only slightly diminished. All he knew now was that he wanted to see her again and soon. Neither of which details he intended to share with his brother.

'What are you doing here, Lance?'

'Looking for you. I came by after lunch, as if happens, but there was no sign of you. I presumed you were off sowing seeds or something.'

'It's July.'

'Harvesting, then?'

'Not quite yet. I've been down on the shore.'

'Really?' Lance's gaze sharpened. 'Taking some time off? That doesn't sound like you.'

'Helping to load lobster pots, if you must know.'

'Ah.' His brother looked disappointed. 'In that case, you can take a break with me now. Only stay downwind if you don't mind. No offence, but between the lobsters and the pigs, you've developed something of a potent aroma.'

Arthur sniffed his sleeve self-consciously. He hadn't considered the smell of the lobster pots when he'd wandered over to join Frances. Had she wanted him to sit downwind, too?

'Shouldn't you be at the mine?' He propped his spade against the fence and climbed over.

'I was. Only I forgot something so I had to go back to the house.'

'What was that?'

'Just a document, nothing important now. What *is* important is who I found there.'

Arthur felt a distinct sense of apprehension. 'You don't mean...?'

'Tenacious, isn't she?' Lance made a claw-like gesture with one hand. 'Though ostensibly she came to call on Violet and thank me for rescuing her sister. She said she'd wanted to visit for, and I quote, *simply an eternity*, but hadn't been able to on account of her mourning. Apparently she thought recent circumstances warranted an exception.'

'Did she ask about me?'

'I believe she was hoping that I would leave the room so she could, but I wasn't about to abandon Violet. We had tea and biscuits. All terribly civilised.' Lance gave him a pointed look. 'You might need to start barricading your front door.'

'I'm not hiding. Shall I make some coffee?'

'I'd prefer something stronger.'

Arthur lifted an eyebrow. In their youth, Lance had regularly drunk to excess, but since his marriage to Violet he'd become a changed man. The fact that he wanted alcohol now suggested he wasn't quite as relaxed as he liked to appear.

'I've got a bottle of whisky somewhere. Take a seat.' He gestured to a bench by the front door and went inside, returning a few minutes later with a bottle and two small glasses.

'I could drink the lot.' Lance tossed back the contents of his tumbler the moment it was in his hand.

'Anything you want to talk about?'

'Nothing new.' Lance placed a hand on his forehead and squeezed. 'Do you think there's a way to make the baby come early?'

'I'm not the person to ask. Have you spoken to a doctor?'

'Several. They all tell me not to worry, but I can't help it.'

'I know.' Arthur refilled his glass and put the bottle aside. There wasn't anything else he could say, nothing but empty reassurances.

'So let's talk about something else.' Lance rested his head back against the wall. 'Seen the little sister again?'

'Why would I have?' He felt himself tense instantly. 'She lives in Whitby and I live here.'

'With only the fields and the shore in between. I'd have thought it would be easy to meet if the two of you wanted.'

Arthur gave him a sideways look, but Lance's eyes were closed. 'I suppose it would be. *If* we wanted.'

'You know that Violet thinks you ought to go and apologise?'

'I believe she's mentioned it seven or eight times, yes.'

Lance chuckled. 'Well, I'm not telling you to do anything, though it occurred to me that the younger Miss Webster might be just the answer to your problems. Even Lydia would have to give up pursuing you if you married someone else.'

If he'd had any hair, Arthur thought that his eyebrows might have vanished into it. 'It might be somewhat insensitive to choose her own sister.'

'That couldn't be helped. All's fair in love and war, et cetera. It wouldn't be your fault if you really liked her.'

'Which I never said I did.'

'Not out loud, no.'

Arthur narrowed his eyes. 'It still sounds a somewhat extreme way of solving the problem. I'm perfectly happy on my own.'

'Or maybe you've just got used to telling yourself that.'

'Not everyone wants to get married.'

'Haven't I made it look appealing enough?'

'It's not that and you know it.' Arthur lowered his glass slowly. 'I'm just better off on my own. I'm not fit to be someone's husband. My mind isn't stable enough.'

'Don't be absurd. You're as sane as I am, for whatever that's worth.'

'At the moment, perhaps, but remember what happened before.'

'It was only once.'

'Once for nine months and look at the consequences! If it wasn't for me, Father would still be alive.'

'You didn't kill him, Arthur.'

'No, the shock did that, but I caused it.'

'Because he pushed you. He was always pushing you, him and Lydia Webster together. The pair of them would have driven any man—'

'Mad?' Arthur curled his lip. 'It's all right, you can say the word. It's the truth, after all.'

'No, it isn't. You only lost your way for a while. I've seen it happen in the army.'

'That's still no excuse. Father and Lydia might have pushed me, but I managed the mad part all by myself.'

'Just because it happened once doesn't mean that it'll happen again.'

'I still won't take the risk. That feeling of powerlessness, of being out of control…' He shook his head. 'I never want to feel that way again and I'm damned sure nobody wants a husband who feels that way either.'

'And if the lady in question thought otherwise?'

'The lady in question only knows that I jumped overboard and spent some time on a fishing boat. I've no intention of telling her anything else.'

'Well, it's up to you.' Lance sighed and stood up. 'And now that we've each thoroughly depressed the other, I ought to get on to the mine. For the record, though, I still think you're punishing yourself too much. The past is the past. You shouldn't let it spoil the future, too. Violet taught me that and she's a hundred times smarter than I am.'

'No arguments there.'

'In any case, I presume you won't be bringing a dinner guest this week?'

'No, but you can put Violet's mind at rest about Miss Webster. As it happens, I *did* see her this afternoon.'

'Is that so?' Lance's expression was too smug for its own good.

'Yes. She was having a picnic on the beach.'

'What a fortunate coincidence.'

'So I apologised, but that's all.'

'That's what I'll tell Violet then.'

Arthur watched as Lance mounted his horse and rode away, still wearing a self-satisfied grin. Not that there was anything to smile about, not really. He'd told his brother the truth. He had absolutely *no* intention of getting married, not ever—although if that was the case then he really shouldn't be arranging picnics with young, unmarried ladies. All things considered he probably shouldn't see her again at all—and if she ever found out the truth about his past then he doubted she'd want to see him again either. What self-respecting woman would? But then it was *only* a picnic, a kind of extended apology, nothing special, just some light conversation over lemon buns…

So why was he already looking forward to it?

Chapter Nine

'Moat good enough for you?'

Arthur sat back on the sand, awaiting the verdict as Frances tapped her chin thoughtfully.

'It's not bad and I must say Georgie's turrets are excellent. Well done, Georgie.'

'Not bad?' Arthur pushed himself to his feet as the little boy grinned. 'That's all you can say after I wrench every muscle in my body?'

'I don't hear Georgie complaining.'

'He's closer to the ground. My back may never recover.'

'Oh, very well. If it means so much to you, I think it's an excellent moat. For a first attempt anyway.'

'Harumph.' His expression turned decidedly grumpy. 'Well, since I'm not going to get any credit for my labours, let me look at yours.'

'No!' She took a step forward, wrapping her arms around her easel protectively. 'It's not finished yet.'

'So you can give criticism, but you can't take it?' He folded his arms. 'Fair's fair, Miss Webster.'

She hesitated for another moment and then took a step backwards to reveal the canvas. It was a bit like removing her veil again, she thought nervously, though she'd barely noticed that garment's absence today. She was actually getting used to not wearing it around Arthur, even if at that moment she would have liked a little protection from the intensity of his gaze. The painting was a seascape in watercolours, but she'd added both him and Georgie to the foreground, the pair of them crouched side by side as they built a chain of sandcastles along the length of the beach. Despite her teasing, their endeavours were really quite impressive. A little boy's dream, in fact, though looking again at her canvas, she realised that she'd lavished far more attention upon them than on the sea itself.

'You know I thought you had some talent six years ago.' Arthur tipped his head to one side, looking speculatively between her and the painting. 'Now I see I was mistaken.'

'What do you mean?' She bristled at once.

'And I thought I was the sensitive one.' His lips twitched. 'If you'll let me finish, I was about to say that you've become an exceptional artist. The way you've captured the rainbow in the water is stunning.'

'Oh...thank you.' She felt her cheeks flush, as though his words were warming her up from the inside.

'Of course that's just the opinion of an inept moat-digger, but this one is duly impressed. Now...' He settled down on the blanket and stretched his legs out. 'Is it time for our picnic yet?'

'Yes.' She turned away to beckon Georgie and cover her paints, glad of an excuse to hide her expression. 'I suppose you've worked hard enough for one day.'

'Kind of you to say so. What do we have this time?'

'These.' She reached into her basket and pulled out two pieces of shortbread. They were square-shaped and covered with a thick layer of caramel and chocolate. 'They're called Apollos.'

'They look delicious.' He shifted over, making room for her on the blanket as Georgie collected his rations and toddled happily away. 'You'll be having a lemon bun again, I suppose?'

'Naturally.' She sat down beside him.

'And planning on taking an hour to eat it?'

'I like to savour things.'

'So I've noticed.' He swayed slightly, bringing his head close to hers in a way that made her feel even warmer. 'Aren't you ever tempted to have something different?'

'No.' She sat very still, trying to ignore the tingling sensation of his breath on her cheek. 'I know what I like.'

'Then I admire your loyalty.' His gaze dropped to her mouth before he sat back again, taking a big bite of his shortbread.

'Mmm.' He rolled his eyes appreciatively. 'This is the best so far.'

She laughed aloud, glad to have a release for her confused emotions. His proximity was disturbing enough, but the way he'd just looked at her, as if she were the cake, even more so. His eyes had certainly lingered on her mouth longer than a gentleman's should have. 'You always say that. Last week the strawberry tart was your favourite.'

'I know. I wouldn't have thought it possible to beat that either, but…'

'This does?'

'*That* was excellent. *This* is sublime. From now on, I'd like an Apollo every time. Two or three of them, preferably.'

'The bakers will think I have a very sweet tooth.'

'Say they're for Georgie.'

'They're already supposed to be for Georgie!'

'Well…' he winked at her '…he's a growing boy.'

She turned her face away quickly, looking towards the sea with the most artistic expression she could muster. The fine weather showed no signs of waning and the waves were still gentle, breaking on to the shore with only the faintest of whispers. It was almost *too* placid. When Arthur winked at her like that, she felt as though there ought to be giant waves and breakers, something to justify the sudden rush of blood to her head.

This was the fourth time in three weeks that they'd met on the beach, halfway between Whitby and Sandsend, and he spoke as if he wanted to carry on meeting her, as if he enjoyed her company as much as the cake. Since his apology they seemed to have taken up where they'd left off six years before, falling back into their old sense of camaraderie, though she was acutely aware of everything that had happened during the intervening years, too. Their conversations were familiar and yet unfamiliar. Sometimes she felt as if no time at all had passed, but then other times a shadow would cross his face like a cloud over the sun and they'd be almost strangers again. She caught glimpses of the *old* Arthur, but they'd both changed. She wasn't the same girl who'd felt an adolescent yearning for him back in her mother's parlour either. Now she felt intensely aware of him as a man, not to mention of herself as a woman.

Not that he would ever think of her in that way, she was sure. It had been bad enough when he'd been engaged to her sister, but now there was even less chance of him seeing her as anything other than a friend. Which was all she wanted, too, she reminded herself. After

Leo, she'd taught herself not to expect or even want romance. Arthur might not seem to care about her scar, but she certainly wasn't going to risk any more rejection. Besides, there were other, far more important things in her life. Her new jewellery venture for a start, something a man—she avoided thinking the word 'husband'—doubtless wouldn't approve of. After all the heartache and pain her independence had cost her, there was no way she was giving it up now, not for anyone. Still, there were times when the expression in Arthur's eyes made her insides feel strangely fluid.

Then there were days when she thought she ought not to see him again at all. As nice as it was to have a friend, especially one who seemed blissfully unaware of her scar, she couldn't help but feel guilty about betraying Lydia. Not that she was betraying her exactly, but still… She was only grateful that Georgie seemed more interested in telling his mother about cake and sandcastles than anything else, such as who they met. She didn't want to consider how her sister might react if she knew the whole truth.

'I have a present for you, too.' Arthur's voice broke into her thoughts suddenly. 'In exchange for all the cake.'

She turned around just in time to see him pull an egg-shaped chunk of black stone from his pocket. 'I found this in the cliffside the other day. I thought it might make a nice pendant or something.'

'It would.' She let him place the jet in her palm. 'Or a brooch, maybe.'

'Something to match your eyes.'

'Oh, no.' She shook her head as she rubbed her fingers gently over the surface. 'It wouldn't be for me. I told you, I don't wear my own pieces.'

'Why not?'

'Because…' She lifted her shoulders evasively. 'I like to keep my outfits plain, that's all.'

'Because you don't want anyone to look at you?'

Yes. She let her shoulders fall again. *Yes*, that was exactly the reason, though she preferred not to hear it spoken out loud.

'You know I hardly notice your scar any more.'

'Hardly?' She didn't mean to sound so sceptical, but his expression was kindly.

'I mean that I notice it in the same way I notice you have brown eyes and hair. It's a part of you, that's all.'

'The part everyone stares at.'

'Maybe at first, but you're assuming that it's all anyone would ever look at. There are plenty of other reasons to look at you, believe me, Frances. But…' he reached a hand out as if he hadn't just given her the most unexpectedly touching compliment '…if you're not going to wear it yourself then I want it back.'

'What? No!' She closed her fingers around the stone possessively. 'You just gave it to me.'

'Exactly. *To you.* On condition that you make something for yourself.'

'All right,' she conceded defeat. 'I'll think of something.'

'Good. You know, I wouldn't normally tell a lady that I saw a lump of stone and thought of her, but…' He swayed towards her again. 'A simple "thank you" would suffice.'

'Oh!' She clapped a hand to her mouth in embarrassment. 'Of course, thank you. It was very thoughtful of you.'

'You're welcome.' He bowed his head and then gave her a quizzical look. 'If you don't want to wear it, why make jewellery at all?'

'Because I like creating things. It makes me happy and it's nice to earn some money of my own. It's good to know that I can be independent if necessary.'

'*Is* it necessary?'

'No, but sometimes it's hard, feeling like a burden to others. At least my jewellery has value.'

He lifted an eyebrow, regarding her in silence for a couple of moments before mercifully changing the subject. 'How do you go about turning jet into jewellery anyhow? It just looks like a rock to me. It's not even shiny.'

'That's what's so wonderful about it. The potential is all there, only most people don't notice. It just takes a while to bring out the true beauty beneath. First you have to cut the stone to the size and shape that you want, then you smooth the edges with sandpaper, then you carve the detail.'

'Using?'

'Anything I can find. Darning needles, hairpins, things like that. I have some miniature chisels and files, too.'

'Then you polish?'

'Yes, with jeweller's rouge mixed with paraffin and linseed oil, only I have to be careful since it stains so easily. I've turned my hands red a few times.'

'Red?'

'Yes. That's why the men in the workshops are called red devils.'

'Huh, I'd never thought of that. But how do you cut such a hard stone in the first place?'

'With a grinding wheel.'

'Which you just happen to have in your bedroom, I suppose?'

She gave him an arch look. 'No, I take my pieces to

Thorpe's workshop in the harbour. They do all the cutting and grinding for me.'

'They don't think it's something of an odd request from a young lady?'

'No. I asked Mr Thorpe and he agreed.'

'Just like that?'

'Not exactly.' She took a bite of her lemon bun, stalling for time before she answered. She didn't talk about her accident very often—never, in fact—but she could hardly explain her arrangement with Mr Thorpe without mentioning it. Strangely enough, however, she didn't feel particular anxious about telling Arthur. To her surprise, a part of her actually *wanted* to tell him.

'Mr Thorpe thinks that he owes me a debt. He doesn't, but I'm glad for his help anyway. You see, that was where my accident happened, in his workshop.'

'A jet workshop?' Arthur drew his brows together.

'Yes. You see, a grinding wheel revolves about nine hundred times a minute. It needs a lot of water and sometimes the stone cracks under the pressure.'

'That's what happened?'

She nodded. 'I was standing next to the grinding wheel when a piece splintered off and hit me in the face. Right here.' She pointed to the arch of her cheekbone. 'I was lucky it missed my eye.'

He looked sombre for a moment and then reached a hand up. 'May I?'

'If you want.' She nodded, fighting the instinct to retreat as he pressed his fingers against the damaged skin.

'Did it hurt?' His voice sounded softer.

'Very much at the time.' Her mouth turned dry as his thumb trailed a path down the side of her face. Apart from her mother and the doctor, no one else had ever touched her scar. 'But not any more. Except sometimes, when I sleep on that side, it wakes me.'

'I don't understand.' His brows were drawn together so tightly he looked almost fierce. 'What were you doing so close to a grinding wheel? Accidents like that shouldn't happen.'

'But they do, far more often than they should. It's a dangerous process, but we shouldn't have been there in the first place.'

'We?'

'Yes.' Her heart started to race all of a sudden. 'My fiancé took me.'

Chapter Ten

Frances tipped her head to one side so that Arthur's hand fell away from her face. For some reason, she didn't want him to still be touching her when she told him about Leo.

'You were engaged?' His expression didn't alter though his gaze seemed to darken.

'Yes, for all of a month. It was several years ago.'

'Who to?'

'Leo Fairfax.'

'Fairfax?'

'Yes.' She blinked at the sudden strident tone of his voice. 'Do you know him?'

'I used to.'

'Well, we were engaged. I was only seventeen, but it was a very good match. Everyone said so. His father was a merchant like mine.'

'So it wasn't a love match?'

'No-o...' she hesitated '...although I tried to persuade myself otherwise. I was young and I still believed in romance, but really it was all arranged.' She swallowed, feeling as though there were a knot in her chest that was tightening as she spoke. 'He knew all about my interests, though he called them my funny little hobbies just like everyone else. We got engaged very quickly, too quickly, but it made my parents happy, and then…well, he decided it would be fun for us to visit a jet workshop on my birthday. Mr Thorpe didn't want to let us in, but Leo insisted. We were only there five minutes before it happened.' The knot was painfully tight now, but she fought against it. 'I think perhaps the boy at the wheel was nervous about us standing so close, but it was an accident. I didn't blame him, but Leo…'

He lifted an eyebrow when she faltered. 'He did?'

'Yes.' She swallowed. 'He blamed everyone except himself. Poor Mr Thorpe was horrified by what had happened, the poor man, but at least he had the good sense to summon a doctor. Leo wanted a policeman instead. He just stood there ranting, threatening to prosecute everyone, but I refused to allow it. That was the beginning of the end for our engagement.'

'Surely he didn't break it off because you disagreed with him?'

'Oh, no, I was the one who broke it off. To my mother's enduring dismay, I might add. It wasn't because we argued either. He was just so horrified by my scar, so much that he could barely stand to look at me. I think he was trying to find a way to break our engagement without seeming dishonourable, but in the end the whole situation became too embarrassing for both of us. He was relieved when I offered him a way out.'

'I'm sorry.'

'Why?' She looked up at him in surprise. 'You didn't have anything to do with it.'

'I'm still sorry it happened to you.'

'But if it hadn't then I'd be married to a man who never really loved me and who valued my appearance more than he did my *self*. How could I have ever been happy with a man like that?'

He lifted his chin, holding her gaze in stony-sounding silence for a few moments before muttering a string of particularly vehement swear words.

'Arthur!' She didn't know whether to be shocked or to burst out laughing. 'Georgie might hear you.'

'Sorry.' He looked unrepentant. 'But Fairfax deserves them.'

'I know. Twice over!' She opted for laughter. 'I didn't say you were wrong.'

'How can you be so cheerful about it?'

'Because it is how it is. Wishing it were otherwise won't do any good and I still have my sight. If I'd lost that, then I wouldn't have been able to paint or make jewellery or do any of the things I love. And in a funny way, it's given me more freedom than most women. Nobody expects me to marry or follow the rules any more. The ordinary rules don't apply because I'm different, or at least people see me differently. Even my parents do. If my accident hadn't happened, then I couldn't devote so much time to my art. I wouldn't be able to come to the beach like this without a chaperon. I wouldn't be able to...'

She stopped mid-sentence. She'd been about to say that she wouldn't have been able to come and meet him, but she couldn't say that without implying too much about her feelings and she didn't understand those herself. She and Arthur were friends now, sort of, but that was all. Even if, in some ways, they felt like kindred spirits. Their meetings on the beach were a kind of escape from the real world, a place outside rules and conventions and judgements, one where they could both be themselves. Or at least that was the way it seemed to her.

'What I mean is that now I'm free. Leo's rejection hurt, but I'm a realist now. I know what people think when they see me and I know who really cares about me. I've learned the hard way, but at least I know.'

She leaned back on her elbows. Although whether that last statement was entirely true… She'd found out how much Leo cared about her, but what about her family? They'd all made a point of saying how much they still loved her and yet it was her parents who'd first suggested she wear a veil out of doors. They never insisted on her accompanying them to social events either, letting her wander wherever she liked instead, in stark contrast to Lydia. *Could* they really still love her if they were so embarrassed by her?

'Not all men are the same.' Arthur's tone was gruff as he lay down beside her, folding both arms behind his head.

Frances took one look and sat up again quickly. It felt too intimate, lying side by side on a blanket with only a three-year-old as chaperon. 'I think a lot of men would have reacted like Leo.'

'Perhaps, but we're not all so shallow.'

'You fell in love with Lydia.'

She could have bitten her tongue out the moment the words were out of her mouth. They sounded bitter and jealous and faintly accusing even to her. Instead, she wrapped her arms around her knees, feeling chilly all of a sudden.

'So I did.' She sensed rather than saw his face turn towards her. 'But not just because of her looks. Or do you think I'm so superficial?'

'No, but I think men value physical beauty more than women do.'

'That doesn't mean they can't admire other attributes, too. Things that often outweigh it.' His tone shifted abruptly. 'On the other hand, maybe you're right. Maybe I was that shallow once. Maybe I was so dazzled by your sister's beauty that I saw what I wanted to see in her character.'

'Lydia has a lot of good qualities,' she answered defensively.

'Perhaps, but I'm not sure I ever got close enough to find out. I admit I was flattered by her attention, by the fact that she favoured me, but she was always surrounded by other admirers. I thought that I loved her, but when I look back, there were so few times when we actually talked. I'm not sure I ever had more than a dozen private conversations with her.'

'Lydia said you had to keep your engagement a secret until you could convince your father to accept her.'

'True, but we still could have talked once in a while. I thought so anyway, but she always kept me at a distance, as if she were afraid of getting to know me. We were engaged for three years, but at the end of it, I barely knew her.'

Frances didn't answer, couldn't even think of an answer, as she watched Georgie start work on another sandcastle. It didn't sound like Lydia to be shy, but then in retrospect, perhaps Arthur was right. *She'd* spent more time talking with him than her sister ever had. What did that say about Lydia's real feelings for him?

'Maybe it's simply a matter of time and perspective. Take these two shells, for example.' Arthur pushed himself upright again, scooping up a couple of shells from the sand. 'One is smooth and shiny and catches the eye. The other is rough with jagged edges. Which is the more beautiful? The answer seems obvious at first, the shiny one, but the longer you look at the rough one, the more you start to notice other, more interesting features about it. Look at the intricate pattern here on the underside. Look at all the dints and scratches. You can tell that this shell has been through a lot. It's been beaten and battered by the sea, but it's still strong and resilient and captivating in its own way. It's a less obvious beauty, but it's still beautiful none the less.'

She found herself leaning sideways, leaning across him to peer at the shells in his hand. 'But you still think the smooth one is the most attractive?'

'Objectively, yes. It has all the qualities that we're supposed to admire. It's smooth and regular and a good size. But since I've come to admire other, less tangible qualities, I prefer the second.'

'So beauty's in the eye of the beholder? Are you a philosopher now?'

'Viscount, sailor, farmer, philosopher...' His eyes sparked with humour, though his expression remained serious. 'I'm not trying to belittle the first shell, but true beauty comes from within, from what something *is*, not simply how it appears. Maybe true beauty *needs* to be tested and weathered, to prove itself through all the tempests that life can throw at it.' He looked faintly sheepish. 'That's what I've come to believe anyway.'

'But perhaps you're not being fair to the first shell either.' She drew her brows together. Despite the warm glow his words gave her, as metaphors went, they felt downright disloyal. 'Maybe it just hasn't had a chance to prove itself yet. Besides, the shells didn't ask to be compared. They were just lying there together on the sand.'

'True.' The look in his eyes seemed to grow warmer. 'Then shall we say they're both beautiful in different ways?'

'Yes.' She gave a soft sigh, feeling as though a weight

were being lifted from her heart, even if it was all too good to be true. It was all very well claiming such idealistic sentiments with *her*, but would he say the same thing if it were Lydia sitting beside him? Or would he be dazzled again? And how would she know until he was actually in the same room as her sister again? And yet, he *seemed* to mean what he said… And he was adamant about *not* wanting to see Lydia…

'Do you *really* think that anyone can be beautiful?' She couldn't help herself from asking the question.

'If they are on the inside, then, yes, I really do.'

'Even if they have a scar on one side of their face?'

'Frances.' He put the shells aside and reached for her face instead, cradling her cheeks between his fingers. 'I just told you, I hardly notice it any more. I only see you.'

She felt her heart leap and realised that she was holding her breath. His fingers were warm on her skin, though she could feel the callouses on them as well. They were what made him beautiful, too, she thought. Or handsome at any rate. *Very* handsome, especially now, sitting beside her on the blanket as if he were perfectly content in her company. He'd been tested as she had, too, though she still didn't know his whole story, only pieces of it. He'd told her that he didn't find it easy to talk about his past, but then neither did she. And she *wanted* to know his story. Even though his face was only a few inches from hers and his amber eyes were smouldering with an intensity she sensed was reflected in hers, too.

'Arthur.' She blinked deliberately, pulling her head back as his own moved infinitesimally towards her. 'What happened to you?'

Chapter Eleven

Arthur heaved a deep breath, bracing himself to answer. With his hands on her cheeks, he couldn't see Frances's scar at all. It made her look quite uncannily like her sister, though the thought hadn't occurred to him until that precise moment. Metaphorical shells aside, he certainly hadn't been thinking about Lydia.

They'd been having a pleasant afternoon, or so he'd thought. He'd been enjoying himself, just as he'd enjoyed himself every afternoon he'd spent in her company over the past three weeks, and not just because of the cake. He'd enjoyed talking, sitting, watching, just being with her, but now the fact that she wanted to know what had happened six years ago made him feel as if storm clouds had suddenly appeared overhead.

It had been hard enough hearing the story of her broken engagement. It wasn't just *what* had happened that bothered him, though that had made him angry enough. It was simply the idea that she'd been engaged at all, to a man she must have cared about, even if she'd been disillusioned fairly quickly. Not that it ought to bother him, he chided himself. After all, he had a former fiancée, too—her own sister, of all people!—but still, hypocrite as he was, it did.

He hadn't been particularly well acquainted with Leo Fairfax, though he remembered him clearly enough. Tall, athletic and, in retrospect, annoyingly good looking with blond hair and blue eyes that made him look like a Greek hero. He and Frances together must have made a strikingly attractive couple before… He stopped himself from completing the thought. It seemed disloyal somehow to imply that she wasn't attractive any more when she definitely was. Not in her own eyes, perhaps, but certainly in his…

Even the way she'd been savouring her lemon bun had been altogether too distracting. So much so that he'd been contemplating a swim in the bracingly cold waters of the North Sea before returning home. It was a strange sensation altogether, this feeling of being drawn to a woman again. Strange and vaguely alarming, as if he were losing some part of his hard-won independence.

For a while he'd assumed that the feeling was simply desire. He'd made a point of looking at other women to see whether they provoked the same reaction, but they didn't. Inconvenient as it was to find himself drawn to his former fiancée's own sister, he didn't find any of them half so attractive as Frances. And inconvenient wasn't a remotely strong enough word. He didn't *want* to be attracted to her. It would be much easier if he could see her as the girl he remembered, a bright-eyed young woman with a happy face and a welcoming smile, nothing more.

He'd always liked her, but now he was starting to like her a little too much for comfort. She'd told him the story of her accident in a matter-of-fact way and yet he'd sensed the anguish behind every word. He admired her strength, though it was obvious her emotional scars ran as deep as the one on her face. Still, her bravery and resilience impressed him. They made him want to be stronger, too. He felt drawn to her on some profound, soulful level. She wasn't the kind of woman who would lie or betray him. And so here he was, cupping her face in his hands, wondering whether she might feel the same way, whether she might want to be kissed as much as he wanted to kiss her, and this was the moment she chose to ask about his past.

He couldn't have asked for a clearer answer than that.

'It's a long story.' He pulled his fingers away from her cheeks, unable to resist tucking a stray tendril of hair behind one ear before he finally let go.

'I've told you mine.' Her voice sounded faintly breathless, though the intensity of her gaze didn't falter. She looked serious, but sympathetic, too, as if she were trying to draw the story out by sheer force of will.

'So you did.' He resisted the urge to touch her again. The rest of her hair was coiled into a bun at the nape of her neck and he found himself itching to unravel it. 'Did it make you feel better?'

'A little. It's never pleasant reliving any painful experience, but it was a long time ago.'

'So was mine, though in some ways I feel as if it was last week. What happened, what I did to my father, that's a burden I carry with me every day.'

'If you don't want to tell me…'

'I don't, but you were honest with me. I owe you the same in return.'

He pulled one knee up and rested his forearm on top, wondering where to begin as he watched Georgie dig a second line of moats around their sandcastles. Had he ever been as young and carefree as that? Perhaps, a long time ago, though he had little memory of it now.

'My father was a difficult man.' He started talking almost unconsciously. 'As far as I can remember, he always was. Even when Lance and I were boys he never smiled or played or spent any time with us unless he was forced to. He was cold and remote, but our mother made up for it. She was the complete opposite, kind and gentle and loving. We adored her, but then she died when we were eleven.'

'I'm sorry. What happened?'

'A fever. I was there at the end. She called me to her and asked me to look after Lance and my father.' He reached down and trailed a path through the sand with his fingers. 'They were both so stubborn and hot-tempered, whereas I was calmer like her. She knew that they were going to butt heads and she wanted me to prevent it somehow. I promised her I would try, though I didn't have the faintest idea how. Maybe I ought to have tried harder. Maybe the effort was doomed from the start. In any case, whatever I ought to have done, I failed. Our father became even more intractable and Lance...well, that was when he started to go wild. I felt trapped in the middle.'

'It must have been awful.' She placed a hand over his and he twisted his fingers around, lacing them through hers.

'It was. Father didn't do anything to stop Lance's behaviour, almost as if he wasn't interested in him. Whereas I... I was the heir, the one he wanted to mould, to shape as his idea of the perfect Viscount. My life was one long series of lectures, but I never argued, never stood up for myself. I left that to Lance. He argued all the time, right up until he ran away to join the army without even telling me. That was the very worst time in my life. I was completely alone with my father, but I still never rebelled. I did what he wanted, behaved the way he wanted me to, but I hated my life. I know it sounds ungrateful when I had so much—a home, a comfortable existence, a title at some point in my future—but I wanted more. I wanted to *do* something with my life, too, but my father thought a gentleman shouldn't soil his hands with anything like work. I felt so helpless and weak and...*crushed*. I wanted to be a good son and my own man, too, but the two were incompatible. Then I met your sister.'

'Oh.' Her fingers twitched as if she were about to pull them away, but he closed his own around them.

'I thought she was the most beautiful woman I'd ever seen, like a ray of sunshine in my miserable existence. I couldn't believe that she liked me, too. I thought that if I married her then somehow everything else would be all right.'

'So you proposed?' Her voice sounded flatter than before.

'No. It was never my intention to keep anything from my father. I would never have asked Lydia to wait for so long either, but then one day I said something about the future and she must have misunderstood. To this day I've no idea how it happened...' He lifted an eyebrow as she gave him a strange look and then pressed her lips into a thin line. 'What?'

'Nothing.'

'It's not nothing. What?'

'You honestly don't remember proposing?'

'I don't remember saying those exact words, no, but I must have...' He frowned. 'Mustn't I?'

'You know for an intelligent man...'

'I can be remarkably naive about women?' He sighed. 'You think she tricked me?'

'No-o, I wouldn't put it quite like that. She might have anticipated you a little, but you *were* in love with her. I saw the two of you together.'

He clasped her hand even tighter. 'I suppose I was, inasmuch as I knew her. I thought that I did, but now... Now I wonder if it was all just wishful thinking. Maybe that's why I didn't try to talk with her more often either. She was my ideal. Maybe I didn't want to risk spoiling the one good thing in my life...' He grimaced. 'That doesn't reflect very well on me, does it? My only excuse is that I didn't like myself very much at the time, but I wonder if it's even possible to love another person under those circumstances? What kind of love is it when we expect the other person to make up for some unhappiness in ourselves? Love should be about giving, not taking.' He shrugged. 'Anyway, I thought that if I did everything else my father expected of me then he'd allow us to marry, but he wouldn't even discuss it.'

'Not at all?'

'I tried persuasion at first. I told him that I was in love, but he refused to listen. Then he told me about the agreement he'd made with Violet's father—without consulting either of us, I might add—for a marriage based solely on money. I thought about an elopement with Lydia, but there was the promise to my mother... I felt as though I'd already failed her in regard to Lance and I didn't want to fail her with my father as well. I couldn't let the whole family fall apart.'

'I doubt she would ever have asked if she'd known the strain it would cause.'

'I don't think she would have either. You know it's funny, but on that last day she told me that I was the strong one.' He laughed as if the idea were genuinely amusing. '*Me*...as if I had some quality my father and Lance didn't!'

'Maybe she was right. You lived with all that pressure for a long time.'

'But I failed in the end. I ran away, too.'

Her fingers tightened around his. '*Why* did you?'

He drew in another deep breath and exhaled slowly. 'There came a day when I decided enough was enough. I'd been to your house that afternoon. You were painting in a corner—a picture of horses, if I recall correctly— and I was just one of Lydia's many admirers. I couldn't bear for things to go on like that any longer so I made a decision. I went home determined to speak with my father, to demand that he let me live the life that I wanted, but he wasn't in his study as usual. He was in the drawing room in his armchair by the fire, drinking whisky and looking at miniatures of me and Lance as boys and crying. I'd never seen him cry before. I sat down and asked him what was wrong and we talked. It was the only real conversation we ever had, all about Lance and my mother and me. I realised that he wasn't such a monster after all, not deep down. He had feelings, only most of the time he had no idea how to open up and show them. That was his tragedy, I think. I told him that I wanted to marry Lydia and he agreed. He even gave me his blessing. It was the best night of my life.'

'Then what happened?'

'I went to bed happier than I'd felt in ten years. When I came downstairs the next morning I was filled with a new sense of joy and purpose. It was a beautiful summer's day and I was going to propose, properly this time, to the woman I thought I loved.'

'And?'

'And he denied everything. He refused to accept the conversation had ever happened. He was so convincing that I even started to wonder myself. He told me that if I married Lydia then he'd disown me as well as Lance and disinherit us both. That was when I saw red, I suppose. I told him that I didn't care about the title or the house or the money, any of the things he thought were so important. I said that I'd marry Lydia without his consent and marched out of the house determined to do just that.'

She lifted her eyes to his with a look of sadness. 'And that was when you saw her with somebody else?'

'Yes. I realised then what a fool I'd been.'

'But why didn't you speak to her?'

'There was no point. She wasn't the woman I'd thought she was, perfect or otherwise. If my heart broke, it wasn't over her. It was over a figment of my imagination.'

'Oh.' There was a strange look on her face. 'But then I don't understand. Why didn't you go home again? If you realised all that, why did you still run away to sea?'

Chapter Twelve

Arthur lifted both of their hands and looked at the interlaced fingers. He'd told Lance and Violet what had happened to him that day, but was he *really* going to tell Frances, too? Did he trust her so much?

'That morning…' he forced himself to speak '…something inside me just seemed to snap. I was afraid that if I went back to my father then I'd never be able to break free from him again. I'd be under his control for years, possibly decades. I found myself at the harbour even before I realised where I was going. I'd always loved sailing so I climbed into our boat and took it out by myself. It was a clear day. There were gannets and puffins and cormorants on the cliff tops, screeching loudly enough to drown out all thought. I remember sitting on the prow, looking out at the water and feeling a strange sense of peace, as if all of my worries, all of the strain I'd been under didn't matter any more. Lance was gone, my father had renounced me and Lydia had found someone else. I'd done my best, but it was over. I'd failed, but I didn't owe anything to any of them any more. So I stopped thinking and just felt…*peaceful*. And then, somehow, I was in the water. It felt soft and comforting, as if I were being embraced by the waves.'

She leaned sideways, rubbing her shoulder against his as if to comfort him. 'Did you want to drown?'

'No. I can see why you might think so, but, no. I wanted to be free, but I never wanted to die. I was just moving by instinct, swimming and swimming further away from the shore. I had this strange idea that it would all be all right, that somebody would find me, which luckily they did.'

'The fishing boat?'

'Yes, on its way back to Scotland. I was half-conscious by then and they probably thought I was either mad or a criminal on the run, but they let me work on the deck anyway. It was hard labour, but I enjoyed it. Bizarre as it sounds, it felt like a kind of rebirth. I was a man without a past, without a name, but it was who I wanted to be.'

'Because you were free?'

'Yes. For nine months, it was as though the rest of the world didn't exist. Then one day, we made port in Newcastle and I decided to join the others for a drink in the harbour. We sat outside a tavern and listened through the open window to the owner telling a story about a family near Whitby, a viscount and his twin sons.' He ran a hand over his head at the memory. 'I heard the truth by chance, all about my father's death and Lance being shot in Canada.'

'Oh, Arthur...' there were tears in her eyes now '...that must have been terrible.'

'It was. I felt as if I'd been living in a dream and I finally woke up to find all the things I'd put out of my head for months crashing down on me like a wave. That time, I really did feel as if I were drowning.'

'But you came back.'

'Yes…' He cleared his throat as his voice cracked. 'I didn't want to, but I had to find out whether Lance was still alive. I hurried back as quickly as I could and broke into Amberton Castle in the middle of the night. It scared him and Violet half to death. They thought I was a ghost at first—understandably, I might add. It wasn't easy, explaining that I'd gone mad for almost a year.'

'You weren't mad. That's not the right word.' She tipped her head, laying her cheek against his shoulder.

'That's what Lance says.' He turned his own head slightly, breathing in the scent of her hair. 'But most people would say I belong in an institution.'

'Most people don't understand what it's like to go through something like that, to feel as if your whole world has been turned upside down.'

'So they're all wrong?'

'They're all judgemental. Anybody might have snapped.'

'Not anybody.'

'How do you know?' She lifted her head again indignantly, narrowly avoiding head-butting him in the chin. 'How does *anybody* know how they'll react in any situation? None of us do, no matter what we might say or think about ourselves. The main thing is that you came back. That *proves* that your mother was right about you.'

He smiled half-sadly, half-affectionately. 'Frances, how can it be strong to lose your senses?'

'Because you regained them! And when you did, you came back and faced what you'd done. Listen to me!' She glared at him as he started to shake his head. 'You were the one who just said that beauty isn't real beauty until it's been tested. Well, maybe strength and courage have to be tested as well. Some people would have given up completely. Some would have kept on running and never come back. Maybe you're stronger now *because* of what happened.'

'At the cost of my father.'

'Your father was as much to blame for the situation as you were! Yes, you gave him a terrible shock, but you never intended to hurt him. Whereas he must have known the pressure he was putting on you. He was the one who refused to let you live your own life!'

'You sound like Lance and Violet.'

'Well, doesn't that tell you something? We can't all be wrong. You should listen to at least one of us.'

'I know. Rationally, I know it, but if I could go back...'

'If you could go back, then you'd still be faced with all the same choices. You'd still have to choose whether to live your life his way or your way. And if you'd chosen his way, then everything would be different. Lance and Violet wouldn't be married and you wouldn't have a nephew or niece on the way.'

'No, I suppose not.' He drew his eyebrows together thoughtfully. He'd never looked at it that way before...

'And who's to say that your father wouldn't have collapsed if you'd stayed? It might have happened anyway.'

He drew his brows even tighter. She was right. His head knew she was right, but knowing and feeling were such different things...

'He was still my father. I loved him despite everything. I wish I could have told him that much at least.'

She squeezed his fingers again. 'Is that why you won't go back to Amberton Castle? Because you feel guilty?'

'In part. It's not easy going back to a place with so many memories, but it's more than that. It's because...' he paused, wondering how *much* of the truth to tell her

'…it's because I made a choice. I made it the moment I got into that boat. I could have gone home after I saw Lydia, but I didn't. I can't go back now as if nothing ever happened.'

'And that's why you won't sit in that armchair by the fireplace?'

He nodded, surprised by her acuity. 'It was his chair. I don't belong there.'

'But—'

'No!' This time he lifted his spare hand to forestall her. 'I've made up my mind about this. I've inherited the title, there's nothing I can do about that, but I want Lance to have everything else. His family, too, after I'm gone. I don't deserve any of it.'

'But what about *your* family? Your future children?'

'We've already established that I've been a bad son, bad brother and bad fiancé. Something tells me I'm not cut out for marriage and parenthood either.'

'Well…' she gave a cynical-sounding laugh '…that makes two of us.'

He nudged his boot into the sand, feeling even guiltier than usual. He'd told her the truth, though still not all of it. Self-reproach and a need to punish himself were only two of the reasons he couldn't go back to Amberton Castle. But how could he tell her the third, the *biggest* reason—that he was afraid of losing his mind all over again? She'd revise her opinion about him being the strong one then… But if they were being truly honest with each other…

'The tide's coming back in.' She broke the silence before he could decide. 'And Georgie looks as if he's finally finished his masterpiece.'

'So he has.' He looked at the chain of sandcastles and

smiled appreciatively. 'What a shame the water has to come back and destroy it.'

'I don't know. He'll be sad for a while, but then he'll forget and start all over again with even bigger plans next time. Isn't that what we all have to do when things get knocked down and broken? We mend them and carry on.'

'Why do I get the feeling you're trying to tell me something?'

'Because you're not the only philosopher here. Besides, friends support each other.'

'So we *are* friends, then?'

'I'm afraid so.' She paused for a moment and then turned serious again. 'Thank you for telling me what happened, but you should know that Lydia never meant to hurt you. She has no idea that you saw her that day.'

'I know. It's strange, I've been angry at her for years, but now I wonder if it was more at myself. I think I wanted to be in love with her more than I actually was. I wanted something good and positive in my life, but it wasn't fair to use her like that. No matter what she thinks, she had a lucky escape.'

'Maybe you ought to tell her that. She has too much time to think at the moment, trapped in the house like a prisoner. It might help her.'

'Maybe I will.' He looked down at her fingers, still held between his. They felt long and delicate and fitted perfectly between his own, as if they belonged there, as if the two of them belonged together. And what on earth made him think that?

It must be the situation, he told himself. The shared confidences, the murmur of the sea in the background, the little boy playing happily beside them, the warm sun and gentle breeze, not to mention those large, almost-black eyes, so deep that a man could drown in them if he wasn't careful, which in his case was a dangerous metaphor indeed… All of those things were conspiring against them, forcing them into a romantic situation that neither of them wanted. They weren't made for romance. Hadn't they just spent the last hour deciding that, telling each other the various reasons they didn't want or believe in it any more? They were both carrying deep scars in that regard, had both decided on solitary, independent futures without romantic entanglements. She might be holding his hand, but she'd been offering him comfort, that was all. And he *was* comforted. Her words were like a balm to his soul. So why did friendship not seem like enough any more? Why did he still want to kiss her? And why did the idea of living on his own seem so less appealing suddenly?

'Are you going to Lance and Violet's garden party?' He surprised himself with the question.

'Me?' She looked equally startled. 'No, I told you, I don't go to social engagements.'

'Neither do I usually, though if it's because of your scar then that's ridiculous.'

'No more than becoming a recluse to punish yourself for something you couldn't help.'

He let one side of his mouth curve upwards, acknowledging the hit. She made a good point. 'Then shall we both make an exception?'

'You mean go to the party?' She turned her face sharply towards the sea. 'I think that my family will be shocked if I do.'

'So will mine. And the rest of Whitby won't know which of us to talk about first. Only I wonder if it's time for us both to face the world again.'

'Why?' She kept her gaze averted. 'Why should we? We don't need to prove anything.'

'No, we don't need to, but I suppose I want to.' He gazed at her profile in the sunshine, resisting the urge to draw closer. 'You've made me want to join the world again, Frances.'

'Oh.' If he wasn't mistaken, her cheeks darkened again.

'You can wear your veil if you want to, but...'

'I don't want to.'

'Good. Then we can go and support each other and if anyone stares, they'll have me to deal with, not to mention Violet.'

'What about Lydia? My parents won't let her attend parties yet, but if anyone tells her that we're friends...'

'I'll speak to her. Soon, I promise. Only let's go to the garden party first.' Despite his own better judgement, he felt suddenly determined to persuade her. 'Will you meet me there, Frances? Will you face the world with me?'

'Yes.' She turned towards him again at last, smiling so widely it took his breath away. 'Yes, I will.'

Chapter Thirteen

'I'd like to come to the Ambertons' garden party with you.' Frances broached the subject with her mother as they walked through Pannett Park the next morning.

'Pardon, dear?' Her mother could hardly have sounded more startled if she'd just announced her intention of running away to London and becoming an actress. 'Did you say that you *wanted* to come?'

'Yes. The invitation was for all of us, wasn't it?' After one swift glance sideways, Frances kept her gaze fixed firmly on the pavement ahead. Her mother's cheeks were a luminous shade of pink, as if she were already embarrassed by the idea of being seen with her. Fortunately, the closest pedestrians were a good ten feet ahead and, as far as she could tell, those approaching from the opposite direction weren't acquaintances. Hopefully that would give her mother sufficient time to recover from the shock, or at least appear to, before she bumped into anyone she knew.

'Of course.' Her mother's voice sounded conspicuously high-pitched. 'I just didn't think you cared for parties any more.'

'I don't, but since Captain Amberton rescued me the other week, I thought it might be churlish to refuse.'

'Oh, I'm sure he wouldn't think so, but if you'd really like to come...' There was a telling pause. 'Well, then, I'll write and accept.'

'Thank you.' Frances took a couple of deep breaths. That was item one out of the way. As for item two, she had a feeling that wasn't going to be quite so easy. After four years of *not* talking about her scar, it was hard to know where to start.

'There's something else.' She found herself blurting the words out. 'I've decided to stop wearing my veil.'

This time her mother's response was less verbal than a high-pitched squeak of alarm.

'My cheek is much better than it was,' Frances pressed on determinedly. 'And once people get used to it, they'll stop looking, don't you think? Hiding it away only makes it more mysterious.'

'Perhaps, but...are you certain, dear?' Her mother looked visibly distressed. 'People can be so cruel. They might say things...'

'I know and, yes, it might be upsetting at first, but I don't want to spend the rest of my life hiding away.' She stopped walking to pull the lace back from her face. 'It's time I faced the world again, Mama.'

'Yes...' her mother's expression softened as she reached up and pressed a hand tenderly against her cheek '...perhaps it is.'

'I don't want—' Frances started to argue and then stopped, the unexpected words of acceptance sinking slowly into her consciousness. 'You mean...you *don't* mind?'

'Not if it's what you want. I'll support whatever decision you make, darling.'

'But what about Papa? What will he say?'

'I imagine he'll feel the same way I do. He loves you, too.'

'But you were the ones who suggested I wear a veil!'

'Only because we didn't want you to be hurt. We thought it might make you feel better, just until you were ready to be seen again.'

'So it wasn't because you were embarrassed by me?'

'Embarrassed?' A pained expression swept across her mother's face. 'Never! Is that what you thought? Oh, my darling, I'm so sorry if we ever made you feel that way. We were only trying to help.'

'But I…' Frances blinked, struggling to readjust her ideas. All this time she'd assumed that her parents were embarrassed, but now it seemed they'd only been trying to protect her.

'I'm so sorry, Frances.'

'Don't be. I should never have assumed anything so horrible. I'm sorry, too, Mama.'

'Oh, my darling.' To her surprise, her mother wrapped her arms around her, pulling her close in the middle of the park, heedless of the scandalised expressions of passers-by. 'You'll always be my beautiful girl, no matter what happens. You're beautiful because of what's in here.' She tapped her chest over the place where her heart was. 'You have to know that.'

'I do now.' Frances hugged her back, vaguely aware that she was crying. The words were so close to the ones Arthur had said and if it hadn't been for him then she might never have heard them. He was the one who'd convinced her that she didn't need to hide any more. He was making her believe it, too, slowly but surely, and now her mother's words seemed to be healing some wound inside her. A wound that had been even deeper than she'd realised.

'Thank you, Mama. If you don't mind, then I don't care what anyone else says about me.'

'Good.' Her mother's eyes were bright with tears, too. 'You've always known what's best for you. You've known that better than I have.' She sniffed sadly. 'Do you remember what you said about Leo the first time he came for dinner? You said that you had a funny feeling about him, as if he couldn't be trusted. Considering what happened afterwards that struck me as very observant. But then you were always a good judge of character. You saw through him straight away.'

'But I thought you liked Leo!' Frances jerked backwards in surprise. 'That's why I agreed to marry him. You and Father said it was a good match.'

'It was.'

'You begged me not to end our engagement!'

'I know. Only I was afraid…' Her mother's voice trailed away.

'You were afraid that after the accident, no one else would ever want me?'

'Yes.' Her mother looked shamefaced. 'But it was wrong of me, I know that now. I should have listened to you in the first place, never mind the second. I should never have encouraged you to marry Leo at all, not when your heart wasn't truly in it, and I certainly shouldn't have tried to stop you from ending it. I should have trusted your instincts then as I do now. That's why your father and I have allowed you have so much freedom over these past few years, because we trust you and we know how much you enjoy your art and jewellery-making.'

'About my jewellery, Mama… I've been selling a few pieces.'

'Yes, I know.'

'What? How?'

'Whitby's a small town, darling. Mr Horsham asked your father before he offered you any money.'

'And Father didn't mind?'

'No. He wants you to be happy, just as I do. We only wondered *why* you wanted to sell it.'

'I suppose…' Frances chewed on her bottom lip for a moment, debating whether honesty really was the best policy '… I suppose I thought I could be independent one day. I never wanted to be a burden to you.'

'A burden?' Her mother looked horrified again.

'But it also makes me happy,' she carried on, hurriedly. 'I don't want people feeling sorry for me. I want to achieve something. My art makes me feel as though I have some value again.'

'You're invaluable to us, darling.'

'Thank you, Mama.' Frances pressed her face against her mother's neck to hide her expression. She'd assumed that her parents thought her reputation and value were as irreparably damaged as her face, but apparently that wasn't true either. *We trust you…* And all this while she'd been deceiving them, not just by going into trade, but by meeting an unmarried man on the beach. Was it possible that her mother already knew about Arthur, too? No, surely they'd been too discreet, but what would she say if she told her? Would she accept that they were just friends? Even if, during that last meeting, they'd felt like more?

'You never know…' she cleared her throat awkwardly '…maybe one day I'll meet somebody who doesn't care about my scar.'

'Of course you might. Somebody worthy of you, my darling.' Her mother dashed a hand over her face and started walking again. 'Maybe at this garden party. I wish there was time to order you a new dress, but perhaps we can alter one of mine. It'll have to be black, of course, but we can still make it pretty.'

'Just nothing too fussy, please.' Frances laughed at her mother's eager expression. 'And not too many frills either. Otherwise, I'm in your hands. You know a lot more about fashion than I do.'

'Yes.' Her mother's face fell again. 'I always did know a lot about that sort of thing. I've been a bad mother in that way.'

'You've never been a bad mother!'

'Yes, I have. I was always too concerned about my own appearance and it's affected both of you girls. I raised Lydia to believe that looks are all that matter and I hurt you by making you feel even worse after your accident. But you see, looks were all I ever had. They were the reason your father married me.'

'Not the only reason, Mama. Father loves you.'

'Does he?' Her mother looked dangerously close to crying again. 'Perhaps he does still, but he fell in love with my appearance. When we were younger, he always enjoyed showing me off. I was his prize and, to my shame, I enjoyed it. I thought it meant that he loved me, but now we barely talk any more.' She sighed. 'Forgive me for saying this, darling, but it's not easy getting old when you've been beautiful.'

Frances squeezed her mother's arm sympathetically. There was something so melancholy in her voice, as if her beauty truly were a double-edged sword.

'Do you think it was the same for Lydia with John Baird? He treated her like some kind of prize, too.'

'Yes, I'm afraid that your sister and I are alike in that way. She always needed to be admired, as I did, and

John Baird set her up on such a pedestal. Although between us…' her mother looked around surreptitiously
'…I don't believe he was her first choice of husband.'

'You don't?' Frances felt her heart start to thump.

'I always thought she favoured Arthur Amberton. I
believe there might even have been some kind of understanding between them.'

'You *knew*?' Frances was too surprised to dissemble.

'So did you?' Her mother's eyes widened like giant
orbs. 'Well… I suppose it doesn't matter now, but I've
always known how your sister's mind works. Only in
Arthur's case, I was afraid he might genuinely care
for her.'

'What do you mean, afraid?'

'Because I knew his father would never allow the
match and he always seemed so unhappy. Falling in love
with your sister would only have made things worse
for him.' She looked pensive. 'When I heard about his
disappearance, I was afraid there was more to it than
simply an accident.'

Frances gazed at her in surprise. Of all people, she
would never have expected her mother to have been the
one who guessed the truth, though her words gave her
a sick feeling, too.

'So you think he was really in love with Lydia?'

'I don't know. With the version he saw of her perhaps,
but I think she was afraid to let him get too close. Your
sister is less secure in herself than you think. Beauty is
all well and good, but admiration isn't the same thing
as love and she knows that, deep down. John, on the
other hand, was content to marry her for beauty alone,
and after Arthur he was the next obvious candidate. Not
a viscount, but wealthy and successful enough to give
her the life she thought she wanted, the life she thought

her beauty deserved, as if she had something to prove to the world. You know with Arthur gone, I think she was genuinely afraid of being left on the shelf. That's why she married so quickly.'

'But if you thought all of this at the time, why didn't you say something?'

'Because I find that most wisdom is only learned in retrospect. I wish I could go back and raise you both differently. I'd set a better example, teach you both there's more to life than how you look.' She smiled fondly. 'You learned that lesson despite me, but as for your sister, I'm afraid it's too late. Do you know, as a girl she was so loving and thoughtful. She never gave a second thought to her appearance. Wherever we went, she always managed to find a patch of mud or some puddle to jump in. I used to despair, but now I'd give almost anything to see that side of her again. I thought that maybe this year in mourning might help, might give her a chance to start again and think about what she really wants from life, but if anything she's only become more self-obsessed. I worry for her. It's as though she's afraid to look any deeper than her own reflection.'

Frances threaded her arm through her mother's as they made their way through the park gates and back on to the street. She'd never thought of Lydia's vanity in that way before, but now she wondered if her mother was right and it *was* really a symptom of some greater fear.

'I'm sure she's all right, Mama.'

'I hope so, but of course she wants to come to this garden party, too, which obviously your father and I can't allow.'

'Yes.' Frances felt a mixture of guilt and relief, glad for once of the strict rules of etiquette that prevented her sister from attending. If Lydia were going to come to the garden party, then she'd have to warn Arthur and he'd doubtless change his mind about attending. Or maybe he'd still come, take one look at Lydia and forget about her own existence altogether. Although if that were going to be the case then surely it would be better to find out sooner rather than later...

No, Frances gave a small secretive smile, *surely* he wouldn't forget her. After everything he'd told her about his past, *surely* he wouldn't do that. He was going to the garden party because he said it was time for them both to move on and face the world again—together—as if they were somehow a pair. As if perhaps they might be more than friends one day. *Was* it possible? Could she risk believing in love again?

'In any case, it's only another few weeks.'

'Hmmm?' She'd lost track of what her mother was talking about.

'It's only a few more weeks until it's been a year and a day since John's funeral. That's the very least expected for full mourning. After that, Lydia can go into half-mourning and I won't restrain her any more.' Her mother heaved a long sigh. 'Not before time either. This last year has been exhausting, like trying to hold back the tide. Just a little longer and then your sister can visit whoever, whenever she likes.'

Chapter Fourteen

'There. Will she approve, do you think?'

Arthur looked at Meg's reflection in the mirror just in time to see the dog tip her head to one side and yawn.

'Well, that serves me right for asking a dog. I appreciate the support.'

He bent down to ruffle the sheepdog's ears and then straightened up again, adjusting his cravat for the fifth—or was it sixth?—time as he tried to judge his appearance for himself. The suit Lance had lent him fitted perfectly and he'd let his hair grow longer over the past few weeks so that he actually resembled the old version of himself today, even if he still refused to grow a fashionable set of whiskers. Loathe though he was to admit it, if it wasn't for that one omission, he might actually pass muster as a gentleman.

'Come on.' He whistled to Meg and started purposefully down the stairs. He'd got out of bed even earlier than usual to see to his chores and he had a boy from the village coming to keep an eye on the animals, but if he didn't hurry then he was still going to be late. It was the first time he'd taken an entire afternoon off in years and he wasn't sure that he wasn't making a huge mistake.

But it wouldn't be so bad, he reassured himself. Most of the guests would be family and close friends of Lance and Violet, though it was inevitable that there'd be a few members of Whitby society as well. Doubtless it wouldn't take them long to report back on a sighting of the reclusive Viscount Scorborough, which meant that he'd have to get used to being an object of gossip again. If he had any sense, he'd turn around, go back upstairs and take a well-deserved nap instead. Damn it all, what the hell had he been thinking, accepting the invitation? And not just for himself, but encouraging Frances to attend, too...

Frances. The thought of her made his heart flip over in an utterly uncharacteristic fashion. She'd agreed to go to the garden party and unveiled, too. Whatever irritations he had to contend with, they paled into insignificance besides that. He wouldn't let her down by backing out now. Being stared at, gawked at and generally speculated upon as if he were some kind of rare zoological exhibit would be irritating, but he could walk away from those. What he couldn't walk away from was Frances, his friend, his *good* friend, his *good friend* who he found increasingly attractive and whose company he found himself craving more and more.

It wasn't an ideal situation. In fact, given the identity of her sister, it was a very long way from ideal, but the need to see her again was becoming an ache, one that he knew he ought to ignore, but couldn't. Over the five days since he'd last seen her, hardly a minute had passed when he hadn't thought about her—and had it really just been five days? It felt like an eternity. He wanted to meet her in public formally, to show her around Amberton Castle, to speak with her parents...

The latter thought drew him up short. Why did he

want to speak with her parents? Surely only a proper suitor would do that and he wasn't one of those…was he?

He sat down on the bench at the front door to pull on his boots. Over the past few days, on those few occasions when he *hadn't* been thinking about Frances, that was, he'd let himself consider what Lance had said about his 'accident' and the other similar cases he'd seen in the army. He'd started seriously to consider the possibility that it might have been an isolated occasion after all, one brought on by an unbearable situation.

Painful though it had been, he'd even allowed himself to think about what had happened to his father. Lance and Frances were both right about that. Yes, he might have contributed to his collapse, but it hadn't been intentional. He'd always feel guilty about it, but he hadn't known what he'd been doing. And if everyone else thought he was punishing himself too much, then why shouldn't he put the past behind him and move on? He didn't feel in danger of another episode again now. On the contrary, he felt happier than he had in a long time. So why shouldn't he banish his fears and lead a normal life? Why *shouldn't* he pay court to Frances?

He wasn't quite sure when he'd started to change his mind about himself and his future, only he sensed that it had been happening for a while, starting around the time when she'd first shown him her scar in his kitchen. He'd thought that his heart was untouchable, but now he realised it had only lain dormant. In any case, now that he'd opened his mind to the idea of being a suitor, he seemed unable to stop thinking about it. At the very least, he needed to speak with Frances since there was the strong possibility that she only thought of him as a friend. The way that she'd rested her head on his shoulder when he'd been telling her his story had *felt* intimate, but perhaps she'd only meant to comfort him. There was only one way to find out…

He closed his front door and strode across the yard, aware of a tingling sensation in his chest that felt, annoyingly, like excitement. As if he were a youth in the throes of first love and not a jaded farmer who was ten years older than the object of his affections… Then he stopped abruptly, caught off guard by a high-pitched squealing sound followed by a commotion coming from the direction of the stable. What the…? He spun quickly towards it, noticing as he did so the open gate of the pigsty, and broke into a run. He must have been so distracted earlier that he'd left the sty open after filling the trough and now the location of his two sows and their twelve piglets was becoming increasingly, and loudly, obvious.

He burst into the stable just in time for five of the piglets to rush past him, leaving his horses jumping and kicking their hind legs in outrage.

'Whoa.' He put a hand on the nearest horse's neck and looked around. The rest of the piglets were already fleeing, leaving a trail of commotion as they trotted back to the yard.

He muttered a string of epithets, pulling his jacket off and draping it over the stable door as he closed it firmly behind him. Then he rolled his sleeves up, surveying the scene with dismay. The piglets were spread out all over, their little pink bodies covered with varying amounts of muck and other substances he preferred not to think about. His suit would never survive the chase, let alone be in a fit state to be seen afterwards, but there was no time for him to go and change or who knew what fresh turmoil he might find. Meg was barking at the top of her lungs, the usually somnolent cats were scattering in all directions, the chickens seemed to be in fear for their lives and the boy from the village still hadn't arrived yet. There was chaos and uproar everywhere he looked. Which meant that he had no choice but to catch them himself. More than that, he had to hurry.

He muttered one last imprecation and charged in.

Frances stood beside a bed of purple-blue hydrangeas at Amberton Castle, feeling as self-conscious as if she were naked. She'd deliberately not brought a veil with her so that she couldn't change her mind and now she felt as though every eye in the garden was upon her.

It wasn't true, of course. The rational part of her brain knew that. On the contrary, most people were busy playing games amid the flower beds, exploring the strange, rose-shaped maze or drinking chilled wine under a canopy that appeared to have been specially erected for the occasion. Her parents, meanwhile, were standing on either side of her like a pair of sentinels ready to do battle so that, although a few people had looked at her face a little longer than was strictly polite, no one had reacted in horror or outrage. Some of her old friends had even smiled as if they were actually pleased to see her out in society again.

Despite that, every introduction had been painful. She'd *felt* every look, felt them as though she were being pummelled by hundreds of tiny, invisible fists. When she undressed for bed that night, she had the vague suspicion that her body would be covered with a patchwork of purple bruises.

Worst of all was the fact that Arthur hadn't come. After the way he'd encouraged her, the way that he'd promised to support her, he'd failed to keep his end of the bargain—a bargain *he'd* initiated! She'd been a fool to think he might actually care about seeing her, to think that he was any more reliable or had any more depth than Leo either. So much for friendship. The next time she saw him, she'd find the biggest stone on the beach and hurl it straight at his head.

'Mr and Mrs Webster?' Violet Amberton approached them with a good-natured smile. 'Would you mind if I borrowed your daughter for a while? My husband keeps insisting I sit down, but I'm afraid that if I do then I won't be able to get up again. A gentle stroll would be just the thing and I'd like a companion. If you don't mind, of course, Miss Webster?'

'Why, I'm sure she'd be delighted.' Her mother looked both startled and pleased at the same time. 'Wouldn't you, darling?'

'Yes, thank you, I'd like a walk very much.' Frances inclined her head politely, temporarily suspending all thoughts of violence against Arthur. His sister-in-law was a far better actress than she would have expected. Nobody witnessing her behaviour would have had any idea that they'd met before.

'There now.' Violet led her towards a gravelled path that meandered its way through the centre of the garden. 'Now that we've officially met and become friends, you'll be able to visit whenever you want, if you want to, of course.'

'Of course. You know I wanted to come before, only under the circumstances…'

'Oh, yes, Arthur explained the difficulty.' Violet squeezed her arm. 'But I'm happy you're here now.'

'So am I.' Despite Arthur's absence, at that moment, Frances realised she felt genuinely happy. 'Your garden is beautiful. What a lovely idea to hold a party outside.'

'Yes, just as long as it doesn't rain. But Lance was right, I could never have coped with a ball. Carrying a baby is more tiring than I expected. I get exhausted even when I'm not doing anything.'

Frances smiled sympathetically. Violet *did* look tired, not to mention at least twice the size she'd been when they'd last met. There was a note of worry in her voice that hadn't been there before either.

'I'm sure everything will be all right.'

'Thank you.' Violet's smile wavered uncertainly. 'Although I have to admit I'm a little nervous.'

'If you want to talk about it…'

'Oh, I wouldn't want to burden you.'

'It wouldn't be a burden. Sometimes talking about a worry can help.'

'Yes, and the truth is…' she looked around with a distinctly guilty expression '… I can't talk to my husband about it. He's worried enough for both of us.'

'Then tell me instead. I'm a good listener.'

'I will. Not today, but another time…' Violet smiled gratefully. 'You know that dress looks very fetching on you.'

'Thank you.'

Frances dropped her gaze shyly. She'd been pleased with the gown her mother had picked out for her, too, albeit somewhat alarmed by the light fabric and low-cut neckline, so different from her usual modest garments, though her mother had argued that in summer, anything else would look ridiculous. It was slightly out of date, with less bunching at the back than was currently fashionable, but they'd made a few alterations together, removing every last trace of flounce and frill so that the long, form-fitting bodice gave her a sleek, elegant line. The only concession to mourning was the colour, but regarding herself critically in the mirror that morning, Frances had been pleased to see that, for the first time in years, she didn't look like a ghost. Her time on the beach had given her cheeks a healthy colour and she had to admit, the combination of tanned skin, dark eyes and black dress did look striking. At the last moment, she'd picked up a black ribbon and slid the pendant she'd carved from the stone Arthur had given her along it, tying it around her throat to complete the effect.

'Is this one of your pieces?' Violet noticed the pendant, too.

'Yes, it's supposed to be a shell.' She felt herself blushing, not that the words themselves were incriminating. Only Arthur would have understood their significance.

'I can tell. It's quite beautiful.'

'I was just thinking the same thing about your house.'

'Oh, yes, it's a lovely place, although it might not be ours for much longer.'

'What do you mean?'

'We're thinking of moving. Not far, only I'd like to be closer to the ironworks so that Lance isn't traipsing about the Moors in all weathers. And this is Arthur's house, after all, no matter what he says.' Violet looked around, her tone a little too uninterested. 'I can't think where he's got to. He definitely said he was coming.'

'Maybe he changed his mind.'

'Oh, I doubt that. Lance took him a new suit this morning.'

'What have I done now?' The man in question came up behind them, wrapping an arm around his wife's shoulders. 'And speaking of *doing*, I hope you're not over-exerting yourself.'

'I'm walking around a garden.' Violet sounded exasperated. 'I haven't jumped over any hedges or climbed any trees. Honestly, if it were up to you I'd spend the next three months in bed being pampered.'

'Isn't that how wives want to be treated by their husbands? I could lie at your feet reciting poetry and feeding you delicacies.'

'Then I really would look like a whale.'

'You know it's hard for a man to discover that his company isn't sufficiently scintillating.' Lance heaved a sigh. 'But then I suppose I always knew this day would come. My wife keeps sneaking away from me, Miss Webster.'

'But I always come back.' Violet smiled mischievously.

'True, but in this case, I'm afraid I really have to steal you away. Your Aunt Caroline and Uncle Ben have just arrived from York. Apologies, Miss Webster, but family duty calls.'

'Why don't you come and meet them?' Violet offered, but Frances shook her head.

'Perhaps in a while. I think I'd like to walk a bit more first.'

'Of course.' Violet squeezed her hand. 'Then we'll see you soon for the dancing. I've asked the band to do a few sets out here, just for fun.'

Frances watched the Ambertons walk away, no doubt debating the wisdom of whether or not Violet should be allowed to dance, then turned her footsteps towards a small woodland area. It still amazed her that two brothers, twins especially, could be so completely different. The contrast between Lance and Arthur was as stark as that between the garden and the Moors beyond. One was cultivated and urbane, the other harsh and rugged. One fitted into society with apparent ease, the other didn't. One was here now, the other... She pushed the thought from her mind. Clearly she'd read more into her friendship with Arthur than actually existed. She'd thought she could trust him for a start. She'd thought she could rely on him, too. She'd even thought that he might care for her a little. All foolishness.

She pushed on through the woodland, trailing her hands against the sides of the trees and letting herself relax away from the crowds. There were a few apple trees, she noticed, laden with such an abundance of fruit that some of the branches drooped almost to the ground. The apples themselves were large and juicy-looking, almost ready for picking. She stopped and slid her back down one of the trunks, listening to the rustle of the leaves above her head. They sounded a lot like the sea, like waves on the shore...two other things that were similar and yet different...

She closed her eyes, letting a shaft of stray sunlight warm her face. Arthur hadn't come. She'd been so sure that he would, but now her disappointment was fading, replaced by a sleepy torpor. He hadn't come, but she was used to rejection...and she was still there, surrounded by warmth and beauty and a feeling of peace that was lulling her into a gentle slumber. The light caress of the breeze on her cheeks felt wonderful and her nook against the tree trunk was surprisingly comfortable. She gave a wide yawn and folded her hands in her lap. Surely a brief nap wouldn't hurt.

Chapter Fifteen

The warm glow dissipated as a shadow fell over her.

'You're a damnably hard woman to find!'

'What?' Frances opened her eyes, momentarily alarmed by the sight of a dark silhouette looming above her. Fortunately, she recognised the voice almost at once.

'I've been looking for you for an hour.' Arthur sounded half-annoyed, half-aggrieved.

'Well, I've been here for…' She frowned. How long exactly *had* she been there? Had she really fallen asleep? She felt slightly groggy. 'Longer than you, anyway! I thought you weren't coming.'

He folded his arms as if he were offended. 'I said that I would.'

'*Eventually*, you mean?'

'I was detained.' He unfolded his arms again. 'By some pigs if you must know.'

'Pigs?'

'Yes, two whole litters of them. They chose a particularly inconvenient time to escape and cause havoc. I was just on my way out of the house.'

He ran a hand through his hair and she narrowed her eyes to take a closer look at him. He was dressed in a plain dark suit, smart enough, but showing some signs of wear, and hadn't Violet said something about Lance taking him a new suit that morning? Besides, his story sounded too ludicrous not to be true.

'So you're late because you've been chasing pigs?'

'Yes. Chasing, shoving and a spot of wrestling, too. Sows are heavy and piglets are slippery, little b—' he grimaced '—creatures.'

'I can imagine.' She pressed a hand to her mouth to cover a giggle.

'I'm glad that you find my travails amusing, but if you've quite finished…' he reached a hand out '… I need a drink. It's thirsty work hunting pigs, not to mention women sleeping in orchards.'

'You haven't had a drink yet?' She took his hand, warmed by the idea that he'd come straight to find her.

'No, we had an agreement, didn't we?' He hoisted her to her feet with one quick tug. 'I didn't want you to think I'd gone back on it.'

'Oh!' She came up so quickly that she bumped straight into his chest with a thud and he caught her elbows to steady her, his gaze intent suddenly.

'You thought that I had, didn't you?'

'Had what?'

'Gone back on my word.'

'Not for the first hour, but after that…' She shrugged. 'Well, what was I supposed to think?'

'So you ran away and hid?'

'I wasn't hiding! I was taking a break and plotting revenge.'

'Indeed?' His eyes glittered with amusement. 'And what particular form of vengeance did you come up with? I doubt it could be worse than chasing piglets.'

'I was going to put sand in your next cake.'

'Is that so?'

'And throw a few rocks at you.'

'That's more like it. Then it's a good job I *did* come to find you. Now, shall we get back to the house before I collapse from dehydration?'

He offered an arm and she looked at it in surprise for a few seconds before finally threading her hand through the crook of his elbow and letting him lead her back to the path, all the while trying to maintain an outward appearance of composure. It felt strange to be touching him. Strange and decidedly unsettling. They weren't doing anything wrong. On the contrary, they were simply walking side by side like any other respectable lady and gentleman. Except that in all the weeks they'd been meeting on the beach, they'd never linked arms before, had barely even touched except by accident. Now she felt acutely aware of her body, of the thump of her heartbeat against her ribcage and the too-fast sound of her breathing, not to mention the thrilling sensation in her side as his muscular arm pressed against it.

'I hope none of the piglets were injured.' She felt a sudden need to keep talking.

'Mmm?' He sounded distracted. 'Oh, no. The only injuries were to my pride and Lance's suit. I was actually managing quite well until one of the sows got into the house. Apparently she wanted to take up residence in the parlour.'

'Oh, dear. What's her name?'

'Whose?'

'The sow's?'

He looked amused. 'I've called her a variety of names today, though none of them would bear repeating in public. Nuisance is probably the politest word.'

'Well, you can't call her that. She needs a name.'

'I believe I mentioned that she's a pig?'

'Even pigs deserve names. Maybe she wouldn't want to escape if you were nicer to her.' She gave him an arch look. 'What was the name of the heroine in the last book you read?'

'I have no idea. I don't get much time for reading any more.'

'The last play you saw?'

'Same answer.'

'I suppose poetry's out of the question then?'

'I know a few sailor's shanties, but I probably shouldn't repeat them to a lady either. Mostly about a girl called...' his lips twitched '...never mind. You'll have to answer the question for me. What was the last book you read?'

'*Alice's Adventures in Wonderland* by Lewis Carroll. I bought it as a bedtime story for Georgie, but then ended up reading it myself.'

'What's it about?'

'Well, there's a girl called Alice who follows a white rabbit down a hole and ends up in a strange hall filled with lots of different-sized doors. Then there's a magical potion and some cake and she grows and then shrinks and there's a dodo and a talking caterpillar and the Queen of Hearts who wants to chop everyone's head off...' She saw his expression and stopped. 'It's hard to explain, but Alice is a pretty name. Or Dinah. That's her cat.'

'Dinah.' He nodded decisively. 'My grandmother's name was Alice. I can't in all conscience name a pig after her.'

'Why not? Pigs are lovely. I'd flattered to have one named after me.'

'You wouldn't have said so if you'd seen them earlier, but I can't allow that either. It would be too confusing if the two of you ever met.'

'Are we likely to?' The question was out before she could think better of it.

'You're welcome to visit whenever you like.' His hold on her arm tightened perceptibly. 'Only you might want to give me some warning so I'll know to put some clothes on.'

'Oh.' She felt her cheeks flood with colour at the memory of their first meeting. 'Yes.'

'In any case, I *won't* name a pig after you. She'll just have to be named after some ridiculous story about dodos.'

'It's *not* ridiculous!' Frances felt indignant suddenly. 'It made perfect sense to me. It's about dreaming and imagination and not being confined by everyday rules. It's about growing up and how hard it is.' She sighed. 'Imagination is a wonderful thing, don't you think? It's an escape.'

'I suppose so.' He gave her a sideways look. 'Is that what your art is, an escape?'

'Maybe in part, but it's also what I love. It's a part of me. And maybe…' she chewed her lip for a few seconds, thinking '… I suppose in some ways it kept me sane after I was injured. It was a link to the past, to the person I was before my accident. Everyone looked at me differently afterwards and for a while I wondered if I really *was* different. I thought that everyone saw me the way Leo did so I hid myself away. I wore my veil so that I wouldn't have to face anyone and because I thought my parents were embarrassed by me. Art was my one constant, the way I kept hold of my *self*. Only now it turns out that I made assumptions I shouldn't have. My parents weren't embarrassed by or ashamed of me so maybe I was wrong about the way other people saw me, too. Maybe *I* rejected everyone else, not the other way round.'

She smiled. 'Which is a roundabout way of saying that I'm glad I came today. You were right about it being time to face the world again.'

'Then I'm glad, too.' He stopped walking to look at her. 'And for what it's worth, in my humble opinion, you haven't changed all that much. There was always something special about you as a girl. Now there is even more.'

'You think so?' She couldn't seem to tear her eyes from him.

'I do.' The hard lines of his face looked softer than she'd ever seen them. Even his eyes looked softer, though there was warmth in them, too, a flickering heat that made her own temperature suddenly soar. 'I don't know how you do it, Frances, but you make me feel calmer somehow. Remember what I told you about my father?'

'Yes.' She nodded, though at that moment she could hardly have felt any less calm. Her heart was hammering so painfully that she was half-afraid it might beat its way through her chest. She wouldn't be surprised if he could actually feel the shockwaves through her arm.

'Sometimes I feel as if he's still here, berating me. I know all the things he would have said, all the ways in which I would have disappointed him, but when I'm with you, all of that goes away. You soothe my spirits, Frances.'

'Oh.' She felt vaguely crestfallen. It didn't sound very exciting. On the contrary, it made her sound like some kind of sleeping draught.

'Judging by your expression, however, I'm even worse at giving compliments than I thought. Did I say something wrong?'

'No.' She lifted her chin a little higher. 'It's just… I'm not a medicine.'

'*Med…*' His brows snapped together again. 'What?'

'It's not much of a compliment, saying that I send you to sleep.'

'Damn it, woman, I never said that! I might be bad at giving compliments, but you're even worse at taking them. I meant that I enjoy your company.' He frowned and then continued more slowly as if he were working out his thoughts as he spoke. 'You make me feel like my old self again, too. Not the one you met in your parents' parlour, but the one before that, from when my mother was alive. You make me feel young and happy again. So what I'm trying to say is that I like you. Very much, in fact. Is *that* better?'

Frances nodded mutely. *Yes*, she wanted to say. *Yes*, put like that it sounded much better. Only she couldn't seem to answer. She couldn't seem to form any words at all. His chest was rising and falling faster than usual as well. Too fast for talking, as if he were as much affected by her as she was by him, as if he'd meant everything that he'd said. And he'd said that he liked her very much...

He lifted his hands slowly, sliding one under the rim of her bonnet to cradle her face and the other around her neck, tilting her head back so that he could look deep into her eyes. She opened her lips, trying to catch her breath since the whole process of breathing seemed to have become increasingly difficult, but his hands were already moving again, distracting her. Both hands were beneath her bonnet this time, his fingers rough but warm, trailing lightly over her cheeks while his thumbs brushed the swell of her lower lip. At last they met in the centre and he leaned forward, his face coming slowly but steadily towards her as she closed her eyes and felt the pressure of his lips against hers...

Oh.

She didn't respond at once, caught off guard by the

sudden rush of exhilaration. *Oh*... For a few moments, it was the only word she could think of, since coherent thought seemed beyond her. *Oh*... She didn't know what else to think since the potent combination of his words and touch seemed to have stunned her as effectively as if she'd been hit over the head. She could only *feel* and what she felt was beyond description, as though her heartbeat was speeding up and slowing down at the same time. Neither did she know how to react since she had so little experience to draw on. Leo was the only other man she'd ever kissed and he'd never seemed to require any kind of response from her. Quite the opposite—on those few occasions, she'd had the vague impression that he'd been trying to crush her.

Arthur's kiss, on the other hand, was completely different, gentle and tender and searching, as if he didn't want to frighten her. Only some instinct told her to move her lips, too, and so she did, pushing her mouth back against his and revelling in the feeling of warmth that seemed to rush all the way down through her body to her toes, as if her very insides were turning to hot liquid.

She heard herself moan out loud with pleasure, her body responding ahead of her mind. Arthur's kiss was everything she'd imagined a kiss ought to be, back in the days when she'd imagined being kissed, that was. If she hadn't been quite so concerned that she was doing it wrong, she might even have called it perfect.

Slowly, he pulled his hands from her face and transferred them to her sides, sliding them down to her waist as she lifted her arms and draped them around his shoulders. She was squeezing, she realised after a few moments, possibly enough to hurt, though he didn't seem to object. He was still kissing her, after all, and his own hold on her waist was far from relaxed. In fact, it seemed to be tightening, too, drawing her ever closer towards him, if such a thing were possible when they were already so close that she could feel the full length of his chest pressed, solid and strong, against hers.

She moaned again, giving herself up to the feeling that his touch aroused in her, a new feeling she'd never experienced before, but that she recognised instinctively. Desire. A surging, rushing torrent of it that seemed to strip away all her inhibitions and consume her whole body. She hardly cared any more whether she was doing it right or wrong. She only did what her instincts told her, what she *wanted* to do. Which was to press even closer, to leave not the tiniest sliver of air between their two bodies, to feel the pounding of their heartbeats and try to quell the ache that seemed to be building and pulsating between her thighs. It was strange how the more she kissed him, the more intense the ache became, as if kissing him would never be enough, as if they were building towards something else… If only she could press harder and—

'Uncle Arthur?' a small female voice interrupted them. 'Aunt Violet's looking for you.'

Chapter Sixteen

Arthur pulled his head back, counting to ten while he arranged his features into an expression suitable for an almost-five-year-old. As attempts went, he thought he ought to deserve some kind of medal. A distinguished one to boot. When he finally managed to speak, his voice sounded almost civil, despite the fact that Frances had leapt so far out of his arms that she was standing on the other side of the grove, looking like a startled deer.

'Harriet.' Somehow he managed a smile. 'You can tell Aunt Violet we'll be along in a moment.'

'All right.' The little girl looked between them with unabashed curiosity. 'Shall I tell her you were kissing?'

'No!' They both uttered the exclamation together.

'But they won't mind.' Harriet blinked innocently. 'Mama and Papa kiss all the time.'

'I'm sure they do.' Arthur threw an amused glance towards Frances, though she looked anything but amused. On the contrary, her skin was a particularly vibrant shade of scarlet. Clearly the moment between them had passed.

'Frances…' He decided to make some introductions before the child could tell them any more about her parents' domestic habits. 'Allow me to introduce Miss Harriet Felstone.'

'Felstone?' She looked confused. 'But she called you uncle?'

'It's an honorific title. Harriet likes to think of us all as one big, happy family.'

'I see.' The red in her cheeks faded somewhat. 'Then I'm very happy to meet you, Harriet.'

'Very pleased to make your acquaintance.' The little girl had clearly been paying attention to adult conversations, too. 'What's that on your face?'

'Harriet!' Arthur started to remonstrate, but Frances waved a hand.

'It's a scar.' She crouched down to give the girl a better look. 'I had a nasty accident and it left me with this mark.'

'It looks sore.' Harriet leaned forward to get a closer look. 'Shall I give it a kiss? That's what Mama does when I hurt myself. She gives me a special kiss to make it all better. I can give you one, too, if you like?'

'Would you? That sounds lovely.'

Harriet nodded seriously and then puckered her lips, pressing them gently against Frances's cheek. 'There. Is that better?'

'Do you know, I really think it is.' Frances looked delighted. 'That *was* a special kiss, thank you.'

'Maybe Uncle Arthur should give you one, too.'

'Maybe he will. *Later.*' He strode forward as a fresh wave of colour washed over Frances's cheeks. 'Only let's find Aunt Violet first, shall we?'

'All right.'

'She's quite a character.' Frances was still blushing as Harriet scampered off ahead of them.

'Four years going on fourteen, but she's a sweet girl, when she minds her own business, that is.'

He gave her a sidelong look. She didn't take his arm this time, which was probably a good thing since he was feeling somewhat hot under the collar himself, his body in only marginally less turmoil than his mind, which was still reeling from the shock of so many mixed emotions, coming one after the other. Anxiety about being late, irritation at not being able to find her, relief when he finally had and then a rush of pure, unadulterated desire. He'd behaved somewhat recklessly in kissing her, but then she was looking particularly fetching. Most of the time her clothes seemed designed to cover as much of her body as possible, but today he could see her arms as well as the long column of her throat, ornamented by a single thin ribbon and…he peered closer… a single black-shell pendant, nestling in the dip between the twin curves of her breasts… If only he'd kissed her *there* when he'd had the chance!

He cleared his throat instead, though his voice still came out husky. 'You didn't mind what she said about your scar?'

'No. She didn't mean anything by it and her kiss was very sweet.'

'Just hers?'

'Not *just* hers, no.' She looked shy all of a sudden. 'Only I wouldn't call yours sweet exactly.'

'Salty?'

'No…' her lips curved upwards '…but something stronger than sweet.'

'Not unpleasant, then?'

'Not that either, although it did take me by surprise.'

'Really?' He lowered his head so that his mouth

skimmed the side of her ear. 'Because I've been wanting to do it for a month at least.'

'You have?' She peeked up at him, looking so incredibly kissable that it was all he could do not to haul her
up against a tree and prove it to her. If it hadn't been
for their small companion just a few feet ahead, then
he would have.

'I thought when you invited me here it was to support
each other...' she paused significantly '...as friends.'

'I thought so, too. Only as it turns out, I've been deceiving myself. Much as I appreciate your friendship,
I believe I like kissing you even more. I'd like to do it
again. *Soon.* Harriet Felstone has a lot to answer for.'

She dropped her gaze again, which was just as well
since the looks directed at them as they emerged out
of the woodland were more than a little speculative.
He really ought to have taken more care with her reputation, he supposed, though fortunately at this end of
the garden, the only witnesses were Lance and Violet.

'I found them!' Harriet announced their arrival
proudly. 'They were...'

'In the orchard.' Arthur spoke over her quickly, relieved when Violet came forward to greet them, albeit
smiling a little too brightly.

'Well, that's a relief. We thought we'd lost you. Frances, I have a dear friend I'd like you to meet, if you
don't mind?'

'Oh...' She tensed visibly and he didn't move, ready
to support her whatever the answer. She looked as if she
were already considering a flight back to the woods, but
then she seemed to rally. 'Of course. I'd be delighted.'

'So...' Lance's expression was positively gleeful as
the two women moved away. '*Still* just friends? I no-

ticed you went rushing off to find her the moment you arrived. And what on earth are you wearing? What happened to the suit I lent you?'

'Trust me, little Brother...' Arthur put a hand on his shoulder, steering him in the direction of a refreshment table '...you don't want to know.'

'I'll take your word for it.' Lance looked both surprised and pleased by the endearment. Despite being twins, as boys they'd always referred to each other as big brother and little brother, though Arthur hadn't done so for years.

'What's this, champagne?' He reached for a glass and took a deep draught.

'Yes.' Lance looked as if he hardly recognised him. 'By the way, the pair of you were looking very sheepish when you emerged from the trees just now. It's a good thing nobody saw you but Violet and I. You'll have her father coming after you if you're not careful.'

'I don't care if he does.'

'Really? Does this mean that you're finally seeing sense?'

'It means that it's my business—and hers.' Arthur took another mouthful as he looked out over the lawn. It was a bigger gathering than he'd attended for years, bigger than he'd expected. 'How many people did you invite?'

Lance rolled his eyes. 'About a hundred and fifty, give or take. Violet's trying to restore the family name.'

'After we both did our best to destroy it?' Arthur took another swig. 'Well, hat's off to Violet for trying.'

'There's something we've both been wanting to talk to you about, actually...' Lance started speaking hesitantly, then stopped mid-sentence as Arthur gripped his arm. 'Ow! What's the matter?'

'I thought I recognised someone…' He narrowed his eyes. In fact, he was almost positive he recognised someone, though at this distance it was hard to be sure… 'Did Violet invite Leo Fairfax by any chance?'

'Probably.'

'Damn!'

'Why?'

'Frances was engaged to Leo Fairfax.'

'*Your* Frances?'

This time he didn't object to the possessive pronoun. 'Yes. It was years ago, after you came back from Canada.'

'Ah.' Lance frowned. 'No, I didn't know. He's over by the trees, paying court to some heiress or other.'

'I don't want Frances being upset.'

'I could ask him to leave.'

'No, she wouldn't want a scene, but I'd better warn her. Where did she and Violet go?'

'To the rose garden, I think.'

'Good. Keep an eye on Fairfax for me. Don't let him go that way.'

Lance nodded purposefully. 'You can count on it, big Brother.'

Frances took a few deep breaths as Violet led her along a pathway lined on each side by sweet-smelling rose bushes, as if breathing deeply would somehow stop her from feeling so self-conscious. Personally she thought that she'd met more than enough people for one day and she felt more nervous than ever after Arthur's kiss, as if everyone would take one look at her and guess what she'd been doing, though surely they couldn't…

'Ianthe?'

Violet called out to a woman in a turquoise gown and plain bonnet, walking arm in arm with another lady

who resembled nothing so much as a wedding cake. She
was wearing an old-fashioned crinoline that looked to
be about five feet across and was clad entirely in white.
Frances blinked at the sight, surprised enough to forget her own anxieties for a few moments. She'd never
seen anyone wear quite so much lace in one outfit and
in broad daylight to boot. It was actually hard to spot
the small face beneath the lace-bedecked parasol and
flowery headdress, though when she did, she saw that
it belonged to an elderly lady who, if she wasn't mistaken, derived great enjoyment from the spectacle she
presented.

'Mrs Ianthe Felstone, Miss Sophoria Gibbs,' Violet
introduced them. 'This is my new friend, Miss Frances Webster.'

'Miss Webster.' The younger lady had doe-like eyes
that sparkled when she smiled. 'How do you do? This is
my aunt Sophoria and…' she gestured behind them towards a strikingly handsome, dark-haired man who was
bouncing a small child in his arms a few feet away '…
my husband, Mr Robert Felstone, and our son, Edward.'

'My Mama and Papa.' Harriet had decided to accompany them.

'Also known as Ianthe and Robert.' The lady laughed.
'My brother Percy and Robert's brother Matthew are
both around, too, though goodness knows where. In any
case, I'm delighted to make your acquaintance, Miss
Webster. Violet's told us so much about you.'

'I'm pleased to meet you, too.' Frances smiled, wondering what exactly Violet had thought to tell them besides the obvious fact of her scar, though neither woman
was staring.

'Are you enjoying the garden party?' Ianthe asked her.

'Yes, very much.'

'I'm sure it will be pronounced a great success.' The older woman spoke this time. 'I never thought a garden could hold so many people.'

'But it's not too busy, I hope…' Violet threw a worried look in her direction. 'Only one invitation always leads to another.'

'I'm having a lovely time.' Frances smiled reassuringly, feeling a sudden urge to prove it as the band struck up a tune. 'In fact, I'd like to dance.'

'You would?' Violet beamed. 'Then we'll have to find you a partner.'

'You'll do no such thing.' Arthur's voice behind her sent a hot quivering sensation racing through her body, as if she'd just touched something scorching. 'Miss Webster's already spoken for.'

He made a small bow and she curtsied back, smiling a goodbye to the others, all of whom looked to be experiencing varying degrees of surprise. Only the older lady looked unperturbed, giving her a knowing wink before she turned away.

'I don't recall us talking about dancing earlier.' Frances looked up at him enquiringly as they made their way back to the lawn.

'I believe it was implied under the terms of our agreement. We're here to support each other, aren't we?'

'So we are. In that case, I'm honoured.'

'There's just something I need to tell you first.'

'You can't dance?'

He gave a snort before his gaze darkened. 'I may be out of practice, but it's not that. It's about one of the guests.'

'Yes?'

'I'm afraid Violet didn't know about your engagement to Leo Fairfax.'

'You mean he's here?' She sucked in a sharp, panicky breath. Not that it should come as a surprise, she realised. The Fairfaxes were pillars of Whitby society, after all. She ought to have guessed he'd be invited.

'We can leave if you want to?'

'No.' She clenched her jaw resolutely. 'I'm not hiding any more.'

'Good. Lance is keeping an eye on him, but...'

'No,' she repeated the word, more firmly this time. 'There's no need for that either. I ought to go and say hello.' She lifted her chin and then faltered. 'Will you come?'

'Try to stop me.'

They made their way through the throng, past a quizzical-looking Lance, towards an attractive-looking couple drinking champagne and talking in the shade of a large oak tree. The lady, Frances noticed, was especially beautiful, with a mass of strawberry-blonde ringlets and vibrant green eyes.

'Leo.' She felt determined to speak first.

'Frances.' His gaze shot straight to her cheek and then past her shoulder. 'How good to see you again.' He cleared his throat as if the words had actually hurt. 'Do you know Miss Braithwaite?'

'I don't believe that we've met, no. A pleasure, Miss Braithwaite.' Frances smiled politely, though the woman seemed to be having as much trouble meeting her eyes as her former fiancé. 'Although I believe you know Lord Scorborough, Leo?'

'Yes, of course. Scorborough.' Leo held out his hand, though for a moment she thought Arthur was going to ignore it. He simply stared at the other man for a few seconds, neither moving nor speaking, before he finally took hold of his hand and shook it. Judging by the sudden grimace on Leo's face, however, it was less of a shake than a crush.

'Well, it was good to see you again.' Frances put a hand on Arthur's arm, vaguely alarmed by the grimness of his expression. 'But I think the dancing's about to begin. Will you excuse us?'

'Of course.' Leo looked visibly relieved.

She pulled Arthur towards the area of the lawn cleared for dancing, waiting until they were in the midst of the gathered couples before whirling on him. 'What was *that*?'

'What?' Arthur shrugged nonchalantly. 'I was saying hello.'

'You didn't *say* anything!'

'Didn't I?'

'No! I think you actually hurt his hand. I never thought I'd feel sorry for Leo, but that looked painful.'

One side of his mouth curved sardonically. 'It's a trick my old skipper taught me. He used it when he didn't like the price he was being offered for his catch. The number would get higher the longer he held on.' He lifted an eyebrow. 'Surely you don't feel *that* sorry for Fairfax?'

'No.' She bit her lip and then couldn't repress a giggle. 'Maybe not.'

'Good. Now, I believe the first dance is a waltz. A little surprising for the outdoors perhaps, but since we're breaking every other rule today…' He winked as he put one hand on her waist. 'If you'll permit me, Miss Webster?'

She wasn't sure when the music started or what the band was playing. She was only vaguely aware of the steps, too, though she seemed to be moving relatively smoothly, Arthur's hands guiding her through a mass of swaying couples. There were other people there, too, gathered around the edges of the lawn watching them, but everyone seemed perfectly good-natured. Her parents were smiling and nobody was staring at her with disgust or derision, except perhaps Leo, who was cradling his hand and looking as though he'd just swallowed a bee.

'I could still go and horsewhip him if you want?' Arthur murmured in her ear and she laughed.

'I think you've done enough.'

'Well, the offer stands. After wrestling a battalion of pigs, I don't think Leo Fairfax should prove too much of a challenge. But I don't want him ruining things. I want today to be special for you, Frances.'

Special... The word reminded her of what he'd said in the orchard and she stumbled, her knees giving out briefly beneath her.

'Are you all right?' Arthur caught her up again instantly, sweeping her round in a circle as if nothing untoward had happened.

'Yes. It's just been a while since I danced.'

'Me, too. There isn't much occasion for it on farms or fishing boats.'

'Do you *still* miss it?' She felt nervous asking the question. 'Being at sea, I mean?'

'No. I did for a long time, as though my body had come home, but the rest of me was still lost at sea somewhere, but now I finally feel as if I'm whole again, body and soul and heart, too.' He looked so intense that her every nerve ending seemed to tingle in response. 'What about *you*? How do you feel, Frances?'

Happy. That was the first word that entered her head. Unexpectedly, incontrovertibly, deliriously happy.

'I feel whole again, too,' she answered simply and then smiled up at him. Whole and happy and not about to let anybody, Leo Fairfax especially, ruin it for her.

Chapter Seventeen

'Is something the matter, dear?' Mrs Webster peered anxiously at Lydia across the luncheon table. 'You've hardly eaten a mouthful.'

'I'm not hungry, Mama.'

'Is there something else you'd like? Shall I ask Cook?'

'No.' Lydia folded her napkin. 'I just need some fresh air. I've decided to make some calls this afternoon.'

'Calls?' Their mother's face blanched slightly.

'Yes. It's almost a year since John passed away. Surely I can set aside full mourning now?'

'But you're so close, darling. Don't you think you could wait just a bit longer?'

'No.' Lydia's tone was adamant. 'I want to go out and I've already asked for the trap to be brought round. I won't be gone long, but if I stay in this house any longer, I'll scream.'

'Oh, dear...' Their mother still looked faintly queasy as Lydia marched out of the room. 'What do you think, darling?'

'I think she's right.' Frances picked up her teacup and sipped at the contents. 'She's been trapped inside long enough. This past year has been very hard on her.'

'I know. I only wish I could speak with your father, but he's gone to his office already... Do you think I ought to send him a note?'

Frances looked out of the window speculatively. After almost a full week of rain, the sun was shining again at last. The Ambertons' garden party had been succeeded by a series of storms that had kept most residents of Whitby trapped indoors so that she'd felt even more empathy for Lydia's predicament than usual. The days had seemed interminable. Not being able to go out, to go down to the shore, to see Arthur...

She sighed as she recalled her last glimpse of him. After their waltz, she'd danced a polka with Robert Felstone, a galop with Ianthe's brother Percy, then played hoop rolling and skittles with Arthur, Harriet and some of Violet's younger cousins until the party had finally drawn to a close. He'd handed her up into her parents' carriage, his fingers lingering on her elbow and even squeezing slightly before he released her, as if he'd been trying to convey some kind of message.

'Frances?' Her mother's voice penetrated her thoughts.

'Sorry, Mama, I was dreaming.'

'So I noticed. Do you know, both you and Lydia have been doing that a lot recently? Sometimes I think I might as well talk to the walls. I asked if you thought I ought to send a note to your father?'

'No. Lydia said she won't be long.' And judging by the sounds of preparation coming from the hallway, she was already halfway out of the front door...

'Well...' Her mother sighed. 'I'm still not altogether sure that she ought to, but at least it might stop her staring into space all afternoon.'

Frances took another sip of her tea. She'd been pre-occupied with her own thoughts over the past week, but now that their mother mentioned it, Lydia *had* been uncharacteristically pensive. In fact, she'd been acting oddly ever since the morning after the garden party. She'd caught her staring in her direction a few times, too, her gaze openly resentful, almost jealous, as if she knew what had happened between her and Arthur, although surely she couldn't. Who could have told her? They'd received a number of callers over the past few days, but she'd been in the parlour with all of them and nothing particular had been said. Which meant that the only person who could have said anything was…

'Mama?' She peered over the rim of her teacup, trying to sound casual. 'I suppose you told Lydia all about the Ambertons' garden party?'

'Why, yes, of course. Truth be told, she overwhelmed me with questions, but I suppose that was only to be expected. I'm sorry she had to miss it.'

'Did she ask about Arthur Amberton by any chance?'

'Well, I told her the pair of you danced.' Her mother threw a swift glance at the door. 'After all, it's been six years since she last saw him and I didn't think that she'd mind. I thought she might even be pleased for you, though I have to say she didn't look it.'

'Did you tell her that we played games afterwards?'

'Well…yes. It was such a charming sight, the two of you playing with the children like that. I must say he was very attentive to you.'

'I'm sure he was just being polite.'

'Perhaps—' her mother's eyes shone '—although I doubt it was *just* politeness. Good manners aren't the first thing one associates with Arthur Amberton these days.'

Frances stood up and wandered across to the window again, her mother's words ringing in her ears. It was true, Arthur *wasn't* known for his gentlemanly behaviour any more, but maybe that also explained why he'd been silent for the past week. Admittedly, it hadn't been safe to walk on the beach due to the size of the waves and she hadn't expected him to call at the house with Lydia living there, but couldn't he have sent a letter? Or even a note, just *something* to suggest that he hadn't already forgotten her! *He* was the one who'd said that he wanted to kiss her again—and soon—so where was he? Was he busy on the farm or was he regretting what had happened? She tensed at the thought. The afternoon of the garden party had seemed so perfect, but perhaps it had all been an illusion, an idyllic interlude with no relation to everyday life. In which case, perhaps his kiss had simply been a passing fancy, too…

She paused with the teacup halfway to her lips, surprised by the sight of Lydia standing on the pavement outside talking to a boy, the baker's boy if she wasn't mistaken. Instinctively, she took a step back, concealing herself behind the curtains as Lydia looked around furtively and then handed him a piece of paper.

Frances watched carefully, struck with a faint prickle of suspicion. Strangely enough, Lydia hadn't uttered a single word to her about Arthur ever since the garden party despite her incessant questions beforehand, which was especially odd considering what their mother had told her. And Lydia was planning to go out this afternoon, with a particularly determined look on her face. The trap was already standing by to take her…

Frances put her teacup aside and ran out of the dining room, across the hallway and down the backstairs, running along the alleyway and emerging into the street just in time to catch the boy before he turned the corner.

Fortunately, there was no sign of Lydia as she called out to stop him.

'Sam?' She ran up, panting. 'It's Sam, isn't it?'

'Yes, miss.'

'Did my sister just give you a message?'

'Not a message, miss, just a note.' He looked anxious. 'But I'm not supposed to talk about it.'

'No, of course not, I understand. Only I wondered if you could tell me who it's for?'

'I don't think I ought to, miss.' He scrunched up his mouth for a moment and then grinned. 'But I'm not to deliver it for another half-hour. That's the important part.'

'I see. Well, that's good to know, thank you.'

'You won't tell her I said nothing, will you?'

'It'll be our secret.' She reached into her pocket and fished out a coin. 'You've been a great help, Sam.'

She ran back to the house, pausing in the hallway to catch her breath and try to unravel the mystery. If Lydia was going to visit Arthur, as she suspected, then why would she send him a note, too? It didn't make any sense. Why send a note to a man you were already visiting? Unless the note was for somebody else. Somebody who might then take it upon themselves to go and intrude upon them… She gasped, half-shocked by the idea of anything so underhand, half-appalled at herself for being so suspicious. If she was right, then it meant she had less than an hour to get to Arthur and warn him, but *surely* she couldn't be right. Surely not even Lydia would do anything so brazen… But what was it she'd said when she'd first asked her to visit him on her behalf? *If she could just have ten minutes alone with him…*

Frances grabbed her cloak and bonnet, pulling on her sturdiest pair of boots before running back out into the street and down towards the beach. At least the tide was out, that was one small mercy, and the damp sand would be easier to run on. If she was wrong, then it didn't matter, but if she was right, then Arthur Amberton was about to find himself caught in a trap.

She only hoped she could reach him before it snapped shut.

Arthur climbed over a low stone wall and trudged back towards the farmhouse, Meg at his heels. He'd been up since dawn, mending fences that had been damaged in the previous night's storm and his stomach was complaining loudly. He needed something to eat, then he needed to check on his animals and then...well, then perhaps he could take a walk down to the beach and see if Frances was there. It had been almost a whole week since the garden party, six days since he'd kissed her, one hundred-and-forty-four hours of missing her company and dreaming about taking a chance on the future after all...

Violet certainly thought that he should. She'd taken him aside after the garden party to tell him as much in no uncertain terms, as he recalled. Lance had shrugged apologetically in the background, though he'd clearly agreed with every word. Neither of them had seemed to think that he was too unstable and for the first time he hadn't argued back. He'd awoken the next morning positively eager to run down to the beach, only to find the Yorkshire weather conspiring against him. It had barely stopped raining since.

He stopped as he rounded the side of the barn, heart leaping at the sight of a trap parked outside the house. Had Frances decided to visit him there instead? He'd said that she was welcome at the farm whenever she wanted, but he hadn't actually expected her to come.

Not that it mattered, he told himself as he hurried towards the house and pushed open the front door, stopping short in surprise when Meg gave a bark.

'Who is it?' he called out, his heart sinking slowly and then plummeting rapidly as a woman swathed head to foot in dark purple stepped out of the parlour to greet him. She was just as beautiful as he remembered, possibly even more so, but he had to fight the impulse to turn round and run at the sight of her.

'Arthur...' She held both of her hands out in greeting. 'It's good to see you again.'

'Lydia.' He ignored the gesture, folding his arms instead and resolving to lock his front door from now on. 'What are you doing here?'

'You didn't respond to my letters.' Her voice sounded faintly tremulous, as he guessed it was intended to. 'I had to come and speak with you face to face.'

'I *did* respond. I thought I made my answer clear.'

'That wasn't an answer, it was simply a refusal! How could you be so cruel?' She rifled inside her reticule, drawing out a frilly handkerchief to dab at her eyes. 'After everything we meant to each other?'

'That was six years ago. A lot's happened since then. Too much.'

'So you won't even talk to me?' The handkerchief dabbed again. 'You won't let me explain?'

'There's no need to explain. You thought that I'd drowned so you married another of your suitors. That's about right, isn't it?'

'Arthur!' Lydia's eyes opened wide. 'You make it sound so sordid.'

He heaved a sigh and gestured for her to precede him into the parlour. After all, perhaps Frances had been right. Perhaps he ought to have met with Lydia when she'd first asked him to, ought to have let her say her piece so that she wouldn't have felt compelled to visit him. Perhaps he owed her that much for old times' sake. At the very least, he ought to hear her out now.

'I apologise.' He took a seat and cleared his throat. 'I shouldn't have said that. I'm not angry, Lydia, not any more.' To his surprise, he really wasn't. Even looking straight at her, he didn't feel the slightest hint of anger. 'Honestly, I think you did the right thing. I truly hope you were happy with John Baird.'

'I...well, yes, I suppose I was...that is, as happy as I *could* have been under the circumstances.' Lydia's eyes seemed to grow bigger and rounder the longer she talked. 'But I always still thought of you. I know that sounds awful, but we were so perfect together.'

'No.' Arthur shook his head firmly. 'We weren't. How could we have been when we never really knew each other?'

'But of course we knew each other! How can you say otherwise?'

'Because we never *talked*, Lydia, not properly anyway. I never knew anything about your hopes or your dreams or interests, nor you about mine. I told you about my father's objections to our marriage, but I never told you how I felt or how unbearable my life was with him. I never thought you wanted to hear any of that. You always had a crowd of admirers about you.'

'But I never cared about any of them!' She paused briefly. 'Except for John Baird, of course.'

'Of course.' Arthur fought to stop his eyebrows from lifting. 'Look, I'm not trying to hurt you by saying this, but I don't believe either of us was ever truly open and honest with the other, or with ourselves for that matter.

We should never have got engaged in the first place. It was a mistake. Doubly so to keep it a secret.'

'But we *were* engaged!' Lydia was starting to sound desperate. 'It was never formally ended.'

'Except by your marriage.' He held a hand up before she could say anything else. 'I don't want to argue. I resented you for a long time, but now I see that I was at fault, too. In any case, it doesn't matter any more. The plain truth is that we would never have made each other happy, Lydia. We were never in love, not really.'

He reached for her hand, trying to draw the sting from his words. She was really quite extraordinarily beautiful, he thought absently, with the kind of face a painter might yearn to immortalise. He'd been utterly besotted once, but now, beautiful as she was, he could look at her and feel...nothing. In fact, when he looked at her face now, he had the strange impression of something lacking...a red scar on the right cheek. Oddly enough, her face looked wrong without it, or at least his idea of the perfect woman's face did. Because his idea of the perfect woman's face was quite simple. It belonged to Frances.

'Not all marriages are based on love.' If he wasn't mistaken, the tears in her eyes were genuine this time. 'We could still be happy.'

'No. *I* couldn't and I doubt that you would be either. You deserve to be with somebody who truly loves you. Only I'm not that man.'

'Have my looks faded so much then?' She looked visibly shaken. 'Am I so unappealing to you now?'

'Lydia, you're still the most beautiful woman in Whitby, in the whole of Yorkshire most likely, but looks aren't everything.'

The tears in her eyes dried instantly, replaced by a flash of anger. 'This is revenge, isn't it? You're trying to hurt me for marrying John. *That's* why you danced with Frances at the garden party, too! Oh, yes, I heard all about the attention you paid her, but I was going to forgive you!'

He dropped her hand. 'Do you really think I'd use her like that?'

'Why else would you dance with her?' Her mouth dropped open and her tone shifted abruptly. '*Why*, Arthur?'

'Why do you think?'

'You mean…you care for her? You're in love with her?'

'Yes.' It didn't occur to him to either hesitate or deny it. It was true, although ironically enough, if Lydia hadn't asked him directly, he might never have realised the extent of his feelings. He didn't just like Frances, he was in love with her. He wanted marriage and a future with her. And he was telling the wrong woman.

'She's my sister!'

'Yes.' He couldn't deny that either.

'How could you? How could either of you?'

'It wasn't intentional. I know it's not ideal, but it's not revenge either.'

'But how did it happen?' The anger seemed to drain out of her face suddenly, her gaze flickering towards the clock on the mantelpiece. 'When? She's hardly mentioned you since…' her voice dropped to almost a whisper '…she took you my message.'

'Yes. We've been meeting on the beach ever since.'

'In secret? But why didn't she tell me?'

'Maybe she didn't want to upset you. We were only friends to begin with.'

'To begin with…' Her eyes drifted back towards the clock again. 'Well, then, I should go.'

'Lydia?' He wasn't quite sure what her expression

was, only that it seemed to contain a hint of panic. 'Are you all right?'

'Yes. I just think that we've said enough, don't you?'

She hurried towards the parlour door and then stopped, uttering a shrill exclamation and whirling around at the sound of hoofbeats and wheels outside.

'Who's that?' Arthur moved towards the window, just in time to see a carriage draw up in the yard. 'Lydia?' He turned around again, narrowing his eyes suspiciously when she didn't say anything. 'What's going on?'

'It's my father,' she answered through white lips. 'He's come looking for me.'

'And how exactly would he know where to find you?'

'Because…' she seemed unable to look at him directly now '…I went to visit my friend Amelia Kitt before I came here.'

'Amelia Kitt, the biggest gossip in Whitby?'

'Ye-es. I arranged for a boy to deliver a note to me at her house.'

'What did it say?'

'Nothing, it was blank. Only I might have implied that it was important and…' she winced '…personal.'

'And then you told her you were coming here?'

'Yes.'

'On your own?'

'Yes, but I begged her to be discreet!'

'Knowing full well that she couldn't be?'

'I…yes.'

'And that she'd think it her duty to tell your parents, not to mention the rest of Whitby?'

'*Yes!*' Her expression turned angry again suddenly. 'But it wasn't supposed to happen like this! I thought that once you saw me and I explained everything in person then it would all be all right. I thought you'd be glad if my father found us.'

'You thought I'd be *glad* to be trapped?'

'Not trapped. Only I thought you might need a little bit of encouragement, that's all, like last time.'

'Encouragement.' Arthur repeated the word flatly, listening to the sound of a carriage door opening outside. Well, all credit to Lance, he'd warned him often enough that this might happen and now it was too late to do anything about it. He wished he'd jumped out of the parlour window when he'd had the chance.

'I'm sorry.' Lydia looked genuinely remorseful.

'Then prove it. Tell your father the truth. Tell him I had no idea you were here.'

'I can't!' All of the blood seemed to drain out of her face. 'He'd never let me out of the house again.'

'Well, if you think that marrying me is the solution then you're mad!'

'Better mad than a prisoner. I've spent the last year trapped indoors. I can't go through that again!'

Arthur stared at her incredulously, hearing the creak of the front door opening, followed by ominous-sounding footsteps in the hallway. *Was* she mad? He'd just told her that he didn't care for her, that there was no future for them, that he was in love with her sister and she *still* wanted to trap him into an engagement? Worst of all was that there wasn't a damn thing he could do about any of it! He didn't want to be trapped, but if he refused then he'd be acting like the worst kind of dishonourable cur, destroying both Lydia's reputation as well as his own chances of paying court to Frances if he could, by some incredible chance, find a way to escape. If those chances weren't utterly destroyed already...

'*Scorborough?*'

Thomas Webster loomed in the parlour doorway, accompanied by the infamous Amelia Kitt, a pretty blonde who was trying and failing to conceal her avid curiosity behind a veneer of concern. Not one, but two witnesses, and not just family members who might be persuaded to stay silent. Arthur swore inwardly. When it rained, it certainly poured.

'Mr Webster, Mrs Kitt.' He made a formal bow. 'What an unexpected pleasure.'

'There's no pleasure about it! What's going on here?' The tone of Webster's voice showed he was in no mood for social niceties.

'It's not what you think, Papa. It's all a misunderstanding.' To her credit, Lydia attempted a defence. 'Arthur and I were just talking.'

'*Talking?*' Her father's bellow filled the room. 'Tell me, what kind of respectable lady comes unescorted to a gentleman's house simply to *talk*?'

'Oh, Lydia!' Mrs Kitt could hardly contain her excitement. 'How could you be so indiscreet? I felt it my duty to warn your father where you were going, but how could you? You'll be ruined.'

'She will not.' Her father strode into the room, hauling himself up to his full height. 'Not if I have any say in the matter.'

Arthur watched as the older man's face turned from puce to dark purple, almost the same shade as Lydia's dress. It was strange, he thought, to discover exactly what you wanted most in life just at the moment it became unattainable. He had a sudden clear vision of Frances beside him, living here in his house, sitting by his fireside, sleeping in his bed, doing more than sleeping... He felt a sharp pang of regret. *That* was the future he wanted. Except that now he was going to have to marry her sister.

'Papa, I know it looks bad…' To his surprise, Lydia was still trying to talk them out of it.

'It looks worse than bad! It's shameful! How long has this been going on?'

'Nothing's going on! This is the first time I've visited, I promise.'

'Then you'd better have a good explanation…'

'She came to find me.'

The voice from the corridor made every head in the room turn around. Was he imagining things now? Arthur wondered, as the very woman he'd just been yearning for appeared in the doorway, looking to all intents and purposes as if she'd just wandered in from the kitchen, without a cloak or a bonnet or any sign of a veil. He blinked a few times to be sure. It was definitely Frances, but what was she doing there? *How* had she got there? If she'd come in through the front door then surely someone would have noticed.

On the other hand, what did it matter when he'd never been so glad to see anyone in his whole life?

'Frances?' It was Mrs Kitt who spoke this time as her father appeared to be speechless.

'Hello, Papa, hello, Amelia. I was just about to make a cup of tea.' Frances gestured behind her, smiling blithely as if she were already the mistress of the house. 'Would anyone else care for a cup?'

Chapter Eighteen

'Will somebody please explain to me what in blazes is going on!'

Frances winced at the sound of her father's roar. She hadn't thought that his voice could get any louder, but apparently she'd underestimated him. He sounded as if he were trying to summon the entire population of Sandsend village to the door. He'd been loud enough from the dining room where she'd eventually managed to force a window jamb open and climb inside without anyone either seeing or hearing her, but now he was positively deafening.

Unfortunately, she wasn't entirely sure that she *could* explain. She'd arrived at the farm just as her father's carriage had drawn up, too late to either stop Lydia or warn Arthur. One glimpse of the trap by the front door had told her everything she'd needed to know about what was happening inside and, if it hadn't, then her father's shouting would have made it clear soon enough.

She'd arrived too late, but she still had to do something. No matter her loyalty to Lydia, no matter her own feelings for Arthur either, she couldn't let him be trapped. He didn't want to marry *anyone*, he'd made that clear early on in their friendship, and she wasn't about to stand by and let it happen. No matter what else, they were friends, and friends didn't let other friends be coerced.

In which case, she'd decided, divesting herself of her outer garments, there was only one thing she could do, something that would make her father's earlier outburst seem like a gentle breeze beside a hurricane, but she had no choice. She only hoped that Arthur understood.

'Of course, Father.' She moved further into the room, smiling with a calmness she was a long way from feeling. 'It's all perfectly innocent.'

'*Innocent?*' Her father sounded on the verge of an apoplexy. 'First Mrs Kitt arrives to say that my eldest daughter is compromising herself with an unmarried gentleman, then I arrive to find not one, but *both* of my daughters alone and unchaperoned? Which part of all that is innocent?'

'Lydia's. She came to *be* my chaperon.' Frances threw a nervous glance at her sister, afraid that she might contradict the statement, but to her relief she didn't utter a word.

'Lydia came for you?' Her father looked suspicious, angry and confused all at the same time.

'Yes. It's all very silly really.' She forced a laugh. 'Only I met Arthur at the Ambertons' garden party last week and he told me all about his piglets. They escaped that day, you see, and it just sounded so comical that I wanted to see them. I suppose it was a bit indiscreet of me to come on my own, but it was such a nice day and I was so eager that I walked here along the beach after lunch. I had no idea of anyone seeing me, but I suppose somebody must have and sent word to Lydia, who came to rescue me.'

'You call that indiscreet? Have you taken leave of your senses, girl?'

'I hope not, but it's really not so bad. Once everyone knows that it was me and not Lydia who came unescorted, then they'll understand it's all just a storm in a teacup.'

'I very much doubt that!'

'You're absolutely right, sir,' Arthur interjected before she could argue again. 'I ought never to have invited your daughter to visit. It was inappropriate and ungentlemanly and I beg your forgiveness.'

'If you want my forgiveness, then you can put the situation right, sir.'

'As I have every intention of doing.'

'What?' Frances spun towards Arthur in alarm. He'd looked as shocked as everyone else when she entered, though she'd avoided catching his eye ever since, afraid of what she might see there. Would he think her brazen, too? 'No! Don't be ridiculous!'

'I don't believe it's ridiculous.' He ignored her protest. 'Miss Webster, would you do me the honour—'

'There's no need for this!'

'—the *very* great honour—'

'You don't have to—'

'—of accepting my hand in marriage?'

'Of course she will!'

'Father!' Frances swung from Arthur to her father and then back again in dismay. The whole situation was spiralling out of control and she couldn't seem to stop it. This wasn't what she'd intended, not at all! She'd come to rescue Arthur, for pity's sake, not to spring another trap. She already felt as though the walls were closing in around them and yet, oddly enough, he didn't look angry. Quite the opposite—his lips were curving in a

smile, a surprisingly serene-looking smile, almost as if he didn't mind at all…

She gaped at him in shock. Arthur Amberton was *smiling*!

'Perhaps you could give us a moment to discuss this alone?' The words were addressed to her father, though she didn't move her eyes from Arthur.

'Absolutely not!'

'But—'

'No buts! You've had too much freedom altogether, young lady, if this is what comes of it. If you think that I'm letting you out of my sight again before your wedding day, then you're very much mistaken!'

'Papa…'

'Lord Scorborough.' Her father held a hand out towards Arthur. 'I know you're a man of your word, no matter what else people say about you. I'll expect you to call on me soon.'

'Gladly.' Arthur shook his hand firmly. 'I look forward to it, sir.'

'Good. In that case, I believe that we've all had enough excitement for one day. Frances, Lydia, Mrs Kitt…' he gave each of them a look that brooked no opposition '…we're leaving.'

Frances sat on her mother's newest purchase, a rococco-style sofa in the parlour, staring at the wall after the worst night's sleep of her life. She'd felt even more disturbed than she had after her accident. Back then she'd lain awake night after night, her emotions in turmoil as she'd struggled to come to terms with what had happened, but at least she'd only had herself to worry about. Now she was afraid she'd managed to ruin someone else's life, too.

Hadn't Arthur understood what she'd been doing

when she'd burst into his parlour so unexpectedly? Hadn't he guessed that she'd come to rescue him, not to trap him for herself? It had taken all of her nerve to go through with it, especially in front of her father, but at that moment it had seemed like the only way to save him from Lydia's trap. Even now, she didn't see what else she could have done.

Except that somehow it had all gone wrong. She'd saved him from one engagement only to shackle him into another—with her! She ought to have known that he'd do the honourable thing and protect her, though surely he must have been fuming inside. No matter how well he'd hidden it behind that enigmatic smile, he must have been rueing the day he'd ever set eyes on her, seeing her intrusion as a betrayal, perhaps even another scheme...

She tipped her head back and threw an arm over her face. She really ought to take a nap. No doubt she looked even worse than she felt, but she already knew that sleep would elude her. Everything she'd thought and expected of her future had been turned on its head. Never mind what Arthur thought of their situation, she didn't even know herself. She was engaged. The whole situation seemed bizarre, incredible even. She had put aside all thoughts of marriage after Leo, so it was hard to open her mind up to the idea again, even harder to work out how she felt about it. She liked Arthur. They were friends. No...she chided herself...after their kiss, they were surely more than that, but as to *what* she had no idea...

In any case, there was a long way between liking and loving. When she was younger she'd always expected to marry for love. She'd convinced herself that she cared for Leo, ignoring the self-centred, shallow side of his character simply because she'd wanted a love story and not a marriage of convenience, but deep down, she'd known it hadn't been real. Was she making the same mistake with Arthur? Ignoring his dark side simply because she didn't want to see it?

No. Despite everything, her lips curled at the thought. She knew all about Arthur's dark side. After just a couple of months, she knew it, knew *him*, better than she knew almost anyone else in the world and she *still* liked him. More than that, she loved him.

She let her arm fall to her side again, struck by the force of her sudden conviction. She loved him. Surely that was the other reason, besides friendship, why she'd run headlong along the beach to rescue him, faster than she'd ever run before, so fast that she'd thought her lungs might burst. It was because she hadn't wanted anyone else to marry him, but what if—her breath stalled in her throat suddenly—what if he might have *preferred* to be caught with Lydia? After all, she hadn't overheard any of their conversation. She didn't even know how long they'd been talking. What if Lydia had been right and ten minutes with her *had* changed his mind? What if one glimpse at her sister's face had undone the bitterness of the past six years and made him forget *her* completely? It was one thing to rescue a man when he needed rescuing. Quite another to interrupt a romantic reunion, possibly even a proposal. Her unexpected arrival had forced him into offering for her instead, but what if, given the choice, he would have chosen Lydia? What if she'd made a terrible mistake and he hadn't wanted to be rescued at all?

She dropped her face into her hands, cheeks flaming with mortification. Was *that* what she'd done? Because if she'd ruined things between Arthur and Lydia, then she'd have to put them right again. She'd refuse to marry him if it came to it. She wouldn't marry a man who loved somebody else, especially her own sister…

She still hadn't spoken to Lydia about any of it. One look at her expression across the breakfast table that morning had put paid to the idea. She hadn't looked angry exactly, only silent and aloof, refusing to meet her gaze no matter how many times she'd asked for the marmalade. It was clear that her sister was in no mood for talking to her about anything, which meant that the only other option was to speak with Arthur himself. Which was easier said than done. He'd said that he'd call soon, but her father had made it clear that a private conversation was out of the question. In which case, who *could* she ask what was going on?

'Ah, there you are.' Her mother swept into the room suddenly, wearing a navy-and-lavender-striped-taffeta day dress. 'Come along.'

'Hmmm?' She looked up in surprise. 'Where?'

'I thought we might do a little shopping. Then perhaps we'll get some lunch, too.'

'I don't know, Mama, I'm not really in the mood…'

'Oh, do come along. It's been for ever since we went shopping together and you'll need some nice things now you're engaged. There's no need to wear full mourning any longer.' She gestured at her own gown. 'We can make a start on your trousseau.'

'Already?' Frances felt a fresh rush of panic. If she started to make a trousseau, then it was as good as admitting her marriage was going ahead. 'Don't you think it's a bit early for that?'

'Not at all. Your father and I think it would be a good idea for you to be seen out buying wedding clothes—'

her mother gave her a knowing look '—just to squash any rumours.'

'Oh.' She bit down on her bottom lip anxiously. 'Do you really think that people will be talking about me?'

'Of course!' Her mother laughed. 'Amelia Kitt is a dear girl, but she's never been remotely capable of holding her tongue. She'll have made sure that everyone in Whitby knows about your engagement by now.'

'Oh, dear.'

'There's no need to look so anxious about it. Personally I think things have worked out rather well.' Her mother walked across to the window and peered through the net curtains. 'I admit it all seemed a bit strange to me at first, but then I remembered the way Arthur looked at you when you were dancing the other day, like a man entranced. It's funny, at the time I thought the two of you seemed quite familiar, almost as if you were already well acquainted, but then I knew you couldn't be since he's such a famous recluse.'

'Mmmm.' Frances shifted uncomfortably in her seat.

'Then I had the most enlightening conversation with Georgie this morning.' Her mother straightened the curtains again. 'Although that still doesn't explain what you were doing at his farm yesterday.'

'Mama...'

'And you know, it also struck me as odd that both you and Lydia rushed there after lunch, separately, too. You in particular must have hurried to get there so quickly on foot.'

This time she didn't bother to say anything.

'Not to mention the fact that whoever sent your sister that warning note must also have known she went to Amelia Kitt's first because nobody called here to ask... But there it is. Some mysteries can't be explained, I suppose.' Her mother gave a sophic-looking smile. 'And sometimes a bit of guesswork is all that's required.'

'Has Papa guessed, too?'

'Gracious, no. Your father deals in facts and figures, my darling. I love him dearly, but imagination has never been his strong suit. Now, shall we go?'

Frances pushed herself up off the sofa. Shopping was the very last thing she wanted to do, but it looked as though her mother wasn't going to take no for an answer and she supposed it was better than lying around worrying.

It took her less than an hour to change her mind. Two more before they were finally free of the dressmaker's and on to the milliner's. By the time three hours had passed Frances was starting to fear that their shopping expedition would never end. She was tired of being measured, of being looked up and down and told what colours would suit her, not to mention overwhelmed by the vast selection of fabrics and designs. If she'd been certain about what her future entailed, then she might have made some attempt to enjoy herself, but as it was she could only feel a sick sense of guilt in case her trousseau proved unnecessary after all. At least her mother seemed to be having a good time, throwing herself into the task with enthusiasm by ordering half-a-dozen new day dresses and a ballgown despite Frances's best attempts to restrain her.

They arrived home mid-afternoon, laden with an impressive selection of gloves, shoes, bonnets and assorted undergarments. Under other circumstances, Frances thought she would have been impressed by her mother's attention to detail. As it was, she wasn't sure where she was going to store everything.

'Well, I think that was a very productive day, don't you?' Her mother pulled off her coat with a sigh. 'I'm exhausted.'

'Shall I call for some tea?'

'I think that would be a wonderful idea.'

'I'll just be a couple of minutes.' Frances smiled at her mother's contented expression. She hadn't seen her looking so happy in years. 'Only I'll just take these boxes upstairs fi—'

She didn't get any further as the door to her father's study opened and he stepped out, accompanied by another man, a gentleman judging by his appearance, starkly and yet elegantly dressed in a black superfine suit and grey-silk waistcoat. Both he and her father were smiling, though it wasn't so much that as his identity that made her jaw drop in amazement.

'Arthur?'

She forced her mouth shut again with a snap, though she still couldn't stop herself from staring. How many more versions of one man could there be? This one looked like a blend of the old and new Arthurs, well groomed, fashionable and yet still somehow ruggedly handsome. He'd been growing his hair over the past month so that he looked less severe and his new clothes—at least she presumed they were new—fitted him perfectly. Almost too perfectly, she thought, forcibly dragging her eyes away, enhancing his broad frame and drawing attention to the muscular body beneath.

'Frances.' He reached for her hand when she made no move to lift it, raising it to his mouth and pressing his lips against the backs of her fingers, holding her gaze with the same intensity she'd seen on his face just before he'd kissed her at Amberton Castle.

'Yes.' She wasn't sure what else to say, struck dumb

by the change in him. Yes, she was Frances... But it hadn't really been a question, had it? It was more of a greeting, not requiring an answer...unless she ought to say his name, too... She took a deep breath, trying to collect her scattered thoughts, which wasn't easy when he showed no sign of releasing her hand...

'I thought you might like to join me for a walk on the promenade?'

'I...' She glanced nervously towards her father. 'I thought...'

'I believe Lord Scorborough and I have come to an understanding.' To her surprise, her father's expression bordered on approval. 'Under the circumstances, I think a walk is perfectly acceptable.'

'You can wear your new bonnet, dear.' Her mother was already enthusiastically opening up a hatbox. 'The cream lining looked so pretty with your hair.'

Frances made a face. After being poked at and prodded for hours, she had a feeling she looked even more ragged than she had that morning. All the new bonnets in the world were never going to disguise that.

'There's no need, Mama. I'm still dressed for outdoors, as you see.' She relented at her mother's crestfallen expression. 'But of course if you think I ought to freshen up first... I'll just be a moment, A—*Lord Scorborough*.'

She grabbed an armful of boxes and fled upstairs to her bedroom, quickly removing her old bonnet and replacing it with the new. To her surprise, the wide brim and cream-coloured lining really did make her look better, so much so that it seemed a shame to wear it with her old grey cloak.

Carefully, she opened up another box and drew out a new, navy-blue paletot. It was one of the few items that she'd chosen herself, a three-quarter-length velvet jacket with gold buttons that she'd fallen in love with at first sight. She caressed the fabric and then pulled it on over her shoulders, smoothing out the sleeves and adding a new pair of navy gloves to complete the ensemble. *There.* She regarded herself in the mirror approvingly. At least now she wouldn't look so out of place beside her handsome fiancé.

Fiancé. The very word made her heart stall, as did the prospect of the conversation she now *had* to have with him. Now that the opportunity had presented itself, she almost wished she could find a way to escape it. Somehow she had to find a way to explain the events of the day before and offer to release him from their engagement. No matter what understanding he'd come to with her father, she had to offer him that. If she could just keep a clear head...

She made her way down the staircase again, surprised to find him deep in conversation with her very animated-looking mother.

'Ah, here she is.' Even her father was smiling by the time she reached them. 'You look very nice, my dear.'

'Shall we?' Arthur offered his arm and she looped her hand through it, wondering just how exactly she expected to keep her mind clear when even that light touch sent a ripple of excitement racing through her. She shifted her body sideways, trying to keep as far away from him as possible without actually leaning.

'Very good.' Her father nodded approvingly. 'Now, tea, I think.'

Chapter Nineteen

'What was all that about?' Frances asked the moment they were out in the street.

'All what?' Arthur gave a small tug, drawing her closer.

'You and my mother.' Her heart skipped a beat as their shoulders bumped together. 'You seemed engrossed.'

'Oh, that. We were discussing the price of lace. I'm given to understand that it's gone up recently.'

'*You* were talking about lace?'

'Yes. Lace is made from yarn. Yarn is a crop. I'm interested in crops. Ergo…' He shrugged. 'Is it so hard to believe I can make polite conversation?'

'No-o, but what about my father? How did you convince him to let us go for a walk? He said that I wasn't allowed out of his sight until we were married.'

'I surmised, correctly as it turned out, that your father had been listening to some of the more bizarre rumours about me. I simply had to convince him that I was still a gentleman.'

'Is that why you're dressed like that?'

'Is it so obvious?' He laughed, tugging at his shirt collar with his spare hand. 'I managed to get the pig smell out eventually, or at least I hope I did. My sister-in-law said I looked rather dashing. Or don't you agree?'

'I didn't say that.' She felt her cheeks blossom with colour. 'It might just take some getting used to, that's all.'

'As might your new coat and bonnet. Both of which look very pretty on you, by the way.'

'You don't have to say that.' She glanced up suspiciously. 'I know I must look a fright. I hardly slept a wink last night.'

'Ah. Then I suppose I can hazard a guess as to the reason.'

He turned his head towards her and she averted her gaze quickly, looking down at the glistening water of the harbour below, at the cobblestoned streets and red-roofed houses, as if the words she was searching for might appear in thin air. They were walking along the promenade already, past the whale-bone arch erected almost twenty years before to commemorate the whaling crews that had set out from, but never returned to, Whitby.

'Arthur, when I burst in on you all yesterday...'

'With your permission, I'll obtain a special licence tomorrow.' He stopped walking abruptly. 'It's not entirely appropriate, given that your sister's still in mourning, but your father agrees it might be best.'

'Tomorrow?' She gasped, feeling slightly winded, as if all the air had just left her body.

'Yes. For some reason I have a prejudice against long engagements.' His lips curved upwards. 'I also think it would be best to marry before Violet has her baby. I'd like for Lance to be my best man and I doubt I'll be able to prise him away afterwards.'

'Oh, yes, I see that, but...' She folded her hands in front of her as if that might help her get her thoughts into some kind of order. 'Arthur,' she said again, 'you don't have to go through with this. When I barged in yesterday I was only trying to help. i'd worked out what Lydia was planning to do, but by the time I arrived, it was too late to warn you. So I climbed in through the dining-room window and made it look as though I'd been there all along. I wasn't trying to trap you, I promise.'

'I know.'

'You do?' She knitted her brows in confusion. He was smiling that enigmatic smile again, the one that had baffled her so much the day before.

'Of course. In fact, I can honestly say that suspicion never crossed my mind.'

'So you guessed what I was doing?'

'Not at first. It only occurred to me later, but the truth is that I didn't care why you did it. I'm only glad you did.'

'So you're not angry?'

'Not in the slightest. There was really only one thing that bothered me.'

'What's that?' She tensed again immediately.

'Just that it wasn't much of a proposal, what with your father and sister and what's-her-name standing there?'

'Amelia Kitt?'

'That's the one. So...' He dropped down on one knee in front of her.

'What are you doing?' She gawped at him, as shocked as if he'd just started undressing in front of her.

'I'd have thought it was obvious.' He glanced pointedly downwards.

'But you don't have to! That's what I'm trying to tell you. I wasn't trying to trap you!'

'I believe we've covered that and, for the record, I don't feel trapped. Not with you. When I thought I might have to propose to your sister, on the other hand...'

'You were going to propose to Lydia?' Her heart plummeted. 'Is that what you wanted?'

He gave her a look that was part-irritation, part-amusement. 'That seems a strange question when I'm down on one knee.'

'But if you only proposed to me because... Why are you smiling?'

'Frances.' His smile spread even further. 'You timed your arrival perfectly. Ten seconds later and, believe me, I wouldn't have been smiling at all. I might never have felt the impulse again. Believe me when I say that I'm deeply grateful to you.'

Grateful? She shook her head, trying to make sense of so many conflicting emotions. He preferred her to Lydia, she felt elated by that, but she didn't want him to marry her out of gratitude either. The very thought made her suddenly, irrationally angry. What kind of proposal was *that*?

'But we're still trapped, both of us, and we don't have to be.'

'I believe that your father might see it differently.'

'My father can see it in whatever way he wants!' She squeezed her hands into fists. 'He only needs some time to recover from the shock. He'll come around if I talk to him.'

'I think not.' Arthur's smile faded as he got back to his feet. 'He's right about Amelia Kitt. All of Whitby will know that your sister came to visit me by now. Your story ought to save her reputation, but not yours and certainly not mine. I don't mind being called a recluse, but I draw the line at being a debaucher of innocents.'

'But no one will think that! Not when it's me. People will assume...'

'People will assume the worst because that's what they do.' He was starting to look angry now, too. 'No matter what you think, your scar doesn't make you exempt from the rules.'

'Well, maybe I don't care about rules *or* reputation! Maybe I'd rather be a social pariah than an object of pity!'

'Pity?' He was scowling openly now. 'Who do you think pities you?'

'Everyone! *Poor* Frances Webster, they call me, that poor, jilted girl with the scar. Well, I don't want to be her any more. I'd rather people thought I was ruined!'

'Personally I'd prefer it if you were Frances, Lady Scorborough.'

'No!' She shook her head furiously. 'I won't be pitied by anyone and that includes you.'

'Is that what you think? Hell, woman, what does a man have to say? I'm not asking you to marry me out of pity!'

'Then duty or honour or whatever you want to call it. They all amount to the same thing. Don't try to deny it. *You* were the one who said that you'd been a bad son and a bad brother and you didn't want to be a bad husband, too. *You* said you didn't want to marry! If it hadn't been for yesterday then you *still* wouldn't. But I don't need you to be honourable and I don't need you to support me either. I'm selling my own jewellery now and I don't need a husband telling me what I can and can't do.'

'I don't want to tell you what to do! I'm not trying to trap you either. We can be independent *together*.'

'Oh.' She blinked, the wind taken out of her sails somewhat. 'Well, that doesn't matter anyway. I can manage perfectly well on my own.'

'So can I!' He grasped hold of her arms, pulling her towards him. 'Only I don't want to any more. You're right, if it hadn't been for yesterday then I might not have changed my mind, but I have. I thought I wasn't suited to marriage, but I still want to give it a try. For some reason, I want to share my life with a pig-headed, stubborn, infuriating woman like you. Now will you let me finish this damned proposal or not?'

'Pig-headed?'

'Yes, if you think that I wouldn't want you just because of your scar. I thought I showed you how I felt last week. Or did you think that was just pity, too?' He lifted a hand to her cheek. Despite the roughness of his words, his touch was gentle, sending a warm pulse through her body. 'Because it wasn't. Now, Frances Webster, will you marry me? Not because your father insisted, but because I do. I want *you*. The only question is whether you want me, too.'

'You really don't care about my scar?' She caught her breath as his other hand slid round her waist.

'Do I need to prove it?'

'Yes.'

She breathed the word on a sigh as he lowered his head and touched his lips lightly against hers. He tasted salty, she thought, though that was hardly surprising when they were stood on top of a cliff with the sea breeze blowing all around them, making the ribbons on her new bonnet flutter like streamers.

She tipped her head back, feeling as if she were being lifted, too, as she reached her arms around his neck and let her lips mould against his, all the yearnings and cravings that she'd ever felt, but put aside, rushing back to her in a raw, unrestrained torrent. His arm tightened around her and she could feel desire building again, even stronger than the first time they'd kissed, so strong she felt as though she were being consumed by it. The tip of his tongue traced a path along the seam of her lips as if he wanted her to open them so she did, then almost leapt backwards in surprise as his tongue slipped inside, stroking and exploring and caressing until finally it joined with her own.

She was vaguely aware of a warning voice at the back of her head, telling her to stop. She doubted that this was what her father had anticipated when he'd agreed to them taking a walk together. First a public argument and then this, a kiss that was pushing the very limits of decency. It was really quite scandalous. She ought to insist that they stop and move apart…which she would, in just a few more seconds. Another minute perhaps…

'There.' It was Arthur who lifted his head finally, his ochre eyes black with desire as they gazed down into hers. 'Now do you believe me?'

'Yes.' She smiled, feeling faintly dizzy.

'Good. Because there's no escaping the engagement now. I believe we've just made a public spectacle of ourselves.'

'Oh!' She looked around, though fortunately there was nobody else in sight. 'No, it's all right. I don't think anyone saw us.'

'Don't be so sure.' He grinned. 'I expect there are tongues wagging behind several drawing-room curtains at this moment.'

She felt her cheeks redden and laughed. 'Well, then, we'll just have to hope they recognise you in those clothes. I don't want them to think I'm engaged to you and kissing somebody else.'

'Good point.' He reached up and swept his top hat away from his head. 'There. I don't want anyone to mistake me for Lance either. Now...' he tightened his other arm around her again '...about that special licence? I want to marry you as quickly as possible.'

Frances bit her lip. She wanted to marry him as quickly as possible, too, but there was something else she needed to do before that.

'Could we wait until next week?' She shook her head quickly when he frowned. 'It's not that I don't want to marry you. It's just that I want to put things right with Lydia first.'

'*You* need to put things right?' He looked distinctly unsympathetic. 'As I recall, you weren't the one who did anything wrong.'

'I know. I know she acted badly, too, but it was partly my fault. I should have told her about us after the garden party, I just didn't know how to. I think she's hurt.'

To her surprise, he didn't argue. 'You might be right. I think she was genuinely shocked by what happened yesterday.'

'She certainly didn't expect to see me.'

'Not just by that. Perhaps I was too blunt in what I said, but I wanted her to understand.'

'What did you tell her?'

He heaved a sigh. 'That our whole engagement had been a mistake and that she deserved someone who would love her for herself, but that it couldn't be me.' He pulled her close again. 'Because I cared for somebody else. *You.*'

'Oh.' Frances felt guilty and elated at the same time. 'I think she really believed that if she had ten minutes alone with you then everything would go back to the way it was six years ago.'

'She said something like that.'

'I still can't help but feel sorry for her. Lydia sets so much store by her appearance, but it isn't her fault really. All our lives, everyone's always told her how beautiful she is, as if that's *all* she is, just a face. It's not surprising she's come to place so much value on it herself.'

'That still doesn't excuse what she did.'

'I know, but maybe now her first year of mourning is over, things might get better. I hope so. In any case, I want to put things right with her before we get married. I'd like for her to come to the ceremony.'

'All right.' He sighed again. 'If that's what you want then I won't object, but I refuse to wait long. I'll give you a week and no more. Next Monday at the latest.'

'Thank you, Arthur.'

'Not a day later, mind.' He made a harrumphing sound and put his top hat back on again. 'Now I'd better get you home before your father comes storming down the street looking for us.'

'Shouting at the top of his lungs again?' She laughed. 'In a funny way it's nice to know he cares so much.'

'He cares a great deal. He told me so in his study this afternoon. He only hopes that I'm good enough for you. As do I, for that matter.'

'And all this time I thought my parents were embarrassed by me.' She curled her arm through his again. 'I misjudged them both.'

'And me, too. Admit it, you thought that ten minutes alone with your sister would change my mind about her, too, didn't you?'

'I…' She chewed on her lip guiltily. 'Not exactly, but…'

'You wondered?'

'Yes.'

He drew her closer so that they were walking shoulder to shoulder. 'Frances Webster, if it takes the rest of my life I'm going to convince you how beautiful you are.'

'Only to you.'

'Do you want anyone else?'

'No.' She laughed. 'I suppose not.'

'Good, because I've always been a one-woman man. It turns out I just needed to find the right woman.'

Chapter Twenty

'I'm going out riding today.'

Lydia marched into the drawing room, looking even more stunning than usual in a tight-fitting, mauve riding habit.

'Are you, darling?' Their mother lifted her head from the game of snakes and ladders she was playing with Georgie. 'On your own?'

'No, with a gentleman friend.'

'I don't think your father…'

'I'm not *asking* Father's permission,' Lydia snapped. 'I'm a grown woman with a son—' she threw a dazzling smile towards Georgie '—and I have my own money. If Father doesn't like the way I behave, then I'll leave and set up my own establishment. I don't know why I didn't think of it before.'

'Lydia!' Their mother's expression was aghast. 'You wouldn't!'

'Wouldn't I? I don't see why I shouldn't, seeing as certain other people get to behave however they want.'

Frances dropped her eyes back to her polishing. After four days of strained silences and a distinctly chilly atmosphere, she'd almost given up hope of having any conversation with, let alone getting through to, her sister.

'Although...' Lydia's voice turned sly '... Frances might want to come and say hello to my escort. She used to be quite fond of him, as I recall.'

'Who?' Their mother's eyes widened.

'Leo Fairfax.' Lydia smoothed her hands over her bodice. 'I met him out walking in Pannett Park the other day and he was *very* solicitous. I'd forgotten how handsome he is, too.'

'Then I hope you have an enjoyable ride...' Frances got to her feet with as much dignity as she could muster '...but I spoke to him the other week at the garden party and I've no desire to do so again, thank you.'

She managed to preserve an expression of calm all the way to her bedroom before starting to cry. It wasn't because of Leo, but that her own sister could be so deliberately cruel was a bitter pill to swallow. No matter how hurt she might be, Lydia's sudden interest in her former fiancé, a man who she'd never shown the faintest hint of interest in before, seemed like revenge pure and simple.

In which case, she decided, sitting up again and wiping her eyes, why shouldn't *she* visit Amberton Castle? She'd kept away to be tactful and not make Lydia feel any worse, but what was the point when her sister was so determined to be angry?

'I've been promising to show Violet some of my jewellery for weeks,' she explained to her mother five minutes after Lydia and Leo had left, the pair of them looking positively resplendent together on horseback. 'Why don't you come, too?'

'Not today, I think.' Her mother glanced anxiously towards Georgie. 'I'm worried about your sister.'

'I know.'

'She's just so bitter. I'm afraid she might do something foolish.'

'She's a grown woman, as she said, and I'm sure Leo will take good care of her.'

'Like he did with you? Oh!' Her mother pressed a hand to her mouth. 'I'm sorry. I didn't mean it like that.'

'It's all right, Mama, I know what you meant, but that was four years ago. I'm sure he's grown up a lot since then.'

She tried to put the whole situation out of her mind and look forward to seeing Violet again as the carriage rolled up into the Moors, but it wasn't easy. The sound of Leo's voice in her parents' hallway had set her mood and her nerves on edge. Was *he* trying to get back at her, too? she wondered. Not just because of the events of the garden party, but because she'd dared to replace him and with a viscount to boot?

The same thoughts kept spinning round and around her head for so long that she was relieved when the carriage finally pulled to a halt outside Amberton Castle and she was able to climb down, almost colliding with a red-haired youth as he came hurtling out of the front door.

'Sorry, miss!' the boy called over his shoulder as he ran in the direction of the stables.

'What's the matter?' she shouted after him, but he was already too far away to hear. Quickly, she went in through the open door, just in time to catch a flurry of maids rushing upstairs with jugs and towels.

'What's happening? Is Mrs Amberton all right?' She was struck with a sudden sense of foreboding.

'It's the baby, miss,' one of the maids answered over the banister. 'It's coming now.'

'Oh!' Frances dropped the box of jewellery she was carrying on to a bureau and followed them, taking the stairs two at a time.

'Violet?'

She ran up a second flight of stairs and burst into a bedchamber to find the tiny woman hunched over with pain, one hand grasping the bedpost while the other clutched at her stomach. Her cheeks were crimson-red and streaked with sweat while the housekeeper, a tall and gaunt-looking woman wearing a frankly terrified expression, stood over her, waving her arms helplessly.

'Frances...' Violet reached out a hand when she saw her. 'I'm glad... Ah!'

'I'm here.' Frances ran across the room, clutching her hand briefly before starting to haul at the laces on the back of her gown. 'Has anyone sent for a doctor?'

'Yes, and Captain Amberton, too.' The housekeeper looked distinctly relieved by her arrival.

'Good.' She pulled Violet's gown away so that she could breathe more easily. 'There. That should feel cooler. Now,' she turned to one of the maids, speaking calmly to allay the growing atmosphere of panic, 'I'd be grateful if you could give a message to my coachman. Tell him to go back to Whitby and say I'll be here for a while helping Mrs Amberton.'

'Yes, miss.'

'Thank you.' Violet threw her a grateful look.

'You didn't think I'd just turn around and leave, did you?'

'No...' Violet bent over the bed, clutching the coverlet tightly between trembling fingers as another spasm of pain racked her body. 'But I'm scared...it's too soon.'

'Not necessarily. My mother says that babies themselves decide when to be born. I was a month early. But if your child's ready, then you need to be, too. You can squeeze my hand and scream as much as you like.'

'You might regret…saying that.'

'I might, but we'll manage.'

'Have you…done this before?'

'Yes, I helped when my nephew Georgie was born.' Not that she'd done much more than fetch and refresh bowls of water, but there was no need to tell Violet that… Frances smiled reassuringly. 'I know exactly what to do, don't worry.'

'What on earth are we carrying?'

Lance panted as he and Arthur heaved an unwieldy and bizarre-looking contraption into one of the farm outbuildings.

'It's called a rouge wheel.'

'It looks like two discs covered in leather.'

'Apparently that's what a rouge wheel is. It's used for polishing jet.'

'And this is your idea of a wedding present?'

Arthur jerked his chin up defensively. 'This and a few other things.'

'Like that workbench and those shelves?' Lance made a face. 'Well, I suppose Frances knows what she's getting herself into. If she's marrying you, then she might even be crazy enough to appreciate all of this. Now if you've finished abusing my ill-advised offer of help, I'm going to make a pot of tea. I need it.'

Arthur rubbed his sleeve over his face. He'd been elated for the first few days after his engagement, but now Lance's words made him feel mildly discomforted. *I suppose Frances knows what she's getting herself into...* But she didn't, did she? He might have told her all about his past, but he hadn't mentioned anything about his fears for the future. He'd *hinted* at them perhaps, but he'd never actually told her just how concerned he was about the possibility of losing his mind again. Over the past month he'd managed to convince himself that he'd put the past behind him, but what if he was wrong? What if there was still a chance of another episode? Shouldn't he warn her? At least give her a chance to change her mind about marrying him?

He grimaced at the thought of how that conversation might go. *Dear Frances, as much as I'd like you to marry me, you ought to know that there's a good chance my mind is unstable and I might run away again. Only try not to worry. It only happened once before for nine months. Hardly any time at all really...* What bride wouldn't want to hear such sweet words?

He slammed a hand down on the workbench. At least the artist's studio he was preparing for her was starting to take shape. Contrary to what she'd assumed, he had no intention of stopping her from making jewellery and hopefully this would prove it to her. There was a new stove and lamp, as well as a rug he'd taken from the parlour to make it more cosy. Of course, they'd need a new one for the parlour at some point, but he'd let Frances choose that. She'd probably want to redecorate the whole house according to her own tastes. That was *if* she wanted to live there at all. Maybe she assumed that they'd move into Amberton Castle. Everything had happened so quickly there hadn't been a chance to discuss it. Maybe there were *more* things he ought to discuss with her?

He ran a hand over his head. The more he thought of it, the more telling her the truth, *all* of it, seemed unavoidable. It would be difficult, painful even, but his conscience wouldn't let him marry her until he had. If she was the woman he thought she was, then she'd understand and at least it would give him an excuse to visit her again, something he hadn't done for the past four days and which he was finding increasingly difficult to bear.

There was a sound of hooves and he went outside to see a horse and rider galloping into the yard. One glimpse of red hair and he recognised Lance's young protégé, a youth he'd taken into his service five years before and was now training as a steward.

'Daniel?' He caught at the horse's reins. 'What's the matter?'

'It's Mrs Amberton, sir. The baby's coming. She wants…'

'The baby?' Lance was already standing on the farmhouse doorstep, his face ashen. 'Now?'

'Yes, sir. It came on very sudden. I got here as quickly as I could.'

'You've done well.' Arthur was already throwing a saddle over his own horse. 'What about a doctor?'

'Mrs Gargrave's sent for one, sir.'

'Good… *Lance!*' Arthur bellowed as his brother showed no sign of moving. 'Come on!'

'It shouldn't be happening yet.' Lance still didn't move. With his grey pallor he looked almost like a statue.

'That doesn't mean it's a bad thing. You said so yourself. You wanted the babe to come early, remember?'

'Yes, but not *this* early!' Lance shook his head. 'I should never have said that. This is all my fault.'

'Don't be ridiculous.' Arthur practically hurled his horse's reins at him. 'It doesn't work that way. Now get on your horse. Violet needs you. *Now!*'

Chapter Twenty-One

Arthur felt as though he'd been pacing for hours, which in all fairness, he probably had. It must have been at least three since he and Lance had arrived and Violet had been in labour for at least another hour before that. He'd paced up and down while several maids had come and gone, carrying fresh supplies, though Frances and Lance had remained closeted inside. The world outside the windows had fallen silent and dark, in contrast to the lights burning and the cries emanating from inside. Time itself seemed to have lost all meaning. If only there were something he could do...

He stopped abruptly, jerking his head up at the sound of a baby's cry, followed by a muffled exclamation.

'Frances?' He called her name out instinctively, breathing a sigh of relief when the door opened and Frances appeared. Her bun had come half-unravelled so that tendrils of dark hair tumbled loose over her shoulders and cascaded halfway down her back. He'd never seen her hair down before and she looked beautiful. As well as half-dead on her feet.

'Is it over?' He stepped forward as she came out into the corridor and closed the door softly behind her.

* * *

'Violet!'

Lance's shout was so loud that Frances thought half of Yorkshire must have heard him arrive. It put even her father's bellow to shame, though it wasn't the kind of call designed to soothe a woman in labour either. Fortunately, the doctor's arrival five minutes earlier meant that she was able to run out into the corridor to greet him.

'Captain A— Oh!' She stopped at the sight of both Amberton brothers. Arthur had an arm wrapped around his usually stubbornly independent twin's shoulders and was half-dragging, half-carrying him up the stairs.

'Frances?' Arthur looked equally surprised to see her, almost dropping Lance as their eyes met. 'What are you doing here?'

'I came to show Violet some of my jewellery.'

'Oh, Captain Amberton, Lord Scorborough...' The housekeeper followed her out of the room. 'Thank goodness you're both here. I'll make some tea. *Captain!*' She gasped as Lance made to push past her. 'Surely you're not going in there? It's not proper.'

'Propriety be damned! Who's going to stop me?'

'Wait!' Frances decided to do just that, taking a firm step sideways. The crazed expression in his eyes was disquieting. 'Take a deep breath first.'

'Why?' His expression turned from surprised to panicked in under a heartbeat. 'What's the matter?'

'Nothing. The doctor says that everything's proceeding as normal, but Violet needs you to be calm.'

'Calm?'

'Yes, calm. You'll be no help at all to her like this.'

'But she's all right? She'll *be* all right?'

'I hope so.' Frances looked towards Arthur for support. Lance's very intensity was alarming, as if he were trying to force her into a promise she had no way of keeping.

'Maybe I shouldn't go in after all.' He looked uncertain suddenly, running a hand through his hair as he half-turned back towards the stairs. 'Or maybe just a drink first…'

'Don't you dare.' Arthur gripped his shoulders, swinging him back round again.

'But I can't…'

'Yes, you can! Lance, Violet needs you, more than she's ever needed you, and if you go anywhere near a bottle tonight then I swear I'll throw you out of this house myself. Imagine what she'll think if you go in there smelling of brandy.' He pushed his face closer. 'Don't make me beat some sense into you, little Brother. Now get in there and be strong for your wife.'

Frances felt as though the temperature in the corridor had just plummeted, the atmosphere turning icy as the two brothers fronted up to each other. She'd never heard Arthur speak in such a peremptory fashion, nor sound so commanding before. Anyone listening would have thought that *he* was the army captain. She waited as the mood seemed to become more and more tense, afraid that they were about to come to blows, but then Lance pulled his shoulders back, clenched his jaw and marched straight ahead into the bedchamber, his face set with a look of stolid determination.

'Well, if you don't need me any more…' The housekeeper gave her a beseeching look.

'No, you've done plenty, Mrs Gargrave.' Frances recognised the plea. 'I think the doctor can handle things now. I'll stay, too.'

'She looks relieved.' Arthur arched an eyebrow as the housekeeper practically ran down the staircase.

'It hasn't been easy.' Frances threw a worried look at the doorway. 'I think Mrs Gargrave is the one who needs a drink.'

'Then she's welcome to raid the drinks cabinet.' He took her hand and pressed it. 'How about you?'

'I'm all right.'

'I'll be here in case you need anything.'

Frances looked into his face, touched by the gentleness of his expression, and then rushed forward, throwing her arms around his midriff and burying her face in his neck. At that moment, all she needed was his warmth and reassuring presence. He held her close, pressing his lips into her hair as she let out a sigh. How could she ever have thought he was a brute?

'This is all I need.' She squeezed her arms. 'Just this.'

'The first one, yes.' She gave a tight smile. 'Twins.'

'Twins?' He drew in a long breath and then released it again in a rush. *Of course* it was twins. They ought to have known by Violet's size. Ironic that he and Lance, of all people, shouldn't have guessed.

'This one's a girl.'

He nodded. 'How's Lance?'

'Better. I think what you said did the trick, only...'

She lifted a hand as if to brush whatever she was worried about aside and he caught it, raising the knuckles to his lips.

'Only what?'

'Only don't go far.' She didn't look him in the eye this time, staring at a point just below his chin instead. 'Just in case...'

Just in case... He felt his throat constrict at the intimation. 'Is it so bad?'

'Violet's exhausted, but the doctor says the second baby is usually easier, so...'

She let her voice trail away and he nodded. 'You look worn out, too. Maybe you should have something to eat?'

'No, I couldn't.' She shook her head and a coil of dark hair unhooked itself from behind her ear and fell over her face. He lifted their fingers together to sweep it back again, before cradling them gently against her cheek.

'Frances...'

'I have to go back.' Her voice sounded ragged and he dropped his hand reluctantly, seeing the effort it cost her to control her emotions.

'Yes. I'll still be here, I promise.'

'I know.'

'Lord Scorborough?' The door had barely closed behind her before Mrs Gargrave's head appeared at the top of the staircase again, though she seemed reluctant to come any closer. 'Any news?'

He forced a smile. The housekeeper looked only marginally less anxious than he felt.

'It's a girl.'

'Oh!'

'But there's another baby on the way.'

'Twins?' The housekeeper's expression turned from joyful to anxious again. 'Can I do anything?'

'No.' It was the question they were all asking. 'Except, perhaps you might prepare a room for Miss Webster? I'm sure she'll be exhausted after...'

He didn't finish the sentence. He didn't need to. The words hung in the air between them, unspoken, unnecessary. *After this is all over...* As it soon would be, one way or another. Only he didn't want to think about the other way.

'Of course, Lord Scorborough. I'll make up one of the guest rooms myself. You know that I like to keep busy.' Mrs Gargrave started back down the stairs and then stopped. 'Would you like your old room made up as well?'

Arthur's brows snapped together at once. Despite his regular visits to see Lance and Violet, he rarely stayed there. The last, *very last* thing he wanted to do was spend a night in his old home, but he couldn't abandon Frances. Now especially.

'I appreciate the offer, but I'll sleep in an armchair.'

'An *armchair*?' Despite the circumstances, Mrs Gargrave was still able to convey a sense of disapproval. 'Very well, Lord Scorborough, as you wish.'

Arthur rested a shoulder against the wall with a sigh. Perhaps he ought simply to have agreed to placate her, especially since he doubted anyone in the house would be getting much sleep tonight. There would be no rest until the ordeal was over, and after that, if all went well, he'd have Frances to take care of. And if all didn't go well…well, then in all likelihood they'd be taking care of Lance together, though if anything happened to Violet he had a feeling his brother would be inconsolable.

He pushed the thought aside as a piercing scream cut the air, followed by a shout that surely had to have come from Lance and then the whole house seemed to fall eerily silent. He stayed perfectly still, hardly daring to breathe, let alone move, and then the door opened and Frances appeared on the threshold, a small bundle cradled in her arms.

'It's over—' she was moving quickly this time '—and you said you wanted to be useful.'

'Is that…?' He was vaguely aware of gawking.

'A baby? Yes.' She smiled. 'Meet your new niece. Your nephew has only just arrived.'

'A boy, too?'

'A beautiful boy.' Her smiled widened. 'The doctor's taking care of Violet now, but he thinks she'll be all right. Here—' she thrust the bundle towards him '—I need to help clear up.'

He took a deep breath and then held his arms out. The baby was lighter than he'd expected, bright pink and wrinkled, but her tiny eyes were already open, their expression faintly bewildered as she took one look at him and started wailing.

'I think she'd prefer to stay with you.' He looked anxiously at Frances as she drew her arms away.

'I think she'd prefer her mother, but you'll have to do for a few minutes.' Frances gave him a supportive tap on the shoulder. 'Don't worry. If you can carry a piglet under each arm, then you can manage a baby.'

She hurried away again, leaving him rocking the child in his arms and wishing he shared her confidence. He'd never held a newborn before, at least not one that wasn't a farm animal, but somehow the swaying movement came naturally. He must be doing something right, he reasoned. The wailing seemed to be quieting.

'Arthur?' Mercifully, Frances's head appeared around the doorway again after only a few minutes. 'You can come in now.'

He moved gingerly towards the room, taking minute steps to avoid tripping, feeling slightly awkward and out of place. Violet was sitting upright in bed, Lance at her side, looking like an even tinier shadow of her former self, with sunken, shadowy eyes and hair that looked as if it had been pasted to her head. He didn't think he'd ever seen a person look more exhausted and yet her smile was breathtaking as she gazed down at the babe in her arms.

'I never pegged you for a nursemaid.' Lance stood up to greet him. He looked almost as bad as Violet, as if he'd aged ten years in one night, but his smile was just as wide.

'Neither did I.' Arthur passed him his daughter. 'This one's a troublemaker.'

'Just like her father.' Violet tore her eyes away from her son to smile at first him and then Frances. 'Thank you, both of you. I'll never forget it.'

'We're just glad you're all right.' Frances leaned over and pressed a kiss to Violet's cheek. 'But now you need to rest.'

'So do you.'

'Soon.'

'Now. You've done more than enough. I'm sure Mrs Gargrave's already on her way to take charge again now the messy part's over.' Violet smiled sleepily. 'Arthur, take Frances and look after her.'

They were the words he'd been waiting for. 'You heard the woman, Frances. Come on.'

He took hold of her arm, leading her silently out of the room and down a floor to the guest quarters. The location of her bedroom was made obvious by the candle left flickering on a chest outside, though he waited until they were standing next to the door before grasping her shoulders and looking deep into her eyes.

'Are you all right?'

'Yes.' She swallowed. 'At least, I am now. An hour ago... I was so frightened, Arthur.'

'I know. So was I.'

'You were?' Her eyes widened. 'But you seemed so calm.'

'As did you.' He couldn't resist any longer, enveloping her in his arms. 'You were magnificent.'

'We must both be good actors then.' She made a sound that was half-sob, half-laugh and then pulled her head back, lifting her hands and wiping the palms over her cheeks. 'The doctor said it was a difficult birth, one of the worst he's ever seen. He doesn't think she'll be able to have any more children.'

'Thank goodness. Lance will be relieved.'

'Your poor brother was beside himself. He was trying not to show it, but you could see the fear in his eyes... He really does love her, doesn't he?'

'More than anyone else in the world.'

'It must be wonderful to be loved so much.' Her face took on a dreamy expression. 'It's what marriage ought to be, isn't it?'

'I suppose so. That and supporting and respecting and—' his tongue almost tripped over the words '—being honest with each other. Those things are important, too. Here.' He reached for the door handle, afraid that the conversation was getting out of his depth after such a long night, and led her into the bedroom Mrs Gargrave had prepared.

'Oh.' She took one look at the four-poster bed and exclaimed in delight. 'That looks wonderful. I think I could sleep for a week.'

'Then you're welcome to. I think Lance and Violet would be more than happy for you to stay. They'd probably let you move in if you wanted.' He picked up a poker and stirred the coals in the hearth. 'Now, are you hungry? You ought to have something.'

'No.' She sat down on the side of the bed and shook her head. 'I'm too tired to eat, but I'd love a cup of tea.'

'Good. I'll be back in a few minutes. Don't fall asleep in the meantime.'

He gave her a warning look and then hurried down to the kitchen himself. Most of the staff were still awake, sitting around a large wooden table and toasting the arrival of the new babies with a bottle of champagne.

'Lord Scorborough!' One of the maids leapt up at the sight of him. 'The master told us to celebrate. He sent the bottle.'

'I'm sure he did.' Arthur chuckled. 'Best drink up, then.'

'Can I help you with anything, sir?'

'No, I'll manage. Don't let me disturb you.'

He walked across to the range, ignoring half-a-dozen surprised expressions as he made a pot of tea himself and then climbed back upstairs, stopping in the bedroom doorway to look at Frances. She was half-lying, half-sitting on the bed, her shoes discarded on the floor beside her, though the rest of her clothing was still intact. Now he looked closer, however, he could see there were several damp patches, as well as specks of blood on the fabric. If she wasn't careful she'd catch a chill.

He placed the tea on the bedside table and laid a hand gently on her shoulder. Tempted as he was to let her sleep, he doubted that anything had passed her lips since the middle of the afternoon and it was better for her to have something than nothing.

'Frances?' He called her name softly and she rolled over, murmuring something indistinct.

'Frances?' He tried again, sliding an arm beneath her shoulders this time and lifting her gently upright. 'You need some tea. Sit up.'

'Arthur?' Her eyelids flickered drowsily.

'The very same. You need to drink and get out of these clothes.'

'I don't care about my clothes.'

'Well, you should. Here.' He lifted the cup to her lips as if she were a child. 'I've been told to look after you and that's what I intend to do.'

'Oh, very well.' She took a mouthful and sighed appreciatively. 'Perfect.'

'Finish it.'

'I hope you're not going to be this bossy when we're married.'

'Worse, probably.' He watched with satisfaction as she drained the last of the liquid. 'Now, do you think you can manage to undress by yourself?'

'I doubt it.' She gave a wide yawn.

'I'll call a maid.'

'No!' She caught at his arm as he started up. 'Don't go. I'll manage, but please don't go. I don't want to be on my own just yet. I don't want to remember...'

She gave a visible shudder and he nodded sympathetically. 'I know. I won't forget tonight in a hurry either.'

'Violet was incredible. She never gave up even when
the doctor thought she wasn't strong enough.'

'Lance always said she was tougher than everyone
thinks.' He sat back down again, wrapping an arm
around her waist and drawing her close.

'He's right. She's indomitable.'

She nestled her head against his shoulder and he
pressed a kiss into her hair, knowing that he should really leave instead. A gentleman, even a fiancé, oughtn't
to be alone with an unmarried woman at night, on a bed,
in the near-darkness...*especially* a fiancé who still had
secrets he needed to share with his prospective bride.
He *ought* to get up and leave, but how could he? She
was warm and soft in his arms and she'd asked him to
stay, for comfort. Just for comfort... But he still had to
undress her. As if the feeling of her in his arms wasn't
tempting enough...

He muttered an oath under his breath. 'We need to
get you out of this dress, Frances.'

'Mmmm.' She burrowed her head closer and he
groaned inwardly. Her hair was tickling his neck, making every nerve ending there seem to tingle and throb
with anticipation. It smelled faintly of jasmine, he noticed, but then that was *her* scent, his new favourite,
the one that made his blood heat and his breath come
in short, increasingly heavy bursts. A tremor of desire
pulsed through him. Damn it all, the evening had been
difficult enough. Now he had a feeling the night was
going to be even more tortuous.

Chapter Twenty-Two

Frances moaned softly as Arthur moved away. She didn't want him to move. Now that he'd woken her up, his reassuring presence was the only thing keeping memories of the afternoon and evening at bay. Violet's pain, Lance's barely contained panic, the doctor's pessimistic expression…

He was right, though, she really ought to get out of her clothes. Despite the fire glowing in the hearth, her body felt damp with sweat and who knew what else. If only her fingers would do what she told them to, but they felt numb, as if they were as wearied as the rest of her.

'I think I've forgotten how to do this.' She laughed softly as she fumbled with the buttons at her neck.

'Here.'

She let Arthur's fingers take over, letting him unfasten the row of buttons at the front of her gown and then slide the fabric lightly over her shoulders.

'Frances?' His voice sounded soft and strangely guttural at the same time.

'Mmm?'

'I need you to stand up for a moment.'

'Oh…yes.'

Reluctantly she forced herself to her feet, swaying slightly as she did so, though his hands were around her waist in an instant, holding her steady.

'I'll be quick.' He sounded positively husky now, untying her belt and the laces of her petticoats before pushing both to the floor, leaving her in just her new lacy undergarments.

'There. You can sit again now.' He guided her gently downwards and then crouched in front of her, rolling her stockings slowly over her legs.

'This is like that first day on your farm.' She laughed, feeling vaguely delirious as the memory drifted back to her. 'Except that I'm not injured or angry with you this time.'

'I'm glad to hear it.' He caught her eye and winked and she felt a rush of tenderness towards him. He was the same man, only he seemed so different from the one she'd confronted in his hallway just a couple of months before. Now he looked kinder, calmer and even more heart-stoppingly handsome, the old and new Arthurs rolled into one perfect whole.

'Just two more days,' he murmured, 'unless you want to marry me tomorrow, that is? I have the special licence all ready.'

'Tomorrow?' She smiled at the idea. It was tempting, but what would her parents say? 'Why so soon?'

'Because I think perhaps we need to hurry.'

'Why?'

'Because of this…' slowly he lifted one of her legs, tracing the arch of her foot with his fingertips '…and this…'

She gasped as he pressed a kiss to the inside of her calf. She'd never imagined that a leg could be so sensitive, but she felt wide awake again suddenly. She wasn't entirely sure what his words meant, but the touch of his lips on her naked skin was giving her a much clearer idea. It was giving her a whole raft of new ideas, each more shocking than the last. The warmth of his breath on her body seemed to be heating her blood, too, sending a hot pulse shooting along every vein, straight to her core, as if he were touching her all over.

'And this...' he murmured again, sliding his lips all the way down from her knee to her ankle in one long, drawn-out caress.

She was panting now, she realised, but she didn't care. It felt too wonderful as his lips and fingers moved over her, taking their time as if he were determined to learn every inch of her body.

'But that's all. For now.' He released her again abruptly. 'You need to get some sleep.'

'Sleep?' She stared at him blankly for a few seconds. What kind of insane idea was that? How could she possibly sleep when he'd just woken her up so effectively? Now that every part of her was throbbing and tingling and longing for more? She didn't want him ever to stop.

'Yes.' He stood up, swinging both of her legs on to the bed as he did so. 'You've had a long evening.'

'So have you.'

'But I was only pacing.'

He leant over her again, stroking a finger down one side of her face and cupping her cheek in his palm before kissing her tenderly on the lips. She kissed him back, feeling the heat in her veins turn into something else, a warm, fuzzy glow that seemed to envelop her whole body and make her feel sleepy again. It made her want to wrap her arms around him and pull him closer, to hold on to the feeling for a while longer.

'I won't go until you're asleep.' He smoothed his

thumb over her cheek as if he'd just read her mind, sitting down on the edge of the bed and pulling the quilt up to cover her. 'I promise.'

'Thank you.' She rolled on to her side, curling her legs up beneath her and regarding him through half-closed eyelids. 'You can lie down, too, if you want.'

Amber eyes seemed to spark as if there were actual candlelight behind them. 'Under the circumstances, I don't think that's a very good idea. *Tonight*, that is. Another time, I believe it might be the best idea I've ever heard. In fact, I can't think of anything I'd like more.'

She laughed softly. 'You know you look like your brother when you smile like that?'

'That's a good sign.' He winked again. 'Women have always found him irresistible.'

'Really?' She yawned. 'Not to me. Which is funny considering that you're twins.'

'You prefer grumpy farmers?'

'I suppose so.' She closed her eyes on the words. She *did* like them. More than that, she loved them, or at least one in particular. She loved *him*. After tonight, she was more certain of that than ever. He hadn't said that he loved her, but she knew that he liked her, that he wanted to share his life with her and now, incredible as it seemed, that he found her desirable, too. She knew he'd never reject her like Leo did because she could rely on him, too. Maybe one day he might care for her the way Lance cared for Violet, but for now, what they had was enough...

It was the last thing she thought before she drifted off to sleep.

'Good morning, Miss Webster.' Mrs Gargrave's shrill voice bore a striking resemblance to a cockerel crowing in her ear.

'Good morning.' Frances heaved herself up on to her elbows, looking around with new eyes as the housekeeper opened the curtains and let in a burst of bright sunlight. In her bone-weary state the previous evening she'd only had eyes for the bed, or more accurately the man beside it, but now in broad daylight she could see the details of the room itself.

It was pale blue and pretty, with a vast mahogany dresser, a matching table and pair of wicker chairs by the window. There was a fresh cup of tea by the bedside and her clothes had been draped neatly over a chair. Had Arthur done that before he left? she wondered. She had no idea what time that had been, only presumably some time before Mrs Gargrave had entered. In which case, where was he now?

'I've brought you a clean dress.' The housekeeper gestured towards a gown hanging on the back of the door. 'It's one of mine, I'm afraid, but there was nothing else suitable. The mistress's would all be too short.'

'Thank you. I'll return it as soon as possible, naturally. How is everyone this morning?'

The older woman's stern features broke into an uncharacteristically wide smile. 'Mrs Amberton's feeling much better, she tells me. She's had some sleep and breakfast, too. Captain Amberton and the babies are with her now.'

'And… Lord Scorborough?' She tried her best to sound nonchalant.

'He's having breakfast downstairs. He also suggested you might want a bath before you get dressed.'

'Oh, yes, please!' Frances sat up eagerly and then frowned. *Arthur* had suggested that? She remembered him insisting that she get out of her stained clothes the night before. Had she looked and smelled so terrible, then? A wave of embarrassment engulfed her. And he'd kissed her legs!

'Very good.' Mrs Gargrave nodded briskly. 'I'll arrange it.'

Half an hour later Frances slid into a tub filled almost to the brim with rose-petal-scented water. Never mind why Arthur had suggested it, she told herself, it *felt* wonderful, washing away all her anxieties from the night before and making her feel human again. Eagerly, she rubbed herself down with soap and then dipped her head under the surface, letting the bubble of the water fill her ears. She was still submerged when she heard a faint knock.

'Yes?' She surfaced again, expecting a maid, only to hear Arthur's voice on the other side of the door.

'Can I come in?'

'Of course.' She rolled on to her stomach and peered over the rim of the bath. 'As long as you don't mind.'

'What would I mind?' He took a few steps into the room, bearing a tray in one hand, and then stopped. 'Ah. I didn't think Mrs Gargrave would have arranged it quite so soon.'

She shrugged, feeling peculiarly unselfconscious, as if the water had swept away the last of her inhibitions. 'It's all right. I don't mind if you don't. You saw me in my undergarments last night.'

'So I did.' He moved closer towards her, though he kept his gaze averted. 'I brought toast. I don't suppose you want it in the bath?'

'Bath toast?' She giggled at the idea. 'No, thank you, but you eat it if you like. I've been promised bacon and eggs later.'

'Much better.' He gestured at the floor beside the bath. 'May I sit down?'

'You may, although Mrs Gargrave might have a fit if she finds you here.'

'Ah, but at this precise moment our fearsome housekeeper is gazing adoringly at my new niece and nephew.' He took a bite of the toast and grinned. 'She'll be there for a while, trust me. Lance has finally done something she approves of.'

'What if one of the maids comes in?'

'Hmmm.' He tapped his chin thoughtfully. 'That *is* a problem. All right, if anyone comes in, you scream and I'll dive under the bed. Or...' he crossed the room again and turned the key '...we could just lock the door.'

'Clever clogs.' She made a face as he sat down on the floor beside her. 'This was a lovely idea, though. Just what I needed.'

'Good. Would you like me to wash your hair?'

'Wash my...' She blinked in surprise. 'What?'

'It's not so shocking, is it?' He raised his eyebrows. 'We're almost married, after all, and I won't look at the rest of you, I promise.'

'Won't it be hard not to?'

'Pull your knees up if you like. Although it really doesn't matter. You saw me practically naked the first day we met, remember?'

'It's not a sight I'm likely to forget.' She gave an exaggerated shudder. 'I've had nightmares ever since.'

'Is that so? Then I'll strive to cover up from now on.'

'Too late. I'm afraid I already know the worst. But you can wash my hair anyway.' She pulled her knees up as instructed and folded her arms around them. 'And that wasn't the first day we met. We've known each other for years.'

'I suppose so, though in some ways all that feels like a different lifetime. We were different people back then.'

'I know what you mean.' She tilted her head back as he ran his fingers over her scalp. 'I wonder where we'd both be if you hadn't left and I hadn't had my accident?'

'I wouldn't be washing your hair, that's for certain. Where's the soap, by the way?'

'I dropped it.' She rummaged in the tub and then passed it to him. 'Here.'

'Thank you.' He rubbed his hands together to make a lather and then stroked them over her head. 'How's that?'

'Perfect.' She sighed. 'Mrs Gargrave says that Violet's feeling better.'

'Yes, the doctor's coming back later this morning, but I think the danger's past. She and Lance are holed up in their room with the babies and the whole house is besotted.'

'Including you?'

'Maybe a little, especially with your little namesake.'

'My what?'

'Your namesake. Only I'm afraid that it's Francis with an i, not an e. It seems that Lance already promised to name his daughter after somebody else.'

'Who?'

'Sophoria Gibbs. Apparently she was instrumental in bringing him and Violet together.'

'So they're Francis and Sophoria?' She felt genuinely delighted. 'I like that. Frank and Sophie.'

'Your nephew and niece when we're married.' His voice sounded huskier again.

'Yes, I suppose so...' She tipped her head back again, giving him an upside-down smile before resting her shoulders on the back of the tub. She didn't care how much of her he saw any more. She felt completely relaxed, as if the previous night's experiences had drawn them even closer together. With his hands in her hair and the heat of the water surrounding her, she felt utterly and completely happy. Maybe today could be her wedding day after all, she decided impulsively.

Chapter Twenty-Three

Arthur had the strong suspicion that he was trying to drive himself mad. That was the only logical explanation for why he'd volunteered to wash her hair. That and the fact that he'd wanted an excuse to touch her. After tucking her into bed the previous night and then settling himself into one of the wicker chairs by the window, he'd woken up positively aching to hold her again. Some particularly vivid dreams hadn't helped...

'Did I smell so bad?'

'Hmmm?' He stilled his hands as they threaded through her hair, taken aback by the question.

'Last night.' She twisted her head, peering over her shoulder at him in such a way that he caught a glimpse of one perfectly formed breast. 'Mrs Gargrave said that a bath was your idea. I wondered if it was because I smelled so terrible.'

'I can't say that I noticed, though if you had then it would have been perfectly understandable. I don't care about things like that, Frances.'

'I know.' She turned her face away again, though from the tone of her voice he could tell she was smiling. 'I've never known anyone like you before.'

'Is that a good thing?'

'Yes, you don't judge people the way everyone else does. You don't care what other people expect of you either.'

'Because what other people expect of me isn't important. Sometimes expectations can be a prison. I learnt that the hard way.'

'Perhaps.' The smile was gone from her voice now. 'Although people having no expectations of you can be lonely, too. Being an outcast isn't easy.'

'Neither of us has to be lonely any more, Frances.' He rubbed his hands tenderly over her neck and massaged her shoulder blades. Perhaps now was the time to tell her about his fears for the future, but it was hard to concentrate with the feeling of her skin beneath his fingertips and he was still distracted by his fleeting glimpse of cleavage. 'Besides, you smell quite delectable now. What kind of a person would judge you by something so trivial?'

'Leo would. He used to tell me if I had so much as a hair out of place.'

'I believe you. His hair's always perfect.'

'You know, Lydia went out riding with him yesterday.'

'With Fairfax?' He was surprised enough to forget about her breasts for a moment.

'Yes. I think it's her way of getting back at me.'

'I told you, you don't have to feel guilty.'

'I know. At least my head knows that, but it's hard not to feel that way. I've tried talking to her, but it's no use, she won't listen. I think she's really hurt.' She heaved a sigh. 'Poor Lydia.'

'*Poor* Lydia who went riding with your former fiancé just to upset you?'

'But it *doesn't* upset me, not in the way that she thinks. She can do whatever she wants with Leo Fairfax. I don't care.'

He dipped his head and pressed a kiss against the back of her neck. 'Then let's forget about them for today. Now dip your head under the water. You need a rinse.'

'Are you going to look away again?'

'Do you want me to?'

She was silent for a moment before spinning around suddenly, allowing him a full view of her bosom before sliding, mermaid-like, beneath the water.

'There.' She bobbed up again after a few moments, surrounded by a swirl of dripping black hair. 'Clean enough for you?'

He cleared his throat, unable to answer as all coherent thought seemed to abandon him.

'Today.' She stood up, droplets of water cascading around her as she looked deep into his eyes and smiled.

'Today?' Somehow he croaked the word out.

'For our wedding. I don't want to wait any longer either. If you'll still have me, we can get married today.'

'If I'll still have you…' He didn't bother to reach for a sheet, hauling her soaking-wet body straight into his arms instead. 'Of course I will.'

'What are you thinking about?'

Frances looked shyly across the breakfast table to where Arthur was leaning back in his chair, regarding her through half-closed eyelids with a lazy-looking smile on his face. It seemed ridiculous to feel self-conscious after she'd just stood completely naked in front of him, but she did. To be honest, it was hard to believe that she'd behaved in such an uncharacteristically forward fashion, although she didn't regret it either. Arthur made her feel safe and accepted and *loved*. He made her feel brave, too—brave enough to show the whole of herself, just as she was—and he hadn't exactly objected. On the contrary, his embrace had been positively bone-crushing, accompanied by a series of kisses so fierce that she'd felt vaguely disorientated, not to mention disappointed, when he'd pulled away again after a few moments, wrapping a sheet around her shoulders and then stepping aside like a gentleman. For the first time, she'd actually wished he *was* the callous brute she'd first taken him for.

Afterwards, he'd helped her to dress and even made an attempt to do her hair, with the result that it was now tied in some kind of knot at the nape of her neck, one that she wasn't entirely sure she'd be able to unravel, not that it mattered. Of all men in the world, Arthur was the very last who would ever judge her on the way she, or her hair, looked. It was one of the things she loved most about him.

'I'm not thinking,' he answered at last, his smile widening. 'I'm just feeling happy.'

'Happy?' She lowered her fork in surprise. It wasn't a word she associated with him, but now that he mentioned it, he *did* look happy, as well as younger and handsomer, too. The look on his face implied it was all due to her and the idea made her feel warm and tingly inside.

'Hard though it may be to believe, yes. *Very* happy.' The smile was a grin now. 'I ought to watch you take a bath more often.'

'Arthur!' She threw a quick look at the open door to the hallway.

'Of course maybe next time I shouldn't just watch. Maybe next time I should join you.'

She looked down at her plate, feeling warm and tingly on the *outside now* as well, embarrassed and excited in equal measure. It was certainly an interesting idea, even if he was just teasing her… But since she was feeling brave this morning…

She pushed her chair back and moved around the edge of the table, wrapping her arms around his neck before seating herself squarely on his lap.

'It's a pity I'm already so clean…' she peeked up through her lashes, teasing him back '…but I'm afraid Mrs Gargrave might think it strange if I take two baths in one morning.'

His gaze darkened instantly. 'Tonight, then.'

'Tonight.' She felt a tremor of anticipation ripple through her body as he slid his hands over her shoulder blades and down her back. 'Isn't it strange to think we'll be married in a few hours?'

'No second thoughts?'

'None, although my mother won't be happy about the lack of time to prepare. The clothes, the food, the…' She paused mid-sentence. 'Where will we even live? At the farm?'

'That was my intention.' His hands stilled on their journey downwards. 'Unless you have any objections?'

'No. I like it there.' She leaned forward, rubbing her nose against his and then touching a kiss to both of his cheeks, trying to ease the look of tension that had appeared on his face suddenly. 'Is it so difficult being here? Are the memories so painful?'

'Not as much as they used to be—' he frowned '—only I suppose I'm afraid of falling back into old ways.' He looked on the verge of saying something else before the sound of a knock on the front door distracted him. 'Besides, it's Lance and Violet's home now.'

'And Francis and Sophie's.' She clambered off his

knee reluctantly at the sound of voices in the hallway.
'In that case, we'll live at the farm, just as long as you
don't expect me to round up any stray piglets.'

'Duly noted. You can take charge of the chickens.'

'Or cats. I like cats.' She grasped hold of his hand,
pulling him up out of the chair after her. 'Speaking of
Francis and Sophie, I'd like to see them again before
I leave.'

'Good, because I doubt you'd be allowed to leave *without* seeing them again, although it sounds as if the doctor's just arrived. Care to join me for a quiet stroll around
the garden until everyone's ready?' He raised his eyebrows. 'There's a maze with some particularly secluded
corners.'

She feigned a look of shock and then giggled, skipping happily towards the door. 'I suppose if it passes
the time…'

Arthur propped a shoulder against the door jamb,
watching as Frances sat down on the bed next to Violet. Even Mrs Gargrave's grey gown couldn't dampen
his desire for her, nor block out his memory of the body
beneath. Not that he wanted to block it out. On the contrary, he *wanted* to think about it, to remember and savour every last curve and detail of how she'd looked *and*
felt, but now wasn't the time or the place. That would
be tonight. Still, he couldn't help but feel a tightening
sensation in his chest every time he looked in her direction, which was all the time since he appeared unable to drag his eyes away.

He'd told her that he was happy and meant it. It was
a strange feeling, like the echo of some emotion he
remembered from a long time ago. Except that echo
wasn't a strong enough word. There was nothing quiet

or restrained about this feeling. It was all-engulfing, a deep-seated sense of contentment and joy. He felt like a new man, a man whose past didn't matter, as if the presence of new life in the house had given him a new sense of optimism. The easy way in which she'd accepted where they would live had made him happier still. If she could be so calm about that, then maybe he could tell her the rest of his worries, too. Soon. Very soon. Perhaps on the journey back to Whitby...

'You slept here, then?' Lance came up to him, clasping his hand in a firm grip. 'I wondered about that.'

'What about you? Have you had any rest yet?'

'No.' His brother shook his head ruefully. 'I've just been looking at them, all three of them. I can't tell you, when I think of what might have happened...'

His voice broke and Arthur put a hand on his shoulder. 'It's all right. *They're* all right.'

'I know and I need to thank you for what you said last night. If I'd started drinking, then you'd have probably found me out roaming around the moors this morning.'

'I don't think so.'

'Then maybe you think better of me than I deserve.' Lance dashed a hand across his face. 'I think I understand how you felt now.'

Arthur lifted an eyebrow quizzically. 'What do you mean?'

'When you ran away. You were desperate, weren't you?' Lance put a hand through his hair. 'I've never felt as desperate as I did last night, not even when I was shot. I'm only thankful you were here to stop me from doing something stupid.'

'The situations are different.' Arthur frowned, struck with a vague sense of disquiet. Somehow the parallel disturbed him. 'You would never have abandoned Violet.'

'I hope not. In any case, I'm grateful.'

'Lord Scorborough?' the doctor interrupted them, lowering his voice discreetly. He'd packed his bag as if he were ready to depart, only there was a sombre look on his face that suggested some unfinished business. 'Might I have a word?'

'With me?' Arthur exchanged a surprised look with Lance before following him out into the corridor. 'Of course. Is something the matter?'

'I'm afraid… That is to say, yes. I was surprised to see Miss Webster still here this morning.'

'Indeed?' Arthur raised his chin, giving the doctor a look that he hoped told him to mind his own business. Surely he hadn't just drawn him aside to deliver an etiquette lesson? 'We *are* engaged, sir, and my brother and sister-in-law were both under the same roof. Not to mention that these are somewhat exceptional circumstances.'

'What?' The doctor looked faintly irritated. 'Oh, no, I wasn't talking about that. Only I take it that Miss Webster hasn't received any messages from Whitby this morning?'

'No. Why?'

'As I thought.' The doctor made a harrumphing sound. 'I wouldn't usually share information like this, but since you're engaged, you should know that I met my colleague, Dr Muggridge, on my way here this morning. It seems that he had a long night, too, only at the Websters' house. Apparently their eldest daughter was involved in some kind of riding accident yesterday afternoon.'

'Lydia Baird?'

'Yes. I understand that it's quite serious. No broken bones, fortunately, but she had a severe knock on the head. From what I gather, she hasn't regained consciousness.' He paused significantly. 'Somebody ought to inform Miss Webster.'

'Of course…' Arthur frowned, already wondering what to say. 'I'll take her back to her parents' house at once.'

'Good.' The doctor nodded, as if he considered his duty discharged. 'In that case, I'll be on my way, too. I believe everything here is as it should be.' He glanced back into the room and shook his head. 'Sometimes my patients amaze even me.'

'Yes. Thank you, Doctor.'

Arthur walked slowly back into the bedchamber. Frances was holding one of the babies, rocking him or her gently back and forth in her arms with a smile that faded the moment she saw his face.

'Arthur?'

'We should be getting you home.' He tried to muster an encouraging expression.

'Oh, but you must come back soon.' Violet beamed as Frances handed the baby back to her. 'And thank you again. I don't know how I would have coped without you.'

'You're more than welcome—' Frances gave her a look that made his chest ache '—and I'll be back very soon. I have to keep an eye on my little namesake, after all.'

They made their way downstairs in silence, Arthur keeping a few steps ahead so that she couldn't see his expression. He could feel her curious glances, but he still had no idea what to say. Anything apart from the truth would feel like a lie, but he dared not tell her the truth just yet. He didn't want to panic her into making a mad dash across the Moors. He had to get her back to Whitby first and *then* tell her what had happened—why their wedding would have to be postponed…

'I'll fetch the horses.'

He left her in the hallway, still avoiding her eyes, and hurried off to the stables, returning a few minutes later to find her already waiting on the doorstep, bundled up in her coat and bonnet, looking out into the distance.

'Red sky.' She pointed eastwards. 'I suppose that means there's another storm coming.'

'Probably…' he helped her up into the saddle '…but we'll get you back home before it hits.'

'Arthur?' She reached an arm out as he mounted his own horse. 'Is everything all right?'

'Why do you ask?' He picked up his reins, pretending not to notice her outstretched hand.

'You just seem different. Is it about our wedding?'

'No.' He risked a glance towards her and regretted it instantly. The anxious look on her face tore at his heart strings. 'I just don't want your parents worrying about you, that's all.'

He set a steady pace over the hilltops, stifling a feeling of guilt mixed with something else, the same discomforting emotion that seemed to have taken hold of him during his conversation with Lance that morning, undermining his earlier happiness. It was intangible but insistent, like an idea hovering at the edge of his consciousness that he didn't want to confront, but couldn't ignore either. What was it Lance had said? That he understood him better, that he'd been pushed to a similar level of desperation… But if that was what marriage entailed, then surely *he* of all people would do better to avoid it altogether. What if his relationship with Frances pushed *him* to the edge again somehow? He already loved her, there was no way back from that, but perhaps he could turn back before he loved her *too* much…

He berated himself for the thought, especially at such a time, slowing to a brisk trot as they joined the main road that led into the outskirts of Whitby, though the change of pace did nothing to ease the growing tension between them.

'Frances…' He couldn't put off the news about Lydia any longer.

'Yes?' Her voice sounded more guarded than before.

'Dr Bennett spoke to me this morning.'

'Oh?'

'About your sister.'

'What?' She pulled on her reins, her voice sharp with panic. 'What about her?'

'Apparently she had some kind of accident yesterday when she was out riding.'

'But she's all right?'

'I don't know. She hit her head and… *Frances!*' he called after her as she spurred her horse on again, but it was too late. She was already turning the corner of the street ahead of them, galloping at full pelt over the cobbles towards her parents' house.

Chapter Twenty-Four

'*Lydia!*'

Frances burst into the house, charging breathlessly across the hall and up the stairs into her sister's bedroom.

'Oh, Frances.' Her mother got up from the bedside and opened her arms when she saw her. 'Thank goodness you're here.'

'Mama.' She flung herself into her embrace. 'I only just found out. What happened?'

'All I know is what Leo Fairfax told us. He said that she wanted to race, that she claimed she was sick of being cooped up and a prisoner and she wanted to feel free. *Free!*' Her mother's face crumpled. 'Then she fell. This is all my fault.'

'No.' Frances clasped her hands tightly. 'If it's anyone's fault, then it's mine. She was upset about Arthur and me. I should never have kept secrets from her.' She forced herself to look down at the bed. Lydia was lying perfectly still, the top of her beautiful face covered with a thick, white bandage. 'How bad is it?'

'She's been unconscious since it happened. The doctor says that if she doesn't wake up soon…'

Her mother faltered, unable to finish the sentence. She didn't need to. The implications were all too obvious.

'I'm sorry I wasn't here.' Frances squeezed her hands again.

'There was nothing you could have done. After we got your message about Mrs Amberton I thought it was better to leave you where you were. How is she?'

'She had twins, a boy and a girl.'

'Oh.' Her mother's eyes filled with tears. 'How lovely. I'm happy for her. Was Arthur there, too?'

'Yes, he brought me back when Dr Bennett told him about Lydia. He's probably taking the horses around to the stables now. I abandoned mine in the middle of the road.'

'Well, I'm glad he's here to take care of you.' Her mother almost managed a smile. 'You should go downstairs now. I'll stay here.'

'No, I want to stay with you, both of you.'

'You can come back soon, but your father needs you, too. This has been a terrible shock for him. Go down and see how he's doing for me.'

'If that's what you want, Mama…' Frances dragged herself away reluctantly, descending the staircase to find Arthur and her father standing by the parlour window together. Both of them looked round when she entered, though for a moment she felt as though she were looking at a pair of strangers. Her father seemed to have developed new worry lines since she'd last seen him, and Arthur…she felt a shiver run down her spine…his face wasn't so much harrowed as blank, without any expression at all. She could hardly believe it was the same man who'd undressed and then kissed her so tenderly the night before.

'Is she…?' Her father started forward hopefully.

'No.' She winced as the gleam in his eyes faded. 'But she doesn't seem to be in pain.'

'Yes. That's something, I suppose.' Her father's voice turned shaky. 'If you'll excuse me, Lord Scorborough, I'll be in my study.'

'Papa...' She made a move as if to stop him, but he was too fast, crossing the room with the speed of a man half his age.

'I think he wants to be alone.'

Arthur's tone was sympathetic, though he made no attempt to approach her either and she folded her arms, feeling cold all of a sudden. 'I've never seen him like this. So...stricken. Mama, too. I should have been here for them.'

'I'm sorry, Frances.'

'It's not your fault. You brought me back as soon as you could. Mama said she didn't send word straight away because she knew I was helping Violet.'

'I see.' Neither of them spoke again for a few moments, as if the air was too heavy for words to penetrate. 'Is there anything I can do?'

'No.'

'If there is...'

'I'll send word.'

They lapsed into silence again, the few feet between them feeling like miles.

'I ought to go back upstairs.' Frances dropped her arms back to her sides, unable to bear the tension any longer.

'Of course.' He straightened his shoulders as if her words had just jolted him. 'In that case, I'll be at the farm...if you need me.'

'Yes.' She felt a lump swell in her throat and cleared it hastily. 'Your animals will be hungry.'

'I have a boy who helps me now.' He frowned as if he'd intended to say something else and then hastened towards the door. He was only marginally slower than her father had been, as if he couldn't wait to get away, too.

'Frances...' he paused at the last moment on the threshold, his face utterly emotionless '... I'm deeply sorry. If I could go back and do things differently, I would.'

She didn't answer, waiting until he'd gone before sinking down into a chair. Somehow those words seemed the cruellest of all. *If I could go back and do things differently...* Which things? His engagement to her? His relationship with Lydia? Both? Everything that had seemed so clear the previous night and that morning seemed thrown into doubt, as if she'd simply imagined their closeness. But surely she couldn't have, not completely. *He'd* come to her room, *he'd* taken her in his arms, *he'd* kissed her leg and asked her to marry him as soon as possible. And yet the news of Lydia's accident had altered him completely. He seemed almost as shocked as her father. Which meant that there was only one conclusion she could come to, one that seemed more and more obvious the longer she thought of it: that he really loved Lydia after all and the accident had finally shown him that fact. Which meant only one thing for them.

She pushed the thought away. Whatever it meant, it wasn't important now. Only Lydia was important. Her own relationship with Arthur, whatever it was, or wasn't, could wait.

The next few days passed in a blur. Frances spent most of her time in the nursery with Georgie, trying to pretend that everything was all right, or by her sister's bedside with her mother who never left, not even to eat or sleep. There were no set mealtimes any more, no semblance of a routine. Everything seemed on hold, as if the whole house was holding its breath, waiting for Lydia to wake up.

Arthur visited punctiliously every afternoon, though she wished that he wouldn't. It wasn't that he did anything overtly wrong. He was polite and solicitous and said all the right words of comfort, but the lack of warmth behind them meant they had the opposite effect. He never tried to touch her either, always keeping his hands clasped behind his back, as if he found the occasions as strained and painful as she did. There seemed to be some kind of wall between them, one made of ice since their meetings left her feeling so cold.

He made no mention of the special licence or their wedding either, not that she would have expected him to, but their shared silence on the subject seemed to grow more and more conspicuous. A casual observer might have taken them for nothing more than acquaintances. She couldn't help but wonder if he was worrying about Lydia and the idea made her feel guilty, angry and humiliated all at the same time. The more she considered it, however, the more she thought that she must have been nothing more than a Lydia substitute all along. Not intentionally, perhaps—she didn't think so badly of him—but still just a replacement, a slightly damaged version of the original.

As if all *that* wasn't bad enough, she had Leo to deal with, too. He called one morning and, with her parents occupied, she was the only one left to receive him.

'You must hate me.' The first words out of his mouth made her want to slap him. Hard. They were typical of Leo. Even with Lydia lying unconscious, he could only think of the situation in terms of himself. She spent ten minutes listening to his excuses and explanations before declaring it was time for her to go to the nursery.

'Oh.' He looked surprised to be interrupted, though he moved to the doorway obediently enough. 'I seem to cause nothing but trouble for your family.'

She had to bite her lip to stop herself from agreeing, though his regret seemed genuine.

'I'm sure there was nothing you could have done. Once Lydia gets an idea in her head, it's hard to stop her.'

'Yes.' He bowed his head morosely. 'But I'm sorry, especially after everything that happened between us... I'm sorry about that, too.'

'That was a long time ago. You're forgiven.'

'Thank you, Frances.'

She showed him out of the house with a bittersweet sense of satisfaction. He still couldn't look her full in the eye, but at least the pain of his rejection was gone. Speaking to Leo face to face hadn't hurt at all. Whereas speaking to Arthur, on the other hand...

The only positive in the whole situation was the amount of time her parents spent together. Her father took to sitting in Lydia's bedchamber, too, side by side with her mother, holding her hand in a way she hadn't seen him do in years. She didn't know which of her parents had reached for the other first, but it warmed her heart to see it, as if something good might eventually come of something so bad.

It was the fourth day after the accident when Lydia finally woke up, just as their mother was raising a glass of water to her lips.

'Mama?' The sound of her voice propelled both Frances and her father to their feet.

'Oh!' Their mother almost dropped the glass of water in surprise, though thankfully their father managed to catch it.

'Lydia.' His voice was tight with emotion. 'How do you feel?'

'My head hurts.' She looked dazed as she shifted slightly and then cried out.

'Don't try to move.' Their mother laid a hand tenderly on her shoulder. 'You've given us quite a scare.'

'I'm sorry.' Lydia's eyes moved around the room before settling on her. 'Frances…'

'I'm here.' Frances leaned over the bed, blinking rapidly to stop herself from sobbing with relief. 'I'm so glad you're awake.'

'What happened?' Lydia's brows knitted together. 'I don't remember.'

'Leo said you wanted to race.' Their mother's tone was faintly admonishing.

'Oh…so I did. That was foolish of me.'

'*Very*, but we won't talk about that now. You need to concentrate on getting better.'

'I will.' Lydia's eyes focused on her again, their expression thoughtful. 'Only I want to speak with Frances first.'

'I don't think…'

'It's all right, Mama, it's nothing bad. Only it's important.'

'Oh, very well, but just for a few minutes, mind.'

Frances looked at her sister with trepidation as their parents moved towards the door and closed it softly behind them.

'I'm sorry.' Lydia's voice was faint, but clear. So clear that Frances jerked backwards in surprise.

'What?'

'I'm sorry. I should never have gone out riding with Leo. I was trying to get back at you for taking Arthur. I *wanted* to make you feel bad. This serves me right.'

'No, don't say that.'

'But it's true…' Lydia managed a tremulous smile '…and you know the worst part is that I never even liked Leo. He cares more about his appearance than I do, which is saying something.'

Frances pressed her lips together to stop herself from laughing. 'He's been worried about you. He called to see how you were.'

'Well, I didn't say he was a complete monster.' Lydia gave a weak laugh and then sighed. 'Just when I thought I could start living again, I had to do something stupid like this. Do I look so very bad?'

Frances shook her head. 'You don't look bad.'

'But…my face?'

'It's bruised, but that's all. You won't have any scars, the doctor has already said so.' She reached a hand to her sister's cheek. 'You'll be just as beautiful as ever soon enough.'

'Oh.' Lydia's dark eyes welled with tears. 'I wish I wasn't like this. I wish I didn't care so much about how I look and what people think.'

'We all care a bit.'

'But I've let it control me.' Lydia sniffed and then lifted her chin up, her voice gradually gaining in strength. 'I know I've been cruel to you in the past, but the truth is, I was jealous. You've always been so content in yourself. You never needed other people's attention.'

'It's all right, Lydia.'

'No, it's not. I should have been kinder to you after your accident, but part of me was relieved that you weren't so beautiful any more, that I wasn't going to be replaced by my younger sister. I knew it was wicked at the time, but I couldn't seem to stop myself. I hated myself for being so shallow, but somehow that only made it worse.'

'You don't have to hate yourself, Lydia. I know that things haven't been easy for you either.'

'Do you?' Lydia gave a sob. 'You know, everyone always said that I was the most beautiful girl in Whitby, that I'd make a great match. They said it so often that I never even stopped to think about whether I actually wanted it. I just went along with their expectations. John didn't have a title, but he was still important and he was kind to me. I loved him in a way, but I was never *in* love with him. Then, after he died, I needed to prove that I was still the most beautiful, that I could make an even better marriage. It's pathetic really, but I think that's why I was so determined to catch Arthur. What I did, what I tried to do to him, was horrible.'

'He's already forgiven you.' Frances drew in a fortifying breath. 'But I'm sorry, too. I never meant to ruin things for the two of you.'

'You didn't. How could you ruin something that didn't exist? Arthur wasn't mine. He didn't even want to see me. I thought he might still care for me, but...'

'No, Lydia, I think perhaps he didn't realise how he—'

'Ahem.' Their mother's face appeared around the doorway again, looking faintly anxious. 'Is everything all right?'

'Everything's fine, Mama.' Lydia smiled and beckoned her in. 'Except for a pounding headache.'

'Then that's enough talking, although I'm glad to see my girls getting along again.'

'*Our* girls…' Their father followed their mother into the room and wrapped an arm around her shoulders. 'Frances, Arthur is downstairs. I've already told him the good news.'

'Oh.' She felt her heart leap and then plummet again almost instantly. It was a feeling that had become all too familiar over the past few days. Now that Lydia was awake, there was no avoiding the reason for it either. She had to confront him, had to call off their engagement so that he'd be free to reconcile with her sister instead. No doubt that was what Arthur wanted, too. She only hoped that she got to speak first so she might hold on to a few tattered shreds of her dignity.

As for Lydia… The plaintive way that she'd spoken, *I thought he might still care for me*, suggested that her feelings for Arthur ran deeper than she'd previously suspected. Was it possible that she might have underestimated her sister and that she truly *did* care for Arthur, after all? Because if that were the case, then she had no choice but to step aside.

She took a deep breath and stood up. Now that the time for confrontation had come, she wanted to put it off a while longer, to give herself a few minutes to gather her strength, but at least she knew she could do it. She'd survived her accident and Leo. She could survive this, too.

'I just need to freshen up first. Papa, please could you tell him I'll meet him on the beach in half an hour?'

Arthur stood on the shore, his black greatcoat billowing around his legs as he stared out to sea and waited for Frances. The weather had taken a distinct turn for the worse again. The towering waves were splashing spray all around him, white flecks that blew into his face like driving rain. The tide was coming in, too, a relentless force that surged back and forth, puddling around his boots. If he didn't move soon, the salt would ruin the leather, but he found it hard to care. He only cared about what he had to do—and say.

He couldn't marry her, couldn't build the life of shared calm and contentment that he'd envisaged. It had all been a dream, one he'd let himself believe because he'd wanted it to be possible, but it wasn't. Not because he didn't care, but because he cared too much, far *too* much to risk losing her the way Lance had almost lost Violet, the way she'd almost lost her own sister, too. He couldn't bear to even contemplate the idea, which surely meant he wasn't strong enough for marriage after all. Now that Lydia was out of danger, he had to tell Frances so and end their engagement. It would be painful, heartbreaking even, but it would save her from hurt in the long run. Hurting people—*failing* them—was what he did. First his mother, then Lance and his father... He'd failed each of them in turn. Frances would be better off without him. She might think him a villain after the intimacies they'd shared, but at least things hadn't gone so far between them that they *couldn't* turn back.

'Arthur.'

He turned around slowly at the sound of her voice. He hadn't heard footsteps, but she was standing right behind him, just out of arm's reach.

'Frances.' He attempted a smile, but she didn't respond. 'Your father told me that Lydia's awake again. I'm pleased.' The words felt woefully inadequate.

'Yes, Dr Muggridge is with her again now. He says it's a good sign that there's no confusion or memory loss.'

'Good.' He resisted the urge to take a step towards her. He was aware, painfully aware, of how cold his behaviour must seem, but what else could he do? He couldn't take her in his arms and hold her one last time, no matter how much he wanted to.

'You should go and speak to her.'

'Me?' He drew his brows together in surprise. 'Why?'

'She says she's sorry for what she did.'

'Tell her it's forgotten. I don't care about that any more.'

'I still think…' she stopped and swallowed, as if she were having trouble forming words '…that you ought to go and speak with her.'

'If you want me to, but—'

'Our engagement was a mistake,' she interrupted, speaking in a sudden rush.

'What?' The words seemed to hit him with the force of a physical blow. 'What do you mean, a mistake?'

'We were both forced into it, but there's no need for the charade to continue any longer. I'll deal with my father and I don't care about gossip.'

'Frances…' This time he *did* move towards her, seized with an acute sense of panic. He *ought* to be glad, he told himself, or at least relieved that she was ending things and saving him from doing it, but all he could feel was dread and an intense sense of loss. That and an incongruous desire to win her back.

'You don't mean that.'

'Yes, I do.' She put a hand up, backing away from him at the same time as he advanced towards her. 'I've made up my mind.'

'Well, I haven't! We weren't *just* forced into it. That's not all there was between us, you know that.'

'That was a mistake, too.' Her cheeks darkened, though her determined expression didn't falter. 'If you're referring to the night when Violet had her twins, we were both exhausted and emotional. People do strange things in those kinds of situations. You know that better than anyone.'

He jerked his chin up as if she'd just struck him. Yes, he knew that, of course he did. It was what he was afraid of. But if he was certain of anything, it was that he hadn't imagined his feelings for her, or his desire either. He'd never felt more certain of anything in his whole life. But then he'd been certain that she cared for him, too...

'You wish to end our engagement, then?'

'Yes—' she nodded firmly '—but I'll make it clear that it was my decision. No one will blame you.'

'I don't give a damn if anyone blames me!'

'None the less, I'll make it clear. Since I'm the one who made the mistake...' She looked past him towards the sea, as if her thoughts were already moving on. 'I hope that we can still be friends.'

'Friends.' He couldn't stop his lip from curling. 'If that's what you want.'

'It is.' She gave another decisive nod. 'Just don't forget to visit Lydia. I know she'll be glad to see you.'

Chapter Twenty-Five

Arthur slammed his axe down hard on to a log, split-ting it down the middle and sending pieces splintering off in different directions. He had a big enough pile of firewood already, probably enough for the whole winter if he didn't stop chopping soon, but he didn't want to stop. He'd finally found a way to vent his feel-ings, the combination of loss, frustration and regret that only seemed to have grown in intensity every day for the past month. His broken engagement was now public knowledge, a feat that had been accomplished without any effort from him, and he was a free man. Alone again, just as he'd wanted. Alone and damned miserable.

'What did that log ever do to you?'

He glowered at the sound of hoofbeats, accompanied by his brother's carefree voice.

'What do you want, Lance?'

'Oh, nothing much. I just wanted to remind you that we're leaving at the end of this week, that's all.'

He dropped the axe with a sigh. 'Not this again, Lance.'

'Yes, this again. You might not want it to happen,

but it is. Our new house is ready and Violet tells me the nursery is a thing of beauty. She can't wait to move in.'

'What about all the money you've spent on Amberton Castle?'

'Considering that the iron mine is on your land and earns me a pretty decent return, I'd say we're even, especially since Francis and Sophoria are the heirs.'

'Which is exactly why you should stay and look after the house for them. How can you just abandon our family home?'

Lance made a face. 'I don't think people in glass houses should be quite so sanctimonious.'

'My situation's different.'

'Actually it's not...' Lance jumped down from his horse with a determined expression '...and it's about time you faced up to your responsibilities.'

'*You're* lecturing *me* on responsibility?'

'Yes. I've become quite the staid gentleman in my old age.'

'You're still younger than me.'

'But quite a bit more mature at this point, I'd say. You've been an absolute monster for the past month. Coincidentally since you ended your engagement to the woman you love.'

Arthur narrowed his eyes. 'What about all the staff? What will happen to them?'

'They're your staff really, not mine. *You're* the Viscount.'

'Only in name. As for the rest, you know I don't want it.'

'Arthur—' Lance sounded uncharacteristically sombre '—hasn't it ever occurred to you that you *need* to go back there? Whatever demons you still have to confront, maybe they're in that house.'

'No! I can't go back as if nothing ever happened. I can't be the man Father wanted.'

'Then go back and be yourself. Be your own man.'

'I *am* my own man. Here on my own.'

'Really? Because I think you're stuck. You think you don't deserve to go back because you feel guilty about what happened to Father, but you won't back down from your last argument with him either. So you're at an impasse. But tell me this, big Brother, what was the point of your running away if you refuse to move on? Make your peace with the past. You didn't mean to hurt Father and you don't have to be the man he wanted either, but you can still go back home. You are who you are, but who you are belongs at Amberton Castle and you *can* let yourself be happy, too. You can still marry Frances.'

'It's not as simple as that.'

'Why not?'

Arthur ran a hand over his newly cropped head in frustration. 'Does Violet know that you're here? I thought she might have forbidden you from speaking to me.'

'Yes, she does and, no, she hasn't and she's not *not* speaking to you. She's just upset for Frances, that's all.'

'Frances is the one who ended our engagement!'

'Because?'

'Because she said we'd been forced into it.'

'Something that didn't seem to bother her before.' Lance lifted an eyebrow pointedly and Arthur sighed.

'It did at first, only I thought we were past all that.'

'What else did she say?'

'Just that it was a mistake and that I ought to speak with Lydia. She was quite insistent about that.'

'And have you?'

'Spoken with Lydia? No.'

Lance rubbed his chin thoughtfully. 'And that didn't

strike you as odd, that she wanted you to speak with her sister?'

'No, it struck me as what she wanted. That's all there is to it.'

'So you let her go that easily?'

Arthur picked up another log and glowered. '*She* wanted to end it, Lance. Believe me, she was very convincing.'

'She was pretty convincing as a woman in love a month ago, too.'

'Well, clearly she changed her mind.' He placed the log on the chopping block as a sign that the conversation was over, but Lance only rubbed his chin some more.

'It just doesn't make sense. Didn't she give *any* other reason?'

'No!' He picked up the axe and then lowered it again. 'Except...'

'Except?'

'I suppose, while Lydia was unconscious, my behaviour might have seemed a bit distant. There's a chance that Frances might have thought I'd changed my mind about marrying her, too.'

'Oh, good grief.' Lance rolled his eyes. 'A normal person acting distant is bad. *You* acting distant... Well, no wonder. Why on earth did you do that?'

'What does it matter now?'

'Because we're trying to work this out!'

'Maybe it's best left alone.' Arthur threw the axe to one side again. 'Look, the truth is I *had* changed my mind. But then I changed it back again and now...now I think this is for the best.'

'Because you're managing so well?' Lance made a cynical face. 'Honestly, I ought to bash the pair of your heads together, though I suppose it might be somewhat hypocritical coming from me. All I know is that Frances cares for you. I might have been somewhat distracted a month ago, but even a blind man could have seen that. And you care for her, too. So leave those poor logs and go and get her back.'

'No.'

'Damn it, Arthur, what are you so scared of?'

'You know what!' He whirled on his brother angrily. 'What if what happened before happens again? What if my mind isn't stable enough for marriage? I saw you that night with Violet. You were desperate, too. I couldn't stand to go through anything like that.'

'You were the strong one that night. You helped me.'

'But what if it had been Frances?'

'Then I'd have been the one threatening to punch you.'

Arthur gave a short laugh. 'You know what I'm saying. What if I end up failing her the way I've failed everyone else I ever cared about?'

'Everyone? You never failed me.'

'I was never able to stop you and Father from arguing.'

'As if anyone could have!'

'But I *promised* Mother!'

Lance's expression looked arrested for a moment. 'I had no idea…but you can't feel guilty about that. It wasn't your responsibility, Arthur.'

'I know. Deep down, I know, but I'm still scared of failing Frances. What if something happens and I have another episode? What if I end up running away again?'

'*What if?*' Lance gripped hold of his shoulders. 'You can't base your life on *what if*. What if I turn out to be as bad a father as ours was?'

'What? Of course you won't be.'

'And you won't have another episode. Funny how we can be so sure about each other, isn't it?' He let go of his shoulders again. 'Anyway, if it's running away that you're worried about, then you're too late. I hate to break this to you, big Brother, but what do you think you're doing now?'

'I'm not running anywhere.' Arthur felt his whole body go tense.

'You're not fighting either. As far as I can see, you're running away from the love of your life and hurting yourself and her into the bargain.'

'I would *never* hurt Frances!'

'But you are. *This* is failing her! So go and tell her what a damned fool you've been. Go and demand to know why she ended your engagement and then propose to her again.' Lance kicked away the log from the block. 'Do whatever the hell it takes to win her back.'

Arthur drew in a deep breath and then let it out again. 'All right, let's just say for a moment that you're right, what do I do? What do I say to her?'

Lance threaded his fingers together, flexed them and then grinned. 'I was afraid you'd never ask…'

Frances climbed up beside Lydia and Georgie on the trap. She'd been vaguely surprised when her sister had suggested a ride out, even more so when their mother hadn't objected, though Frances had eventually agreed to accompany her on condition they didn't go far. She had work to finish, a pair of matching brooches in a pre-Raphaelite design that she personally thought were the best pieces she'd ever produced. Mr Horsham had already offered to take them, as well as anything else she made. Her jewellery was selling so quickly that she could barely keep up with demand. Which was just as well since working distracted her.

'Are you sure that you ought to be doing this so soon?' She glanced nervously at Lydia as her sister took up the reins.

'Perfectly sure and it's not *so* soon. It's been a month and you know what they say about getting back on the horse.'

'The doctor still says…'

'That I'm lucky I wasn't more badly hurt and that I shouldn't overdo things?'

'Yes, so maybe you should listen.'

'I am, but it's such a beautiful day. I doubt we'll get many more like it before winter and Georgie and I want a picnic up on the Moors, don't we, darling?'

'The Moors?' Frances stiffened, belatedly noticing that they were taking the road towards Sleights. 'But I thought you didn't like the Moors?'

'I didn't used to, but I've changed my mind about a lot of things since the accident.'

'Can't we go somewhere else?'

'No, and don't even think about jumping down and abandoning us. I could faint at any moment.'

'You just said you felt fine.'

'For now. Only my head feels dizzy already.'

'Oh, all right.' Frances folded her arms in chagrin. 'Then I hope you've brought cake.'

'Naturally. Some lemon buns from Mrs Botham's. Georgie told me how much you like them.'

'Did he?' She looked askance at her sister.

'Yes. In fact, he's told me a lot of interesting things recently, all about cakes and picnics and building sand-castles on the beach.'

'Mmmm.' Frances twisted her face to one side,

making a pretence of looking at the landscape as they branched off from the main road and on to a smaller track over the moors.

'Speaking of castles...' Lydia carried on blithely. 'I thought it was high time I visited Amberton Castle again.'

'What?' Frances swung round again so quickly that she felt a searing pain in the back of her skull. *'Why?'*

'Partly because I missed the garden party and partly because we've been invited. The grounds there should be lovely for a picnic.'

'No!' She felt her stomach lurch almost painfully. 'Not there, Lydia, please. I mean, I want to see Violet and the babies again, but...'

'Oh, she isn't the one who invited us.'

'You mean Lance?'

'Guess again.' Lydia threw her a smile. 'Though it shouldn't be too hard. There's only one other answer.'

'Arthur? No! Absolutely not. Turn the trap around right now!' Frances made a grab for the reins, but Lydia pulled them out of her reach.

'Did I mention that I met him a few days ago? He called at the house when you were out at the jeweller's.'

Frances felt as though her heart had suddenly stopped beating. 'No, you *didn't* mention it.'

'Silly me. By the way, the hamper's just on the back there. Have a sandwich if you're hungry.'

'Lydia!'

'What?' Her sister's face was the picture of inno-cence. 'We have cheese and pickle and beef and...'

'Tell me the truth, are the two of you in love?'

'Arthur and me?' It was Lydia's turn to look sur-prised. 'Don't be ridiculous. What on earth makes you think that?'

'Because you must have spoken about your past. Your past feelings for each other, I mean... And after your accident, he was so worried. And you said...you sounded...' she cleared her throat awkwardly '... I thought maybe you'd realised how much you still meant to each other.'

'In love...' Lydia burst into a fit of giggles. 'Nothing like. We did touch on the past briefly, but most of the time we talked about you. It was quite galling really.'

'You mean—' Frances felt her heart start to beat again '—you're *not* engaged?'

'*Engaged?*' Lydia sobered long enough to lift her eyebrows accusingly. 'Do you think I'd be taking you to Amberton Castle today if *that* was the case? What do you take me for?'

'I...' Frances stared at her sister, her thoughts spinning. 'I'm sorry.'

Lydia made a harrumphing sound. 'Well, that's all right. I suppose my previous behaviour speaks against me, but that's all over and done with now. I'm a new woman, a better daughter, sister and mother.' She reached behind her to tousle the curly mass of Georgie's hair. 'This is the only man I'm interested in from now on.'

Despite her confusion, Frances couldn't help but smile. The way the little boy was gazing adoringly up at his mother suggested her own days as his favoured companion were numbered. Lydia looked different from her usual polished and preened self, too, with a smile that touched every part of her face and made her eyes crinkle at the corners. She looked less perfect and even more beautiful.

'But *why* has Arthur invited us to Amberton Castle?' She dragged her thoughts back to the situation in hand.

'Not us. *You.* Aggravating as it is, I'm simply your method of transportation. That's why he came to visit me actually, to ask for my help in getting you here.'

'Then why aren't we going to his farm?'

'You'll have to ask him.'

'But I ended our engagement!'

'Yes, I would imagine that has something to do with it all.' Lydia twisted her head towards her suddenly. 'Wait, is that why you broke it off? Because you thought he was in love with me?'

Frances hunched her shoulders. 'Maybe…'

'Oh, Frannie…'

'Well, what was I supposed to think? He started acting strangely the moment he heard about your accident.'

'Not because he was in love with me! Well, that's one mystery solved. Mama and I have been racking our brains trying to work out what happened.'

'It's not the only reason and I still don't want to see him.'

'But…'

'But nothing. It's over. The way he behaved…it was just like Leo all over again. You don't know how it feels to be rejected like that.'

'Excuse me—' Lydia sounded aggrieved '—but do I need to remind you of that scene in his farmhouse?'

'Well, it's happened to me twice! I'd be a fool to risk it again.'

'But maybe Arthur wasn't rejecting you. You could just let him explain.'

'Why?' She regarded her sister suspiciously. 'Has he explained to you?'

'Not exactly. All he said was that he'd made a terrible mistake and he wanted a chance to win you back.

That's *all*, a chance, but he sounded sincere to me. Anyway, we're here now.'

Frances took a deep breath as the ivy-clad turrets of Amberton Castle rose up from the valley below them. It was truly a spectacular place, the grey stone glowing pale pink in the afternoon sunshine, as if it really had jumped straight out of a fairy tale.

'Off you go, then.' Lydia drew the trap to a halt in the courtyard. 'He's waiting.'

Frances looked towards the house with trepidation. Lydia was right. There he was, waiting under the archway of the imposing front porch with his hands clasped behind his back, the same way he'd stood in her parents' parlour on the morning they'd come back from Amberton Castle, the morning after the night when he'd undressed her... The memory made her turn away again, the emotions so raw they felt like an open wound.

'Take me home.' She gritted her teeth. 'Whatever he has to say, I don't want to hear it.'

'Well, it's up to you, but Georgie and I aren't going anywhere until we've had our picnic.' Lydia nudged her son conspiratorially and then threw a friendly wave in Arthur's direction. 'But I'd take pity on him if I were you. He's not Leo and he's not in love with me. Besides, the poor man has been positively miserable for the past month.'

'How would you know?'

'By the rings around his eyes for a start. Not to mention the constant frowning. I do so hate to see a handsome man spoil himself, but I'm afraid you're the only one who can do anything about it. Honestly...' Lydia raised a hand to her head dramatically '...all this tension is enough to make me feel dizzy again. If I don't eat something soon...'

'All right!' Frances glared ferociously as she jumped down from the trap. 'But we'll talk about this later!'

'I'm sure we will. Only be sure to include Mama in your harangue. She's in on the plot, too.'

'You mean you're both in this together?'

'Why do you think she didn't object to our outing? Even Papa thought it was a good idea. Of course, Arthur did say some very affecting things about not being able to live without you and all that kind of thing. I suppose that helped win them over. Now, we'll see you in an hour.'

'An *hour*?'

Frances opened her mouth to argue some more, but the trap was already moving away, leaving her alone with Arthur.

Chapter Twenty-Six

'Frances.' The way he said her name sent an all-too-familiar, all-too-unwelcome *frisson* of excitement racing down her spine. 'Thank you for coming.'

'I wasn't given much choice. For the record, I was tricked.' She turned around, making a point of glaring at him. 'Lydia said you wanted to see me. *Why?*'

'Because I want to show you something. Come with me.'

He didn't wait for an answer, though it hadn't sounded much like a question either, turning on his heel and leading the way inside the house. Frances threw one last look after the departing trap and then followed reluctantly behind, trailing slowly through the great hall and into the drawing room, stopping short in the doorway as he took a seat by the fireplace. Not that she ought to be surprised, she told herself resentfully. He'd told her enough times that he wasn't a gentleman, but still, sitting down first, without so much as offering her a chair, was downright rude.

'I wanted to show you this.'

'You sitting in an armchair?' She didn't bother to disguise her sarcasm. 'I'm impressed.'

'Not just any armchair.' The muscles of his face looked taut with emotion, his brows drawn together in a line. 'My father's.'

'Oh.' She couldn't think of anything to say for a few moments, speechless with surprise. She'd been so wrapped up in her own emotions that she'd forgotten the significance of that particular seat.

'I've sat in it every evening this week. Ever since I moved back here.'

'You've moved back?' Whatever else she might have expected, it *definitely* hadn't been that. 'What about your farm?'

'I found a tenant.'

'But you love it there.'

'Yes—' his brows contracted even further '—but as the landowner, I have other responsibilities and it's time I faced up to them. Lance and I have been dealing with the estate together for the past few years, but what with the ironworks and a family, he doesn't have a great deal of spare time any more. I should never have expected so much of him, but then I never intended to come back here. I intended for all of this to be his and his children's.'

'And now?'

'Now Violet and Lance have bought a new house closer to the ironworks, so I'm back.' He stood up again, his expression resolute. 'And I intend to stay back.'

'You mean you're going to start behaving like a viscount again?' She clasped her hands in front of her, trying to create a barrier between them as he moved closer.

'Something like that.' He lifted an eyebrow sardonically. 'Within reason anyway.'

'Oh.' She pursed her lips, unsure about what kind of expression she ought to be wearing. She felt strangely giddy all of a sudden. He was the self-assured, confident man from the promenade again, the one who'd asked her to marry him, told her she was beautiful and made her believe it, too. The one she still found irresistible despite everything...

'I see.' She cleared her throat, forcing herself to remember how he'd changed. 'How do you feel about it all?'

'Not too bad, surprisingly. The roof hasn't caved in yet and I haven't felt the slightest inclination to throw myself into the North Sea.'

'Don't joke.'

'I'm not, not really. Only I've decided to stop taking myself so seriously. You were right when you said that guilt didn't do any good. So I'm back, living in my father's house and sitting in his chair to make peace with him. I've decided to make things right, as far as I can anyway. I'm taking over the estate like he wanted me to, but I'm doing it my way, not his. That's the best I can do.'

She clasped her hands tighter, trying not to notice how exceedingly handsome he looked, though the resolute look in his eye was strangely compelling.

'Then I'm pleased for you. I hope you'll be very happy here.'

'I won't be, not without you.' His voice held a note of conviction. 'Besides, it's too big a house for one man. It needs a mistress.'

'Well, if you're going to behave like a viscount again then I'm sure you'll have no trouble finding someone.'

'I don't want someone, Frances. I want you.'

'No.' She tensed as he moved closer, his proximity making her pulse start to flutter unsteadily. 'It's too late for that.'

'Why?' He reached a hand out. 'Tell me why you broke off our engagement, the real reason this time.'

'How can you ask me that?' She was almost relieved to feel angry again, batting his hand away accusingly. 'How *dare* you when you were the one who changed your mind about us? I saw it in your eyes. *You* were the one who wanted to end our engagement! Or do you deny it?'

He hesitated for a moment and then shook his head. 'No. I can't deny it.'

'Oh.' She gasped for breath, feeling as though she'd fallen into deep water suddenly. Even though she'd suspected the truth, hearing it from his own lips felt even more painful, as if she were sinking slowly beneath the surface with the force of the waves pushing her downwards.

'In that case, there's nothing else to say.' She started towards the door, desperate to get away from him and out into the open air again.

'There's plenty to say.' Arthur stepped around her, blocking her path. 'Yes, I intended to call off our engagement that day, but I knew the moment you started speaking that it wasn't what I wanted, not really.'

'So it was just a whim?' She gave a brittle laugh.

'No. Look, I was a damned fool in the way that I acted and an even bigger fool not to come to my senses sooner. My only excuse is that I was afraid. I've been afraid for a long time, mostly of myself, of what happened six years ago and the chances of it happening again. I've been so afraid of the past repeating itself that I've been jumping at shadows. I thought I was free, but I was only making another prison for myself. I should have told you the whole truth before. I intended to, but I thought—*hoped*—that I'd moved on, that I was stronger. Then after what happened to Violet and then Lydia, I panicked. I did the very thing I was afraid of and ran away.'

'You were afraid?' She felt as though she were rising to the surface of the water again, her heart aching at the thought of what he must have suffered. 'I thought it was because you still had feelings for Lydia.'

'No. I was worried about her, of course, but that wasn't the reason I behaved so badly. I was scared that I wouldn't be able to cope if anything like that happened to you. I pushed you away because I was afraid of how I might react, of running away again and hurting you. I thought that breaking our engagement was for the best, but I've been miserable every moment since.' He reached for one of her hands, clasping it between both of his and pressing a kiss against the knuckles. 'Frances, if it was my behaviour that ruined everything, then at least give me a chance to mend it…please.'

'No.' She hardened her heart at the imploring look on his face. 'I'm glad that you've found a way to come home, but I can't be part of it. I've moved on. My jewellery is selling well and people value my work. They value *me*. I'm making a life for myself on my own.'

'Frances…'

'No.' She shook her head adamantly. 'I *trusted* you. I thought that you were nothing like Leo, but you rejected me just the same. I won't be hurt like that again.'

'I know.' He squeezed her hand tighter, his gaze darkening. 'I know that I hurt you, but it won't happen again, Frances, I promise.'

She held her breath, looking down at their joined hands and resisting the urge to believe him. Part of her wanted to keep sinking, to fall to the very depths of the ocean and hide, but somehow his words buoyed her up again. He hadn't rejected her because he didn't want her, but because in some strange way he'd been trying to protect her. He'd been afraid of himself and his own inner demons... If she turned away from him and left now, wouldn't she be making the same mistake, letting her own fear of rejection control her? Would *she* spend the rest of her life in a prison, jumping at shadows, too?

'How do I know you won't hurt me?' She asked the question hesitantly.

'Because from now on, I'll be as strong as you need me to be. I can't control the future, but I can stop being afraid of the past. When I left six years ago, it was because I thought my future held only misery and heartache. So I ran and I kept on running until a week ago. It took Lance to make me realise that. Now I know who I am and what I want and I *want* to be here. I won't hide away any more. I intend to face up to my mistakes and be a better man. Because of you.' He closed what was left of the space between them, lifting both of their hands and holding them over his heart. 'I love you, Frances. I might still make mistakes, but I promise that I'll always be here for you. I'll never run away or make you feel rejected ever again, I swear it.'

'Never?' She could see the sunlight sparkling above the surface of the water now as he nodded, his eyes lighting up with a glimmer of hope.

'Just give me a chance to prove myself. You don't have to agree to marry me. Just give me a chance to win you back again.'

'No.'

'No?' The light in his eyes faded, the muscles in his jaw all bunching at once.

'No.' She heaved in a deep breath as she burst through the waves and into the air again. 'You don't need to prove yourself because I already believe you. Whatever challenges we face in the future, we'll face them together. I don't want to hide away any more either. I *want* to be your wife.' She swayed forward into his arms. 'I love you, too, Arthur Amberton. I always have.'

'No veils.' Frances stood in the middle of her bedroom floor, hands on her hips.

'But it's traditional, dear. Brides wear veils, even ones who only give their family a few days to prepare.' Her mother sounded faintly recriminatory. 'Now do be careful where you put your arms. You'll crush the silk.'

'It's no good arguing, Mama.' Lydia perched on a window seat, swinging her legs in a distinctly girlish fashion. 'You know she never backs down.'

'Well, I don't know how I ended up with two such stubborn daughters. It's bad enough you deciding to wear black again just when we said you could go into half-mourning, but now this.'

'I'm wearing black for John out of respect. Since I haven't been particularly respectful this past year, I'm making up for it now. We might not have been the greatest love story, but he was my husband and he deserved better from me. Anyway, it's not as if I'm going into seclusion again. If I've learnt anything from all this, it's that we should all live our lives while we have the chance.'

'Yes, but couldn't you just for today…?'

'And as for my wearing a veil,' Frances interjected. 'Arthur wouldn't like it. He says that he never wants to see me covering my scar up again, so I can't very well do it on our wedding day.'

'Oh, very well.' Their mother threw her arms up in

defeat. 'When you put it like that, I suppose not, but at least let me tie some white ribbon in your hair.'

'You can do whatever you like with my hair, Mama.'

'Well, I think you look perfect already.' Lydia jumped down from the window and kissed her sister's cheek. 'I hope Arthur knows how lucky he is.'

Frances looked into the floor-length mirror and smiled at her own reflection. Her scar was still there, of course, but it wasn't the first thing her eyes went to any more. It wasn't *all* she saw either. Instead, she saw a happy, excited-looking woman on the morning of her wedding day.

'You're sure you don't mind?' She caught her sister's eye in the mirror.

'Not even the teeniest bit. Why would I, when I have my own gentleman escort?' Lydia gestured towards Georgie, playing on the floor with a toy train, and Frances smiled affectionately.

'And such a handsome one, too. Although I hope you'll meet someone else one day.'

'One day perhaps.' Lydia lifted her shoulders and then dropped them again nonchalantly. 'But I'm in no rush. I have nothing to prove any more and I'm determined that I won't be anyone's trophy ever again. If I *do* meet someone then I want him to like me for me, whoever she is.'

'She's my sister...' Frances squeezed her hand warmly '...and I love her.'

'Oh, do stop it.' Their mother was dabbing at her eyes with a handkerchief. 'You'll make me blotchy and swollen even before the ceremony.'

'Well, we can't have that.' Lydia skipped across the room to give their mother a swift hug. 'Now forget about those ribbons. I have a *much* better idea.'

* * *

Arthur paced nervously up and down the pavement outside the church, fiddling with his cravat and lifting his head at every stray noise.

'You know, we *could* wait inside.' Lance stood tapping his foot beside him. 'Considering that it's November and the Yorkshire climate is really best enjoyed in summer, if at all.'

'I'll go in once I see her carriage.'

'Afraid that she'll change her mind?'

'Yes! Do you blame me after everything we've been through? I won't be happy until the service is over.'

'You really are a hopeless romantic, aren't you?'

'You know what I mean.'

'I do. Believe it or not, Violet actually had some reservations about marrying me.'

'You don't say.'

'She even ran out on our first wedding.'

'You're reminding me of that *now*?'

'But Frances will be here.'

'How can you be so sure?'

'Because if there's one subject I know about it's women and Frances loves you, for some bizarre, misguided reason of her own.' He grinned as Arthur shot him a venomous look. 'And because I can see her parents' carriage at the end of the street. Now, I believe that's our cue to go inside. Your days of freedom are over, big Brother.'

'That's where you're wrong.' Arthur drew in a long breath and then released it again slowly. 'They're only just beginning.'

Despite their initial intention to have a small and intimate family ceremony, followed by a small and intimate family gathering, there were at least a hundred people gathered inside the ballroom at Amberton Castle that evening. The Felstones were there, of course, along with Ianthe's Aunt Sophoria, bedecked in more white lace than the bride, as well as Violet's family from York, Mr Thorpe from the jet workshop, the Doctors Bennett and Muggridge, Mr Horsham, the jeweller, and a wide selection of long-lost and newly rediscovered friends.

'Happy?'

Frances laughed as Arthur lifted his wine glass and clinked it against hers. 'Everyone keeps asking me that. Wouldn't it be funny if I said no?'

'Not to me.' He gave her one of his old stern looks. 'It would be a pretty poor start.'

'In that case, it's been a wonderful day and I'm *very* happy. What about you?'

He swallowed the last of his wine and then put the glass down, wrapping his arms around her instead. She looked—*she was*—beautiful, inside and out. The moment when she'd said 'I do' he'd felt as though his heart was full to bursting. The future could never be certain, but what he *was* certain about was his decision. 'I can honestly say I'm happier than I've been for the last fifteen years.'

'Oh.' Her face fell. 'I'm sorry.'

'Don't be. It was a compliment.'

'But to have been unhappy for so long...'

'Ah, but I intend to make up for it now. In fact, I intend to be quite ridiculously happy from now on. You'll hardly recognise me.'

'Oh, dear.' She feigned a look of mock horror. 'I might not have thought this marriage through. I'm not sure how I feel about living with a *ridiculously* happy man. It sounds somewhat alarming.'

'I'll try not to get carried away.' He leaned closer,

skimming a series of small kisses along the side of her cheek. 'Speaking of carrying things away, how much longer do we have to stay?'

She blinked in surprise. 'You want to leave our own wedding celebration?'

'Yes. Immediately, if possible.' His lips continued their progress along her jaw to her earlobe. 'Not that I haven't enjoyed it, but I intend to be happier still today. I've been having visions of you in the bath for the past month and I'm about at the end of my tether.'

'Is that so?'

'It is, although as I recall, the memory of my naked body gives you nightmares.'

'Did *I* say that?' She tipped her head back, her breath coming in short bursts as his lips found her throat. 'Well, I didn't mean every night.'

'Ah. There's still hope for me, then?'

'A little…perhaps.'

'I'm glad you wore our shell.' He lifted his head again, trailing a finger over the hollow of her throat where the jet pendant nestled on its thin, black ribbon. 'It suits you.'

'Unlike this contraption, you mean?' She gestured to the diamond-encrusted tiara on her head, an elaborately wrought silver band in a strawberry-leaf motif. 'Lydia lent it to me. She said John gave it to her and I didn't have the heart to say no. It must be worth a small fortune, but I think she and Mama got carried away.'

'Not at all. It's quite impressive, only…'

'It's not me?'

He pressed his forehead tenderly against hers. 'Diamonds are all very well, but jet is something special. Like you. You'll always be the most beautiful woman in the world to me, Frances.'

She smiled, peering up at him through her lashes. 'What will people think if we leave now?'

'That's we're strange and eccentric and all the other things they've been saying about us for the past few years. We might as well prove them right.'

'They'll know where we're going.'

'And why, too.' He took her face in both of his hands and kissed her full on the mouth, letting his lips cling for a moment. 'Do you know the last time I gave a damn about what anyone thought of me?'

'No. When?'

'It was during our picnics on the beach. I cared what *you* thought of me. I cared because I was already in love with you back then. You opened the door to my prison that first day you walked into my house, Frances. It took me a while to walk out, but you made me want to start over again, to be *me* again. Now I think it's about time I took you upstairs and showed you just how grateful I am. We need to start early because I intend to be thorough. It might take all night.' He pressed one last kiss against the tip of her nose and then stepped back, holding a hand out towards her. 'Do you *really* care what anyone else thinks of us, Frances?'

'No.' She gave the widest smile he'd ever seen, folding her fingers around his and leading the way to the door. 'You're absolutely right. I don't.'

Epilogue

5 years later

'Ow!' Frances winced as something heavy jumped on the lower part of her body and then wriggled its way up the bed. 'Iris?'

'Is it time for the party yet?' Her daughter's face, bright-eyed and framed with a mass of chestnut curls, appeared over the top of the quilt.

'Not quite.' She nudged the shoulder of the man snoring softly beside her. 'Explain to our daughter that it's too early.'

'Hmmm?' Arthur rolled on to his back and gave a wide yawn. 'Explain what to whom?'

'Iris is awake.'

'Ah.' He opened one eye and lifted his head, his shoulder-length hair tousled from sleep. 'It's still night-time.'

'But can I get up now, Papa?'

'No!' This time they spoke in unison.

'But…'

'No buts…' Arthur pulled back the covers and swung his legs over the side of the bed. 'Back to the nursery with you.'

Frances smiled groggily, burrowing her way back under the covers with a sigh of contentment as Arthur hauled their squirming daughter over one shoulder and carried her, giggling, back to bed.

'Remember when we used to wake up all by ourselves?' He climbed back in beside her after a few minutes. 'I've said that if she gets out of bed again before daylight then she won't get any cake later. I know how her mind works. She takes after her mother.'

'Good idea.' Frances rolled towards him, curling up in the familiar warm crook of his arm and resting her cheek against his shoulder. 'Although if you try to take my cake away, you'll be sleeping alone from now on.'

'After five years and two children, I think I know better than that.' Arthur slid an arm down her side. 'Remind me why I'm the one who always puts her back to bed?'

'Because after I gave birth, you were so relieved that you said you'd never ask anything of me ever again.'

'So I did. Well, I stand by it.'

'Besides, I thought farmers liked early mornings.'

'I'm an *ex*-farmer and animals aren't quite as demanding as little girls.'

'But you're so good at dealing with them.' She draped an arm across his stomach, wriggling closer. 'I promise I'll see to Daphne when she wakes up. Then we'll have no peace until tonight.'

'True.' He yawned again. 'It seemed a good idea at the time, making the garden party an annual event.'

'It *was* a good idea. Of course, that was back before we had children and were able to sleep.'

'Back in the days when we used to scandalise Mrs Gargrave by staying in bed until mid-afternoon?' There was a definite smile in his voice. 'That's what I'd really like to do today, just stay here and forget the party. Do you think anyone would notice if we don't make an appearance?'

'Possibly, what with it being *our* party. We're supposed to greet everyone.'

'We could let Iris do it.'

'Good idea, but I'm afraid four still seems a little young for such a big responsibility.'

'Daphne could help.'

'She's two.'

'Mmm.' He made a disgruntled sound. 'Maybe next year, then?'

'Maybe.'

'Do you remember the last party?' She brushed a hand lightly over the sprinkling of hair on his chest. 'When you insisted on taking me for a walk in the orchard just for old time's sake?'

'I do.' His voice sounded faintly husky all of a sudden. 'I remember what happened there, too.'

'Well, it *was* memorable.' She hooked a leg over his thighs, gratified to hear his breathing hitch slightly. 'Although it can't happen again. I'm sure people were looking at us strangely afterwards.'

'That tends to happen when you have twigs in your hair.'

'I did not!'

'No, you were only a little dishevelled. I'm sure no more than a dozen people noticed.'

'Then it *definitely* can't happen again.'

'Spoilsport.' He grabbed hold of her waist, half-pulling, half-rolling her on top of him. 'Maybe we ought to wear ourselves out this morning, then? For some reason, I don't feel remotely sleepy any more.'

'Is that so?' She propped her chin on his chest, looking deep into his eyes as his hands slid over her back and bottom, tugging at the hem of her nightgown. 'That's funny because I'm exhausted. Especially if you're going to call me names…'

'How about *my love*?'

'Much better.'

She pulled her nightgown over her head, revelling in the flare of desire that lit his eyes as she stretched her body out over his. It was pleasing to know that after two children he still desired her. Despite the ups and downs of marriage and parenthood, their love-making had only become more passionate over the years. Arthur was a caring and thoughtful and thorough lover, just as he'd promised, and they knew each other's bodies well enough now to know what they both liked. It was a more emotional, intense form of love-making, less energetic perhaps than in the early days of their marriage, but even more satisfying. She certainly didn't feel like going back to sleep again either.

She shifted her hips over his body and then slid downwards, gasping as his body entered hers. She would never grow tired of this feeling, she thought, of being completely one and whole with the man that she loved, as if they were really one person. He moaned and started to move beneath her and she swayed above him, arching her back and crying out as their rhythm quickened to a crescendo. She felt a rush of heat a few moments before she reached her own climax and then tumbled down on top of him, losing herself in the ripples of sensation that continued to pulse through her body for minutes afterwards.

'*Now* we can go back to sleep,' he murmured against her throat and she laughed softly.

'*Finally.*'

Slowly, she lifted herself away and rolled on to her

side, smiling as he followed after her, curving his body around hers and coiling an arm around her waist.

'Happy?'

'What do you think?' He sounded sleepy.

'*Normal* happy or *ridiculously* happy?'

He tightened his hold, pulling her back against him until there was no space left between them. 'I'm never going to live that down, am I?'

'No. That's why I make a point of asking you every so often.'

'I've noticed. In that case, for the avoidance of any and all doubt, yes. I'm ridiculously happy. As always. How about you, Lady Scorborough? Have I convinced you how beautiful you are yet?'

She twisted her head around to look at him. 'I'm starting to think that you like me.'

'About time.' He seized the opportunity to plant another kiss on her lips. 'No regrets?'

'Regrets?' She was surprised by the very idea. 'How could I have any regrets? I'm in bed with a viscount and there's going to be a party later. With cake. I don't regret anything that's happened in my life. I'm happy.' She closed her eyes, letting herself drift back to sleep. 'Perfectly, deliriously, *ridiculously* happy...'

* * * * *